EVERY HUNTER IS HUNTED

Also available by Barry Lyga

Novels

Time Will Tell
The Hive (with Morgan Baden)
Bang
The Secret Sea
After the Red Rain (with Peter Facinelli and Rob DeFranco)
Thanos: Titan Consumed
Unsoul'd
Goth Girl Rising
Hero-Type
Boy Toy
The Astonishing Adventures of Fanboy and Goth Girl

The I Hunt Killers Trilogy

I Hunt Killers
Game
Blood of My Blood
Before the Hunt
(prequel anthology)

The Mike and Philomel Duology

Unedited
Edited

The Flash

Hocus Pocus
Johnny Quick
The Tornado Twins
Crossover Crisis: Green Arrow's Perfect Shot
Crossover Crisis: Supergirl's Sacrifice
Crossover Crisis: The Legends of Forever

The Archvillain Series

Archvillain
The Mad Mask
Yesterday Again

EVERY HUNTER IS HUNTED

A NOVEL

BARRY LYGA

Published in the United States by Crooked Lane Books, an imprint of The Quick Brown Fox & Company LLC.

Crooked Lane Books and its logo are trademarks of The Quick Brown Fox & Company LLC.

Library of Congress Catalog-in-Publication data available upon request.

ISBN (hardcover): 979-8-89242-555-1
ISBN (paperback): 979-8-89242-557-5
ISBN (ebook): 979-8-89242-556-8

Cover design by Ashton Smith

Printed in the United States.

www.crookedlanebooks.com

Crooked Lane Books
34 West 27th St., 10th Floor
New York, NY 10001

First Edition: June 2026

The authorized representative in the EU for product safety and compliance is eucomply OÜ Pärnu mnt 139b-14, 11317 Tallinn, Estonia, hello@eucompliancepartner.com, +33757690241

10 9 8 7 6 5 4 3 2 1

To Morgan, for her patience

Not Today

PROLOGUE

Patrick woke to the shaky blue dark, his hotel room wobbling and vibrating in the cast-off light of the muted TV. It took him a moment to place which hotel room: a moderately decent airport Hilton. Flying out early in the morning, they had opted for the cheaper wedding night hotel in favor of more money for the honeymoon.

His last solid memory, floating in a sea of bemused and marrow-deep fatigue, was of checking in at the front desk. That must have been hours ago.

He tried to sit up, but a throb at the base of his skull sent him back to his pillow. Walking the fingers of his right hand across the mattress, he encountered not Rebecca, but instead only the cool of her empty half of the bed.

The bedside clock blurred before him. Through sheer force of will, he cleared his eyesight. The clock's display wavered, stabilized, digits melding back into themselves. It was 4:13 AM.

"Honey?" he called. "Honey?"

They were due to fly to Antigua at ten. There was no reason for her to be awake so early.

At no response, he struggled to a sitting position, this time successfully. The bathroom door was open. After a necessary interval to catch his breath and make sure the room would not suddenly upend and hurl him to the floor, he stood. Feeling every inch an invalid, he crept to the bathroom, using the furniture for support along the way.

So utterly silent was the room that he felt he must be wrong, that Rebecca could not possibly be in the bathroom. With the door open, he would hear *something*, and the room was just so damn *quiet*. Maybe she'd stepped out for ice for a headache. Or something. Anything.

But, no, she would be in the bathroom, he knew. She would be in the bathroom, and as he leaned against the doorjamb, he saw she was, in fact, in the bathroom, lying in the tub, face up, one arm flung casually over the side, wearing her wedding gown, its white lace bodice gone almost black with her blood, her eyes staring up at him, staring, staring, and they would never, ever stop.

C H A P T E R

1

HE'D FALLEN ASLEEP on the sofa again and the house was as cold as Thanksgiving leftovers when the sound of the doorbell awoke Jasper Dent somewhere between eleven and noon. The cold hardly surprised him. The house had been frigid when he'd fallen asleep the night before; it had been cold all the previous day and when he'd woken that day, too. The only time the house was not cold was when the air conditioning ran in the summer. Then it was something approximating lukewarm.

He shivered his way off the sofa. The house was old and cranky, and it did not care how he set the thermostat. Its floorboards creaked; its offended stairs groaned at the slightest weight; not a single door within its confines would stay closed, so warped were the frames.

The house had belonged to his grandmother, who had willed it to him. It had little to recommend it save this: It was paid off. Jasper's grandmother had not accomplished much in her life, but by dint of her sheer longevity, she'd managed to leave him a residence free and clear. The old Dent house stood three rickety, drunk-in-a-hurricane stories, flaking its leprous gunmetal paint in great ragged peels. It was, as his best friend Howie had once said, a house haunted by itself.

Jasper had lived there since the age of thirteen, shortly after his father had been arrested and put in prison. For four years, he'd tended to the house and its owner, propping up his Alzheimer's-addled grandmother so that the world thought she was taking care of him rather than the reverse. And then she'd died and he'd inherited. A free residence and the publication of his memoir meant that, for the first time in his life, he had money.

Money could fix things. He knew the house needed serious repair at the hands of experts, but he couldn't decide where to start. So the Dent house groaned and waffled its way into the future like an old beater patched up just long enough to get to the chop shop.

On his own, he'd tried to rejuvenate the house at least a little bit, to resuscitate its potential. The house resisted him at every turn. Everything took three times longer in the Dent house than it should have. The simple act of hanging a frame on the wall more often than not required multiple drill bits, two different stud finders, a can of spackling paste, and nearly inhuman forbearance.

Bulldozing it and starting over seemed the only sane avenue, but every time he decided on that path, some housebound memory would blitz attack him from the cellars of his unconscious and he would determine to renovate the old heap back to life. This was the only home he could lay claim to; he loved it and he hated it in equal measure.

The doorbell rang again as he hesitated between the living room and the kitchen. The kitchen meant coffee, and coffee meant life, but the doorbell was closer. He opened the door and immediately regretted doing so.

The woman standing on his front porch was in her mid-to-late thirties. Attractive. African American with an elliptical face centered around a delicate button nose. She wore a deep-blue Gore-Tex coat, a tartan scarf, and sleek black gloves. Riding an explosion of tight curls, a knit cap perched jauntily atop her head, as though it had grown up there and felt quite relaxed and uninhibited. With a smile, she waggled her fingers at him.

"Hi, so my husband and I just moved into the neighborhood and we—"

As politely and as gently as one could slam a door in someone's face, Jasper slammed the door in her face.

A quick walker, he was almost halfway to the kitchen and the promise of caffeine by the time he heard her protest, "Oh, come on! For real?"

He stopped and chuckled despite himself. "Nice try, FBI!" he shouted back through the door.

She rang the bell again and then started pounding on the door. It sounded like she was hitting it pretty hard and she went on longer than he would have thought possible. Clearly, she wasn't going anywhere.

With a sigh, he went back to the door and leaned against it. "Go away, FBI. Not interested."

She smacked the door one more time, an impressively powerful blow. "Five minutes of your time. That's all."

"Not gonna happen."

"We checked that a moving van was seen in the neighborhood," she said somewhat petulantly. "At least tell me what gave me away."

"A million things."

"Humor me."

He sighed and began ticking them off on his fingers, even though she couldn't see him. "You're wearing gloves, but they're tight enough that I could tell you're not wearing a ring. Married men often don't wear wedding bands, but statistically married women do so overwhelmingly. Ergo, probably no husband. The car parked at the curb is the midsize rental model the Bureau likes, not an SUV or minivan that you would get when moving in somewhere and buying a bunch of new crap for your house. Your coat is puffy, but your left armpit is a little puffier than the right, so that's where your gun is holstered. And last but not least, the FBI knows my girlfriend is Black, too, and one of their shrinks thinks maybe you'd catch me off guard as a result."

Silence on the other side of the door. There were more clues, more slipups, but he didn't feel like elucidating further. Jasper didn't think he was lucky enough to have driven her away with his first salvo.

Sure enough, after a moment, she spoke up. "You're as good as they say you are."

"And your profile has got to include that flattery is the wrong way to go with me."

"Not trying to flatter you," she said. "Just being honest."

She sounded sincere and truthful and earnest, and he took a moment to remind himself that absolutely none of that mattered to him.

"It's been fun, but now I'm going to have my coffee and you're going to disappear back to whatever cubicle the FBI has reserved for you."

In the kitchen, he fumbled around in the cabinets, then heaved out a sigh. His winter coat, a quilted, plaid affair that Howie said made him look like a truck driver, was on a hook near the back door. Slipping into it, he patted the pockets for his phone and wallet, then stepped into a pair of battered kicks. He almost opened the back door, then changed direction.

The FBI agent was sitting on the front stoop that led down into the yard. As he regarded her from the threshold, she wrestled a grin away from her lips before it could fully form.

"What changed your—"

"I'm out of coffee. I'll let you buy me a cup."

* * *

"Take the next left and get on the highway," he told her.

She had introduced herself as Special Agent Maxine de la Croix. He hadn't bothered introducing himself. In de la Croix's inoffensive rental, he directed her off the two-laner that contracted to one lane while bisecting the heart of town. The town of Lobo's Nod had a way of making most things smaller when it absorbed them. Roadways were no exception.

"There's a place closer," de la Croix said. "In town. I saw it on my way. Local joint. Coff-E-Shop or something. Looked nice."

"I don't go there. There's a Starbucks one exit up."

She hesitated only a moment, then signaled and switched lanes. Lobo's Nod, his hometown, his home base, disappeared behind them.

"Do people still call you Jazz?" she asked, glancing over at him.

He favored her with the most withering look in his collection and very deliberately said nothing.

She returned her attention to the road. "OK, look, I'm here because—"

"Because the Bureau sends someone like you every few months. Congratulations—you have the length of the trip to Starbucks and back to talk to me. That's better than anyone else they've sent. They might give you a raise."

"All we want—"

"You guys think that just because my parents were serial killers, I've got some kind of gift for hunting them down."

"You did a fair job of nailing your parents a few years back. And a few of their buddies, too."

He grunted. "I was a teenager. I thought I was invincible. And a lot of people got hurt."

"You're too young to pull off the grizzled veteran routine," she said, her tone tired and snappish. Her face crumpled in self-reproach as soon as she said it. He grinned.

By now they'd pulled into the drive-through lane at the closest Starbucks. De la Croix ordered for them both, handed his coffee to him, and—after a moment's hesitation—headed back to the Dent house. Jasper took a sip of his coffee, even though it was scalding hot.

"Sorry about that before," she muttered.

"Don't be. You finally said something not in the FBI script. Good for you." He saluted her with his coffee.

With a rueful chuckle, she tapped her cup against his. They both drank in silence for a moment as she drove.

"It's not that I want to be difficult," he said, staring out the windshield. "I just don't want to be involved in—"

"We think it's a Crow."

He stopped. He did everything in his power to resist turning back to her, but all his power was not enough. Face-to-face with her, he set his jaw and, with as much testosterone as he could muster, said, "Do not screw with me. Not about this."

"I'm not. I swear."

The Crows. A secret nationwide collective of serial killers. So well concealed that no one who wasn't a member even knew they existed until Jasper, as a teenager, had gone up against the Crow King, Janice. His mother.

And her right-hand man, Jasper's father, Billy.

Together, they had a serial killing career that spanned decades and bodies in the triple digits, but that was only the veneer of their depravity. The Crows were massing power and influence, placing their more agreeable members in positions of social influence and power, all in pursuit of an insane agenda that seemed to revolve around the idea of turning the country into a hunting preserve for serial killers.

The notion was so mad as to be risible, but the fact that the Crows had operated for so long without being discovered smothered any amusement he may have considered.

"Are you sure?" he heard himself ask. Despite his best, most cherished intentions, his temples began to pulse. His breathing had quickened ever so slightly.

They'd pulled into his driveway. De la Croix cut the engine and sighed, turning in her seat to regard him. "This is the end of our trip. I guess you'll never know."

Her lips curled the bare minimum to qualify for a self-satisfied smile. She truly looked nothing at all like Connie, but in that moment he desperately wanted her to. It would make his capitulation a tiny bit easier.

"Let's go inside," he said.

*　　*　　*

"He's called Bridekiller," de la Croix told him, strumming her fingers on a tablet that she had so far not bothered to hand to Jasper.

"What makes you think he's a Crow?"

"There's a passage in your father's book that seems relevant." She consulted a scan on the tablet. "'He takes them in the white. He is pure in ways they are not, so he takes them in the white. In the white he takes . . .'" She broke off and looked at Jasper. "It goes on about taking them in the white for a while."

They were in the living room, Jasper's blanket from the previous night still crumpled on the floor. De la Croix sat in what had been his grandmother's favorite chair, an offensively pale blue recliner gone sweaty-bald-man shiny from decades of use. It reclined no longer on command, but rather at its own whim; it had nearly dumped de la Croix onto the floor when she'd first sat down.

"Go on," he told her.

"So then the text stops in the middle of a sentence, but thirteen pages later, there's a reference to veils in the marginalia that our guys thought was pertinent and seems to be from the same general time period as the stuff about taking them in the white. It seems like your father was describing Bridekiller."

The FBI was in possession of the only thing in the world Jasper could think of as an inheritance from his father: a book Billy had written over his decades-long madness describing the Crows in language alternately lyrical and fuddled, a dense, impenetrable handwritten screed-*cum*-history that followed the rules of logic and syntax as filtered through Billy's diseased brain. Jasper had been led to it by a cryptic comment of his father's and exhumed it from his grandfather's coffin one cold January night when he was seventeen while on the run from the police and on his way to his final confrontation with his parents.

As part of his ultimate plea deal, he'd turned it over to the FBI. They'd spent hundreds of thousands of dollars and some of their best brains on decoding it in the years since.

"Are there historical antecedents?" Jasper asked.

"We have some guys looking into that."

"Because your Bridekiller could be the same guy Billy was describing or someone copying him. These Crows are obsessed with each other. They leave each other little clues, play games, riff on each other's 'art' . . ."

"We know."

"Then what the hell do you need me for?"

"Because he's killed four women in the last seven months and we don't know where to go."

Jasper grunted and held his hand out for the tablet. She brought up the Photos app and gave it to him.

He'd heard of Bridekiller. Serial killer stories had a way of finding him, even when he wasn't trying to find them. Their specific breed of evil and grotesque had a magnetic attraction to his soul, and no matter how hard he tried, the news articles, the roundups, found their way onto his phone and computer as though trained to run a maze that led only to him.

Bridekiller murdered women on their wedding nights. He operated in the Pacific Northwest—of his four victims, three were in the Seattle area, one in Portland. He left the bodies for the new husbands to find.

Jasper swiped through the photos. Four victims. All women, obviously. All white. All brunettes. Each wearing her personal variation on the tried-and-true white wedding gown, that blank map of the future now encroached upon by bloody continents and islands.

Two were in bathtubs. One on a bathroom floor. The last lay face down, crumpled over a hotel toilet as though vomiting up the night's revels had gone pear-shaped.

Swiping further, then back, then forth again. Different angles. Same bodies. Same body type: average. All size eights, maybe, if his eye was accurate.

"What are you seeing?" de la Croix asked with a confidence that grudgingly pleased him.

"Probably not much more than you guys," he admitted. "Look, it's been a while since I've done this. I don't know what you want from me. They're pictures of dead women, OK?" Quite suddenly, he realized he was sweating, a constellation of beads blossoming along his hairline. Ignoring it failed, so he wiped at it with the heel of one hand. It couldn't be the house, still haunted frigid by his grandmother's pissed off, deluded spirit. It was him. Just him.

"You OK?" she asked with something approximating concern.

He didn't answer. Kept swiping. The bodies became a blur of white, red, and black. He'd read somewhere that those were the only colors newborn babies could perceive, and now, unbidden, an image of a baby crawling across a field of bodies crowded into his mind.

"Hates his wife, maybe?" de la Croix ventured, risking a lean forward in the temperamental recliner.

Jasper flipped back and forth, the photos continuing to blur. The baby was crawling, its palms and knees bloodied as it progressed across the red-marred virgin terrain of the brides' bodies. He stood abruptly and threw the tablet down, then strode quickly to the powder room just off the kitchen, ignoring de la Croix's startled shout.

With the door closed, he suffered a sudden and unexpected bout of claustrophobia, but nothing would get him out of this room right now. Braced against the sink, he did not look up into the mirror as he cranked the tap open as wide as it could go, trying to drown the static in his head with the white noise of rushing water.

The baby wasn't in his mind. Not entirely. The baby—blood-streaked and never wholly innocent—was him.

His mother had birthed him solely so that she could kill him. Only his father's twisted interpretative dance of paternal love had saved him. Years later, Jasper repaid the debt by paralyzing Billy and sending him back to jail instead of killing him.

As for his mother . . . he'd tried his best to kill her, something he was still coming to terms with. Not necessarily the effort, but rather the failure.

Shoveling handfuls of water onto his face, he blocked out the world, the dead women, the baby, de la Croix in his living room, prowling and finding who knew what. The water cooled him and slaked him, and eventually he could stop seeing the baby, the bodies. He could stop thinking of his mother, bloody and gasping for breath, her throat caught in the crook of his arm, the throb of his muscles as he choked and choked.

Enough.

There was no towel, for which he could only blame himself and his less than fastidious housekeeping. He stripped off his shirt and used it to mop the water from his face. In doing so, he caught a glimpse of his chest in the mirror. His chest and the tattoo, the damn tattoo he'd gotten years ago, when he'd thought nothing could stop him, nothing could evade him, nothing could hurt him.

Before he'd learned.

He had learned harsh lessons no teenager should have to learn. They echoed still, even in his twenties.

The tattoo dipped along the arc of his clavicle in two-inch-high black Gothic script. Executed backward so that he could read it in a mirror, it said, *I HUNT KILLERS*.

"Stupid," he muttered.

And then, "Shit."

* * *

In his sodden, wrinkled shirt, he stepped out of the powder room. De la Croix stood a few feet away, hesitant.

"Let's go," he told her.

C H A P T E R

2

IT WASN'T RAINING when they landed in Seattle, so the city seemed like a lie from the very start. Jasper disliked it for that reason and also because it was a city at all. Cities were too full of people for him. He preferred his hometown. The Nod was a rusted hulk of an outdated car, but he knew every twitch of its axles and could rebuild its engine blindfolded. That sort of comfort meant a lot.

He white-knuckled the landing, not caring that de la Croix was sitting next to him and noticing. She'd arranged tickets to Seattle before he'd finished packing his bag. At the same time, he'd called Howie to let him know he'd be out of town.

"You're doing *what?*" Howie demanded when Jasper called him, the phone wedged between jaw and shoulder as he fumbled socks and underwear into a beaten-to-hell Lobo's Nod High duffel that had once belonged to his father.

Howie Gersten was Jasper's oldest friend, the only person in the world who'd known him before Billy Dent's depredations became public knowledge and was still willing to remain in his orbit.

"Last I remember," Howie went on, not waiting for an answer, "the FBI is the enemy. They hate you, man. You got one of their agents killed."

It wasn't strictly true, but it also wasn't strictly false. A few years back, on his way to his final and fated confrontation with his parents, Jasper had tried to help catch two Crows in New York City. He'd fumbled badly and as a consequence an agent named Jennifer Morales—who should have known better—was murdered. Leave it to Howie to dredge that up in the most insensitive way possible. One more reason he loved his best friend; Howie never let sentiment or propriety fall as a scrim between Jasper and the truth.

He hadn't thought of Morales in months. Hadn't had the dream where he came across her body in a rented storage unit for nearly a year. There was a part of him that wanted nothing to do with another female FBI agent. He'd have to thrash it out with his therapist at some point.

"I guess they're over it," he told Howie with a lightness he didn't feel. "Look, this is just gonna be a couple of days at the most. I'm going to Seattle to look at the scenes and see what I can see. Then I'm back and we can get back to business."

"Simon'll be pissed."

Simon Dixon. Jasper's business partner, for lack of a better word. Simon was the executive director of WorldVision, an upstart victims' assistance organization. The group did good work under his watchful eye. He was also the only person at WorldVision who knew that Jasper was the organization's founder and source of funding.

He'd called Simon on the way to the airport. "I know I'm going to miss the presentation," Jasper told an exasperated Simon, watching his words carefully in de la Croix's presence. She kept her eyes on the road while pretending not to be listening in. "You can conference me in, if you want."

"This organization either matters to you or it doesn't," Simon said bluntly. Jasper could picture him at his desk, ear-buds in, cupping his face in his hands as he glared straight down at his desk. "You have to commit, Jasper."

"Don't doubt my commitment. Just my poor scheduling skills."

"You shouldn't try to be funny. You're not good at it."

"I've been told that before. We'll talk soon."

As he hung up, de la Croix glanced over at him. "Girlfriend?"

He shrugged. Then he texted Connie. She spent long hours on a theater stage without her cell phone. There was no point calling her.

And now the plane taxied to the gate. Jasper didn't let go of his armrests until the tone sounded that indicated passengers could disembark. He checked his phone. Nothing.

Backstage. On stage. Catching a cat nap back in the dressing room. She could be doing anything at all.

Still, it had been a long flight. He'd hoped to have heard from her by now.

There was no rain in the sky. No smell of it.

By the time they'd pulled onto the highway in another anonymous rental, de la Croix had already contacted the local field office. "We'll hook up with the task force, so you can meet with the local PD, too."

"Don't care about that," he told her. "I don't want other people clouding me up. Just tell me what you know so far. Especially the stuff you've held back from the media."

She licked her lips and hesitated.

"You want me on board or do you want to take me back home?"

"You know, you had the entire flight to look at the file—"

"I don't fly well," he said in his best *are you kidding me* tone.

She nodded. "He roofies the husbands. That's the big thing we've held back."

Jasper leaned back in his seat and stared up at the ceiling. "That makes sense. I was wondering why none of the husbands had anything helpful to offer. You ran blood tests?"

"Of course we did." She sounded truly affronted. "Same drug in every husband. So, it's coming from the same batch. I can get you specifics at the task force, if you want them."

"Not sure I need them, but thanks. Anything else you're holding back?"

"Some minor things. Two of the women had their underwear on. Two didn't. Before you ask: We found the underwear in the hotel rooms, on the floor, so he didn't take a trophy. No evidence of sexual assault, but evidence of sexual activity with one of them."

"Wedding night," Jasper grunted. "Makes sense."

"Did you know most people don't have sex on their wedding night? Either too drunk, too tired, or both."

"That is the least interesting fact I've ever heard."

If she was offended, she didn't show it. "We've confirmed sex/no sex with the husbands, so there's nothing hinky there. All killed by stab wounds. Multiples in some cases."

"Which cases?"

"Second and fourth," she said. "Four stab wounds for victim number two, Rebecca Sizemore. Two for number four, Theresa Van Whitten."

He stared out the window at a perfectly gray, rain-free sky for a long while. Neither of them spoke. At last, he said, "If you're expecting me to say I've cracked it, I hate to disappoint you."

She chuckled and signaled to get off the highway. "We figured it would take you more than the trip from the airport. In fact, we sort of . . ." She darted her eyes at him and slowed as she merged onto the surface street. "We were sort of thinking . . ."

No. He realized what she wanted and mentally slapped himself. Idiot. He should have seen it coming. Should have known from the start.

"We were hoping maybe you could talk to your father—"

"No," he said out loud this time, intending it to be forceful. It came out, instead, as a whisper.

"Just to, y'know, get some intel on the book and that passage," she went on.

"No." Louder. "I don't talk to my father. That part of my life is over. End of story. You want my help, you can have it. You don't get him in the bargain."

"He's the one who wrote the book . . ."

At forty miles an hour, Jasper opened his door. A car in the next lane swerved and honked in surprised anger. De la Croix couldn't slam on the brakes—too much traffic—but she slowed and shouted, "What the hell are you doing?"

"Getting out of the conversation," he told her, and unfastened his seat belt.

"You're—Jesus Christ! Fine! Fine! No more talk about your dad!"

He gave it a heartbeat, then slammed the door.

De la Croix's breath came harsh and fast as she settled back into a driving rhythm. They'd gone maybe half a mile when she spoke again: "You're crazy." She said it without judgment or condemnation.

Jasper shrugged. "Blame my parents."

* * *

The Bridekiller Task Force had set up shop near the Seattle Armory in a part of town called Interbay. De la Croix told Jasper this as she navigated the streets of the city, pointing out the Space Needle every time it peeked above the skyline or popped up between two buildings. Jasper had seen pictures. And

Interbay sounded like a spectacularly bad low-budget science fiction film to him.

The task force lived in an industrial park, in an anonymous two-story chunk of dirty brick with a key-carded set of double glass doors. The only hint of something more intriguing than a medical supply warehouse or rubber gasket distribution facility within was the lack of an overweight rent-a-cop. Instead, just inside the front door was a desk with a severely black-suited man who was doing absolutely nothing to hide the enormous pistol under his left armpit.

"Subtle," Jasper remarked.

"We're not trying to hide," de la Croix told him as she flashed her ID at the sentry. "We didn't have the space we needed downtown, so we moved here."

Jasper flashed no ID. De la Croix had obviously called ahead. He nodded at the guard, who offered a grim little head tilt in response.

They passed through an inner door and into what was clearly a repurposed warehouse space. There were desks arranged in ranks of two down the middle of the floor and temporary office partitions set up in a ring around the perimeter of the facility. Wheeled corkboards, chalkboards, and whiteboards stood at angles to each other, decorated with red lines, circles, photographs, and printouts. Twenty or thirty people—most of them in shirtsleeves and slacks, a few in jeans, a rare two in uniform—rushed and bustled, moving from place to place, from desk to desk, as though tasked with burning as many calories as possible in this one place.

An air of nervous energy and angry intent buzzed, and Jasper thought that if he were Bridekiller and had stumbled on this room, he might just confess on the spot.

"Well done," he murmured.

"What's that?" De la Croix was hanging her coat and hat on a nearby hook.

"You have a nice sense of purpose going here. Get a suspect in here and he'll be terrified."

"Let's hope we get someone to bring in," she said darkly. "Let me introduce you around."

What followed was a blur of faces, names, organizations, and ranks that Jasper didn't bother committing to memory. They seemed too happy to see him. There was hope in their expressions, in their voices. Each of them seemed to come a little more alive. This, he thought, must be how neurosurgeons feel when they meet people with tumors in their brains.

He allowed his hand to be pumped in a succession of annoyingly firm handshakes and managed appropriate expressions of benign interest and muttered platitudes for each new acquaintance. They were all dedicated, as far as he could tell, and also completely superfluous. He wasn't here for them.

Toward the end of the nearly endless meet-and-greet, a self-identified FBI agent held Jasper's hand and attention a little too long, doubtless working up the nerve.

"I've been studying your parents," he said, finally getting to the point and also finally letting Jasper's hand go. "I read your autobiography cover to cover three times. I know you're not in town for this, but I was wondering if I could get just five minutes of your time . . ."

The man had a diseased sort of light in his eyes, a fanatic's tic, a click to his words from too little to drink and too much excitement. Jasper knew a thousand put-downs and shut-downs for this moment, but today he couldn't be bothered. He was, suddenly, exhausted beyond belief. His sofa back in his grandmother's house seemed further than the miles he'd flown, and the frigid Dent house seemed warm in memory.

"I'll see what I can do," he told the agent, then gestured to de la Croix that he was done and it was time to move on.

She ensconced him in an office that had clearly been abandoned on the quick—thumb tacks still pinned shreds of torn-away papers to a wall-mounted corkboard and there was a dregs-fouled mug with a lipstick stain on the desk. He settled into an office chair that still squeaked with newness.

"I'm not here for that," he told her in a low voice, gesturing to the outer area. "I'm not your pet celebrity. I'm here to look at things, ask some questions. If I can help, I will. But I'm not running for office—nix the shaking hands and kissing babies, please, OK?"

She nodded, chewing her bottom lip. "You're right," she said, surprising him. "I'm sorry about that."

"I did stuff when I was younger," he said. "Yeah, I caught some killers. I caught my parents. I was lucky. That's the thing everyone seems to miss when they read my damn book. I got really, really lucky. And even with that luck, my grandmother was killed, my girlfriend ended up with more broken bones than I can count, and my best friend almost bled out on my living room floor."

"And—"

"And Jennifer Morales died," he said before she could. "Believe me, you don't have to remind me. She died. A lot of people died and were hurt. Some good cops lost their jobs. It wasn't fun and games and I'm not the serial killer whisperer. I'll do my best and then I'll leave, and when I go, I won't be walking on water."

She nodded. "Now I get to put you to work?"

"Yeah. Bring me everything."

She arched an eyebrow. "Everything?"

He dragged out the word into its component syllables: "*Ev-er-y-thing.*"

*   *   *

"Everything" turned out to be readily available on a single tablet. Jasper had to hand it to the task force—it was efficient. Every note, photo, test result, impression, and interview had been thoroughly digitized, cataloged, indexed, and uploaded. He sat at the desk he'd been assigned, the office door closed, and swiped through document after document.

At regular intervals, de la Croix—and only de la Croix—would ply him with coffee or water. Around two in the afternoon, she reminded him that he hadn't eaten anything since the plane that morning. He agreed to a chicken wrap and chewed his way through it as he continued studying.

He read an awful lot and learned very little. This was not the fault of anyone on the task force. As best he could tell, the Bridekiller case was a perfect storm of almost everyone in law enforcement doing their jobs to a nigh-perfect standard. They had found every clue, chased down every lead. But there just wasn't enough to go on. He could see why they were stuck, why they were desperate enough to call on a guy in his twenties who'd last chased a killer while in his teens: Bridekiller was going to get away with it. All of it.

Four victims. White. Brunettes. Late twenties/early thirties. Murdered on their wedding nights, left in their gowns to be found by their drugged husbands.

Other than those facts and the geography of the murders, the victims had nothing in common. They hadn't known each other, had had different occupations and hobbies, had run in different social circles. They'd stayed at different hotel chains. There was an exhaustive report from something called the "Social Media/Online Analysis Cohort" (SMOAC—they pronounced it "smoke") that ran to thirty pages before concluding that the four women had absolutely no overlap in their online presences and had never so much as retweeted one another.

He spent some time noodling about with various number replacements for the victims' names, applying the Crows' love of codes and their own peculiar gematria in hopes that something would pop. According to the files, the FBI had already tried this, to no avail, but he figured it couldn't hurt to try again.

Nothing. And despite his assumption, it did hurt: His temples began to throb. Migraine or too much caffeine?

There's no such thing as too much caffeine! It was Howie's voice in his head, mock-horrified. Jasper needed the laugh. Other than horror, the one constant in his life was Howie's ridiculous sense of humor and wholly inappropriate timing.

With a sigh and a rub of his stressed, tired eyes, he leaned back in his chair and stared up at the ceiling. The ceiling stared inscrutably back.

The next time de la Croix eased open the office door, he said, "OK, let's talk."

C H A P T E R

3

S HE BROUGHT ONLY two more people into the office, which he appreciated—he was sure she was tempted to bring more. But the office could barely hold the four of them, and Jasper's comfort level typically maxed out long before the space around him.

Even though he'd met them when he arrived, the man and woman who entered the room were ciphers to him. He remembered nothing except shaking their hands briefly. He thought maybe their names were Sam and Chris. Or perhaps the other way around. He decided not to let it bother him. Sam (or Chris) was the Bureau's behavioral specialist. Chris (or Sam) was the liaison from the Seattle PD. They were both intense and tired, but spoke with minimal formality, which Jasper appreciated.

"We're dead-ended," de la Croix said to begin with. "The last murder was five weeks ago and we have nothing. Not even an estimate on when he might strike again."

"That's the weird thing," Sam (he'd decided she was Sam, the police liaison) admitted. She was leaning against a fragile temporary wall with more confidence in its stability than Jasper would have had. "He's lengthening his time between kills. Makes it harder to predict his next."

"I noticed that," Jasper said. "Usually these guys get more confident as they go along and the high from each kill fades faster and faster, so they have to accelerate."

"There's no pattern," Sam admitted. "He kills the first one. Then three weeks later, the second one. Then it's like five weeks until the third, then almost two months until the fourth."

"It's like he's becoming *less* confident as time goes on, not more," said de la Croix. "He seems to be losing his nerve."

"We think there are constraints on his behavior." Chris, the FBI behaviorist, had unchivalrously taken the last chair. He leaned forward in it, consulting papers on a clipboard. "Something is preventing him from taking action when he wants to or needs to, hence the growing delays. We think he's in a business that requires a lot of travel."

That made sense. "Have you guys done a general Jack Dawes check?" Jasper asked.

Jack Dawes was a cover name and alternate identity shared by the Crows, who thought they were so clever that no one would make the connection between a jackdaw and a crow. Then again, they'd successfully used the name for decades before Jasper stumbled upon it, so maybe they were precisely as clever as they thought. In the years since the capture of Billy and Janice Dent, the Crows certainly should have changed their methodology as a precaution, since they couldn't be aware of what information might have been compromised. Any remotely intelligent criminal would have burned the old identity to the ground. But when dealing with the compulsive nature of serial killers, anything was possible. Jasper had spent much of his life revering a killer named Bobby Joe Long specifically because Long had felt an unalterable and unavoidable compulsion to let his last victim go, a decision that led to his arrest.

The greatest weapon available to the hunter of serial murderers was the irresistible impulse the killers couldn't elude, no matter how hard they tried. It transcended *modus operandi*   it was not a method of operation, but rather a signature, one they could not help but to leave, inscribed in indelible ink.

"The Bureau has been running constant checks on property deeds, driver's licenses, and credit card applications for anyone named Jack, Jonathan, or Jacqueline Dawes since you turned in the book your father wrote," Chris told him, skimming the clipboard. "We've rolled up a bunch of property that appeared to be safe houses and frozen a bunch of credit lines."

"Bet you also pissed off some guys who just happen to be named Jack Dawes, too," Jasper said.

"Well, yeah. But there's nothing connecting that name to this case anywhere in the Pacific Northwest. We've also begun monitoring names that are combinations of your parents', including your mother's maiden name, on the theory that the Crows may begin using them."

For the first time, Jasper found himself caught off guard. That made excellent sense, he hated to admit. The Crows had elevated group solipsism to Olympian levels, and their reverence for their dethroned Crow King and her blood-drenched consort could very well show itself in a new series of aliases.

"Smart," he said with as little begrudging as possible.

If any of the career law enforcement officers in the room took pride or pleasure in his compliment, they didn't evince it.

"That's what we *don't* know," Chris told him. "Here's what we *do* know:

"First of all, Bridekiller isn't his name or even ours. The press gave it to him after the second murder and it's just convenient to use. Anyway, there's a reference in your dad's book—"

"Agent de la Croix enlightened me."

Chris nodded and flipped the page on his clipboard. "Got it. We're feeling pretty confident at this point that the person described in your dad's book isn't the same individual killing women right now. The reference in the Crow Guide—"

"Is that what you call it?"

"Well." Chris shrugged. "We have to call it *something*. Anyway, the reference in the book would have to predate your grandfather's death, since your dad buried the book with him. That would make the individual in the book—let's call him Bridekiller One, OK?—would make him probably something like sixty years old by now. We're not sure he could do this."

He handed over a photo of a scene Jasper had seen already, but from a different angle. Victim number four, Theresa Van Whitten. She lay sprawled in her wedding gown in a tub, yes, but with the new perspective Jasper could see that this was a jetted hot tub, with sides much higher than your standard, run-of-the-mill hotel bathtub.

"Theresa Van Whitten is the heaviest of the victims. Tall girl. Judo teacher. Weighed close to one-eighty. That's a lot of weight, in a long, bulky package."

Not a single person grimaced, objected to, or even blinked at Chris's use of the word *package* to describe a dead woman. It was that kind of room.

"I've known some strong old people," Jasper said.

"We're talking someone in their sixties," de la Croix said. "Maybe even older. And yeah, sure, it's possible to be that fit at that age, but unlikely."

Sam jumped in. "We think the"—she fumbled for the right word—"job—"

"Onus?" de la Croix offered.

"Sure, onus," Sam agreed. "The onus of 'Bridekiller' is sort of like a vocation or an identity passed down from one Crow to another. Or maybe—more likely—taken from one by another. So this new guy, Bridekiller Two, is just picking up where some older Bridekiller left off."

"Do you have stats on women killed on their wedding nights?" Jasper asked. "Instances *not* connected directly to these? From a while back?"

Chris picked up. "We've done a search on similar MOs over the last several years. Nothing there. The problem is when you go back further. The earlier Bridekiller—or Bridekillers; maybe our guy is the third or the tenth—could go back pretty far. Go back far enough and the data isn't tagged or indexed. We have people going through paper records, but it's possible there could have been a guy in the seventies, say, going from small town to small town, killing brides on their wedding nights, and back then no one would have been able to piece it together."

"He'd be a lot older than in his sixties now," Jasper said.

"Yeah, there's no way to know how old Bridekiller One in your dad's book is or would have been."

"Go back far enough and it would have just been a string of disconnected local tragedies," de la Croix put in.

Jasper nodded, pretending to take it all in. In truth, there was nothing *to* take in. He'd looked at all of the information and evidence; he'd absorbed it as best he could. At the end of the day, though, there was a man out there killing women for reasons known only to him, and there was nothing that led to him. Everything else was conjecture and supposition.

"Let's take a look at the crime scenes," Jasper said.

De la Croix startled. She and the others shared a brief, almost intimate look. Jasper thought he detected disappointment in it. *This is the great human radar gun for serial killers?* they seemed to beam to each other.

"It's been a while," Sam said, clearing her throat. "They've all been processed. There's nothing left to see."

Jasper stood. "Sure there is. Whatever *he* saw."

4

WHATEVER *HE* SAW.

The police were always obsessed with what was left behind, clues like the droppings of a predator on the veldt. But Jasper knew that what mattered almost as much was what the killer saw *before* the killing. Environment and action were causally related. He had learned many things at the side of his father—how to dispose of evidence, how to reduce a body to its component parts for quick removal, how to leave false clues to throw the "bastard cops" off the trail.

But he'd also learned how to pick the assault site. How to maximize reward and minimize risk with the proper assessment of the environment and the best possible location. How to avoid leaving clues in the first place by being aware of the setting and everything within.

Whatever *he* saw.

Jasper replayed it in his head over and over on the way to the first crime scene, which also happened to be the closest to the task force's headquarters.

Whatever *he* saw.

He because most serial killers—overwhelmingly so—were men. It was a small and accurate bigotry to assume the killer was a man, even to someone with Jasper's life experience, someone who had witnessed the murder-rage of his own mother and nearly succumbed to it.

On cold days, the spot where she'd driven a knife into his side three times ached. When it rained, his chest throbbed where she'd shot him.

At those times, the only balm for his pain was to think of her where he'd left her: in a bed at Kettle-Herrara Care Institute roughly forty-five minutes from Lobo's Nod, where she lay in a vegetative state. Had since the night eight years ago when they'd tried and failed to kill each other. He visited her often—to be sure, to see with his own eyes that she was still there—and on the days when the pain was great, the temptation to sign the order to terminate her life support oozed over him like a mud bath.

Bridekiller could very well be a woman. A jealous or snubbed or maltreated woman looking for . . . revenge? Satisfaction? Justice?

"We considered it," de la Croix told him when he ventured the possibility. She was at the wheel and they were alone in the car. A surfeit of task force members had offered to accompany them. De la Croix—suddenly and quite scarily adept at assessing Jasper's moods—declined them all.

"We just think the evidence points to a man, with a man's strength," she went on. "I know how sexist that sounds."

"Is biology sexist now?" he asked. "Men are generally stronger than women."

"I could bench-press you." She spoke without hesitation or a trace of boast.

"Oh, so you killed them?"

"Not a chance. I'm just saying: We play the percentages. Most likely a man. But if something seems to point to a woman, I don't think anyone on the task force would ignore it."

"Good to know." He knew the odds, too, and they overwhelmingly predicted a man. Then again, he'd thought the

Crow King would be a man, and it had turned out to be his own mother.

"If you have any particular insight into what might make a woman a more likely suspect . . ." She trailed off into a silence almost as uncomfortable as what she'd just said.

He broke the tension with a short, sharp bark of laughter. "What you mean to say is 'If any of this is making you think of your mommy, let me know,' right?"

She fell silent again.

*   *   *

The crime scenes were familiar to him—he'd seen the photographs and "walked" the spatial video compilations. He had hoped that being within them physically he would notice something that would lead to something else that would lead to something else. But they were just three hotel rooms. Two honeymoon suites, one regular room. Nothing special or extravagant about them. Nothing that screamed, "Hey! I'm a clue! Over here!"

The fourth room was too far away for tonight, down in Portland. They would go tomorrow, de la Croix promised him. If he still wanted to, she'd added, half curious, half discouraging.

Jasper sighed and leaned against the wall in the third of the three rooms he'd examined. This one had been occupied, and the visitors had graciously agreed to step outside and let the police take a look. Jasper hadn't been in the room when hotel management had given them the reason for the interruption, but he imagined the guests would be demanding a new room soon.

Nothing. Nothing. Nothing. It was a litany and a screed all at once. He had absolutely nothing.

"Maybe the only killers I'm good at catching are the ones I'm related to."

"What?" said de la Croix.

He hadn't realized he'd spoken out loud. Embarrassed, he waved her away.

Once upon a time, he'd flattered himself that he could think like a killer, that he could penetrate the bloody fog surrounding their consciences and moralities, drill down into the core of their madness. He didn't necessarily like it, but he could understand it.

A few people had been foolish enough to believe him. Jennifer Morales died for her faith. Detective Louis Hughes lost his badge when in desperation he broke the NYPD's rules and got Jasper involved in a serial killer manhunt. And poor G. William Tanner, long-time sheriff of Jasper's hometown, had thought he was helping Jasper get over his father's depredations by letting him see some case files.

And, yes, to his credit all of those killers had been caught. But the price was high, both to Jasper's fragile sanity and to the people who'd trusted him.

He'd never been able to penetrate that fog, he knew now. He'd just been able to recognize it for what it was, to perceive its footprints and track its spoor.

With a sigh of regret, he realized he hadn't called G. William before leaving town. The old man would miss their weekly Scrabble session.

"This isn't getting us anywhere," he admitted. "How about I talk to the husbands?"

De la Croix hesitated only a moment before checking her watch. "It's getting late. I can have someone round up the locals to meet with you at the task force in the morning. We'll do a Zoom with Portland. Or would you rather see them where they live?"

Intruding on grieving men in the tainted confines of their homes held no appeal for him. He told her that the task force office would be fine and then let her drive him to his own hotel, paid for by the Bureau.

It was too late back east to call G. William, so he sent an apologetic, explanatory text. Then he checked to see if Connie had texted back, even though he knew he would have gotten an alert if she had.

Nothing from her. He told himself that didn't mean anything. Their relationship was like the subatomic particles he'd read about once, the ones that scientists had managed to split and then send on different paths. Somehow, despite their separation, they remained invisibly and intangibly connected. When one experienced a change in direction or spin, the other did as well. No one could explain it. Even Einstein had been reduced to calling it "spooky action at a distance." Very scientific.

Separate, yet connected. She was still connected to him. He had to believe that. It wasn't that he couldn't imagine his life without her; it was that he could do precisely that, all too easily.

Spooky.

He fell into bed and sleep took him quickly.

*　*　*

And that night, he dreamed.

He dreamed of the Impressionist. Fredrick Thurber. The first serial killer he'd ever caught. Thurber had harrowed Lobo's Nod with a series of murders that replicated Billy's own. Jasper had been convinced that everyone in town would assume he was the killer, given that his father had made a life of murder. So he decided that he had to find the killer in order to prove them all wrong. He'd shamelessly manipulated G. William into violating all sorts of protocols and gotten access to some of the case files. Eventually, he and his friends had stopped the Impressionist. But not before more people died.

Howie, Connie, even G. William—they all told him that those people would have died anyway. Most likely along with even more. But Jasper would never allow himself to believe them. If he had kept out of it, if he had let the police do their jobs, maybe those people—Helen Myerson and Virginia Davis—would still be alive today.

But Helen and Virginia did not feature in his dream. Only Thurber. He was aware it was a dream, so even as Thurber approached him, Jasper knew that the man was actually sitting on death row at the Riverbend Maximum Security Institution, waiting for his appeals to run out, waiting for a ride to Nashville and an appointment with a needle.

Thurber grinned at Jasper and spoke with Jasper's mother's voice. "This is where we always end up."

"I don't want to go there," Jasper said. It was a dream. He was aware it made no sense and yet the words seemed hamstrung by some unknowable imperative.

He was in school, at Lobo's Nod High. Ginny Davis told him he was late for play practice, and even though she was dead, he figured he should listen to her. But he couldn't remember how to get to the auditorium. Every hallway he walked down, he could hear the sounds of play rehearsal, but every time he turned, the noise seemed to come from behind him.

Billy strolled out of a classroom. Jasper's nuts tightened in fear, and Billy laughed. "Don't fear me, boy. I'm the one who loves you."

He ran down the hall. If he could get to play practice, everything would be all right. Connie was in the play, too. She would be there. She would help him.

"Someday you're gonna marry that girl," Billy prophesied, keeping pace. He grinned and then disappeared. Jasper kept running, his breath coming faster and faster.

He turned a corner and found himself in bed, on his back. There were severed fingers strewn around him, and Thurber was back, tilting his head back and forth, singing a song that Jasper couldn't quite make out but that he knew he knew.

"You're going to be mine," Thurber said, climbing onto the bed and turning into Jasper's mother, dressed in an ornate white wedding gown.

"No." He was being held down. Something was holding him down. "I'm not yours. I'm going to marry Connie. Even Billy said so."

His mother hiked up the gown and straddled him. When had he become naked? Had he been naked the whole time?

This is only a dream, he reminded himself. Dream or not, though, he didn't want this.

"Yes, you do," she said. "Do you even remember our first time? You were such a little boy."

"Let me go!" he screamed, and looked, and saw that nothing was holding him down, that he was here of his own free will, that he wanted it.

"I don't want this!" he cried as she moved on him. "I'm going to marry Connie!"

"Of course you are," his mother murmured, her hands on his chest, her rhythm increasing. "See?"

And he looked over. There was a bathtub there and Connie in a wedding gown, her throat slit, the gown gone black-red with her blood and his mother intensified her rocking and he couldn't breathe he was choking choking he couldn't breathe and

CHAPTER

5

HE SHOT BOLT upright in bed, clutching at his chest.

"No." His voice was strangled, his breath a hard-fought victory. "No. Damn. No."

According to the clock, he'd been asleep only an hour. He fumbled for his phone and tapped on Dr. Cyrus McCutcheon, his therapist. He hated McCutcheon with a passion, but all of the important people in his life—Connie, her parents, Howie, G. William—had come together and informed him that if he didn't get into therapy and stay in, they would have nothing more to do with him.

He'd believed them. He still did. It was for his own good. Didn't make it any less unpleasant or hateful.

But right now . . .

"I'm sorry," he said when McCutcheon picked up. "I'm sorry to call you so late." He added three hours to the bedside clock. "So, so late. I'm sorry."

"Jasper, it's all right."

"Tell Maria I'm sorry."

"She's still asleep. I'm heading downstairs. Can you give me a second?"

Jasper sank against the pillows. He was painfully, embarrassingly erect. He told McCutcheon he could wait, then lay there, hating himself.

Just a dream, he told himself. Dreams are just dreams. But how many men dreamed about having sex with their own mothers? How many dreamed about wanting it?

How many of them actually had?

It was a mark of progress that he no longer vomited when thinking of his mother's revelation that she'd taken his virginity at age six—a memory he'd blocked out. A chill wracked his body and, shivering, he pulled the covers higher.

"Tell me about your dream," McCutcheon said abruptly. He must have made it downstairs.

Jasper didn't ask how he knew it was a dream. The man could read a clock. He didn't want to talk about the dream. It had taken seven tortuous months of thrice-weekly sessions before Jasper had finally revealed to McCutcheon that his mother had raped him as a child. It had taken even longer to progress to the point that he could actually use the word *rape*.

When he closed his eyes, Jasper could picture McCutcheon settling into a chair in his home office right now, his shaggy gray hair pulled in different cotton candy directions, his bifocals roosting at the very tip of his misshapen nose. McCutcheon had the look of a retired prizefighter, one who stepped down not voluntarily, but rather because no one would let him back into the ring to hurt himself again. He had a bulldog's mien and the forbearance of an angry nun.

"It's your dime," McCutcheon said after a long silence.

"Sometimes it's just nice knowing someone is listening. Even if I'm not talking."

A grunt squeezed its way through the ether between them.

"Fine, then," Jasper said, and proceeded to tell him about the dream. Unfurling the banners of his secrets and fears had become more palatable, but no easier over the years. It took him a while to get through it, with much back-filling and explication.

"Tell me what it means, Doc," he cracked at the end.

"Let me bust out my dream translation dictionary," McCutcheon said with the sort of dry wit that only comes at a roused three in the morning. "Look, believe it or not, I think this is a good thing."

"Oh, sure."

"You've made progress. A year ago, if you'd had that dream, you would have called the Institute to make sure your mother was still in a coma."

"Permanent vegetative state."

"Right. But you didn't."

Someone shuffled by his hotel room door, sending alarm signals through his extremities. A moment later, he heard a drunken giggle, followed by an audible, but incomprehensible slurry of words, then a door unlocking down the hall.

"There's more," he told McCutcheon, and proceeded to tell him about Bridekiller, de la Croix, the trip to Seattle. "I know—it's bad, it's stupid, it's reopening old wounds, but—"

"Actually, I'll surprise you and tell you that I think this is good for you. It's a way of confronting some things you've been burying for a long time."

"I hate when you do that."

"When I say the opposite of what you expect me to say?"

"And when you do *that* and say exactly what I expect you to say." He shifted the phone to his other ear. He was wide awake and the dream seemed like a movie he'd seen once and mostly forgotten. He felt ridiculous for calling McCutcheon. Every time they spoke, he remembered again that he didn't like the guy, something McCutcheon knew and accepted with annoyingly gruff equanimity.

"Normally therapy encourages a cordial if not friendly relationship," he'd said to Jasper during one session. "In your case, I'm OK having you hate me. You don't respect people you like."

Jasper had responded with the sort of heat only possessed by the truly affronted: "You're full of it. I like Connie and Howie."

"And you defy them and ignore their advice at every turn."

If it hadn't been true, Jasper wouldn't have sulked for the rest of that session.

Now, thinking back to that, he wondered how he'd come to this pass, tethered to a man he disliked intensely because, paradoxically, that same man was the only one he could actually listen to, the only one whose advice he considered. The love of his life and his best friend since childhood would face gunfire for him. They had both been grievously injured during and by his teen foolishness; they literally bore scars of that time. Yet he couldn't heed them, only this man he hated.

"So I stick around and help the FBI? Or have I already confronted enough demons that I get to go home?"

"I can't tell you which road to walk. I can only walk it with you."

With that helpful *bon mot*, they wrapped up the call. Despite himself, Jasper had to admit he felt better.

Still, he did not sleep the rest of the night.

6

THERE WAS NOTHING to the men.

They were technically husbands, technically widowers, but Jasper had trouble thinking of them that way. The ink on their marriage certificates had not even dried by the time their wives were dead. He couldn't imagine what that must feel like and was cheered to realize that he had no desire to find out.

They all had the same stories, shifting and changing only in details. In a crime, some details mattered and some didn't. In these crimes, none of the differences manifested any sort of weight or importance.

The story went like this:

Chapter One—Wedding! Yay! Everyone happy! Party! Drinks! Laughter!

(Some began with a Prologue—Met her! Best day of my life! Soulmate!—followed by tears that left Jasper simultaneously annoyed and helpless and guilt-ridden.)

Chapter Two—To the honeymoon suite! Joke about getting lucky from drunk best friend! Stumble to the room! (Two men attempt to carry bride over threshold, a fact they seem quite earnestly to want him to absorb.)

Chapter Three—Too drunk/too tired for sex. Lots of laughter. TV! (Stories varied here as to *what* was watched, with each man desperate to imagine it somehow mattered.)

Chapter Four—Sleep!

Chapter Five—The story takes a dark turn. Husband awakens. Bleary-eyed and groggy. Can't remember where he is or how he got there. Stumbles out of bed to bathroom . . .

The end.

Not a novel, after all. Just the world's shittiest short story.

They all described symptoms of exposure to Rohypnol. All had tested positive for the drug. Three of them had such strong reactions that they had difficulty moving and impaired memory for hours after waking.

They were two white men, one Asian, one African American. Morris Gibson, the Black man, had been convinced the killing was racially motivated, some white supremacist lodging a murderous protest against interracial marriage, until he learned about the other murders. He was the third survivor.

They all wallowed in self-recrimination: They could have done *something*. They shouldn't have had so much to drink. They should have double-checked the locks on the doors. They should have and should have and should have.

They each wanted him to punish them. They each wanted him to assuage them.

He could do neither. He could only listen. He could only walk the road with them, he realized.

*　*　*

Only one of the men stood out to him at all, the second victim's husband, Patrick Olefsky. He'd been the lucky one who'd metabolized the Rohypnol fastest and had pushed through the side effects. In his mid-forties, Patrick had a full head of light brown hair, a pair of too-large ears, and a smallish nose upon which perched horn-rimmed glasses magnifying dull brown eyes. He was the oldest of the husbands and smaller than any of them, yet had recovered more quickly. Proving that science wasn't always an exact science.

His wife, Rebecca Sizemore, had been only twenty-seven. Jasper didn't judge.

At first, he couldn't figure out what made Olefsky stand out to him. But after a few minutes in the man's presence, he came to realize that Olefsky held himself differently, acted in a manner distinct from the other men. He was just as bereft, but there was a level of awareness and self-control that the others lacked, cloaked as they were in the commonality of their anguish. Jasper surreptitiously checked his notes. Mystery solved: Olefsky was a psychiatrist. Of course.

"Did you know any of the other men, Dr. Olefsky?"

Olefsky seemed caught off guard for a moment. "I'm not . . . I'm not practicing any longer. You don't have to call me *doctor.*"

"I didn't realize." He contemplated asking *why* Olefsky was no longer a doctor but decided to hold that back. He repeated his question.

"No. And I still don't. Just their names from the news."

"What about the women? The victims?"

"No."

When people answered questions quickly, Jasper had learned, it often meant they were *too* confident of their responses. "Are you sure?" he asked.

None of the other men had taken the time to reconsider; they'd just issued flat denials again. Olefsky frowned and pondered for a few seconds. "I mean," he said slowly, "I suppose it's possible some of us bumped into each other at some point. Seattle's not *that* big. So, technically . . . But you could show me photographs of them and I wouldn't recognize them."

"How can you be so sure of that?"

He permitted himself the smallest and saddest of smiles. "Because the police did, and I didn't."

"Doctor . . ." Jasper caught himself. "Sorry. Mr. Olefsky—"

"Patrick is fine. Really."

"Fine. Patrick, then. Look, I know you've been through all of this repeatedly with the police and the FBI. I'm not trying to force you to relive your pain. But if there's anything at all you can think of, any detail . . ."

"If reliving my pain would locate the guy who did this, I would put myself back in that hotel room a hundred times," Patrick said resolutely. "No, make that a thousand times." His fury abated, dissolving into a sigh. "But I don't remember anything. The Rohypnol."

Doctor. *Former* doctor. The only one of the men who used the drug's proper name, not *roofie*.

"You got lucky. Recovered relatively quickly," Jasper told him.

"I did?" This seemed to surprise him. "It didn't feel like it. I was woozy for hours. It felt like my head had been used as a tackle dummy."

Jasper nodded. No matter how quickly he'd recovered, that couldn't make up for the blank caesura of memory filled with the murder of his wife.

"I bought your book," Patrick said suddenly. "When it came out, a few years ago."

"My accountant thanks you," Jasper said neutrally.

The book. His memoir. Flashily and predictably titled *A Murder of Crows,* with the glaring and lurid subtitle *My Life Inside the Serial Killer Conspiracy.* Jasper had written it only because his legal bills were enormous, his future job prospects dim after he'd achieved a breathtaking level of national notoriety for someone so young. He loved that the book had made his life possible but hated that it existed.

"I didn't just buy it. I read it. I was fascinated. And I think as a professional, I sort of—"

"Can we talk about something other than me?"

Patrick nodded slowly and cleaned his glasses with a handkerchief he'd produced from his rear pocket. The only other man Jasper knew who actually carried a handkerchief was G. William, back in the Nod. He couldn't help staring as Patrick slowly, methodically brought his lenses to a perfect clarity.

"I'm sorry." He rested the spectacles on his nose again. "It's difficult to talk about that night. I'm deflecting. I'll try not to let it happen again."

Deflecting. Jasper knew the language of therapy too well at this point. It was odd, though, having it aimed at him by someone other than McCutcheon.

"Let's go back to that night. Did you realize you'd been roofied?"

"Not at first." He shook his head like a man who's just been dealt a royal flush with one card off. "I couldn't think straight. Or see straight. And then I saw . . ." He choked a bit, pinched the bridge of his nose. "Sorry. Just need a minute."

"Take your time," Jasper said insincerely. He regretted his tone, but it was lost on Olefsky, who took several deep breaths before continuing.

"I saw her there, in the bathtub, and I just . . . Time just went away, you know?"

"Did you black out again?"

"No. No. I just couldn't make myself move."

"Had you touched her? Did you know she was dead?"

"Of course I did. I'm a doctor. I know a . . ." He pursed his lips. "That much blood. All that blood. No one could . . ."

"I get it. When did you realize you'd been roofied?"

He sighed. "Sometime after the police came. They kept asking me all these specific questions about what we did after we checked in, and I couldn't remember *anything*. And that's when it occurred to me."

"What did you drink that night? And when?"

Olefsky blew out his lips in annoyance. "It was my wedding. I drank all night. Mostly whiskey. From the same open bar as everyone else."

The FBI had interviewed the bartenders and caterers for all four weddings. There were no connections.

Jasper flipped desultorily through Olefsky's file. There were a thousand more questions to ask. But the FBI had asked them all, and before that the Seattle police had asked them all, and before *that* the Seattle police had asked a previous time at the scene. What would be gained by asking the questions yet again?

Olefsky's story hadn't changed. None of the men's stories had changed.

He sighed far longer and far more theatrically than he intended.

Olefsky didn't miss it. "If you don't mind my saying . . . You have all the signs of exhaustion. Have you been sleeping well?"

"I thought you weren't going to deflect anymore?"

Patrick offered a brief chuckle, one that sounded rusty and disused. "I'm sorry. You're right."

"I think we're done here," Jasper told him, and in that moment, realized he was talking not just about Patrick, but about the whole damn task force.

*   *   *

"It's a dead end," he told de la Croix later, in the hovel of an office. "And I'm not telling you anything you don't already know, am I?"

He was still vaguely annoyed at Olefsky's attempts to diagnose him, though he knew deep down that it was just an occupational hazard . . . and that the man was right. Which possibly annoyed him even more.

He refocused on de la Croix, who reluctantly nodded. "We've been at an impasse for a while. We thought you might shake something loose."

"I'm sorry. But every lead you guys have chased down, every shred of evidence . . . It all leads nowhere. I hate to say it because it sounds brutal, but—"

"But unless he strikes again and gives us some new evidence to work with, we've got nothing to go on. Believe me, I know." She had been sipping at a bottle of Coke and now stared at it with disgust, as though it had turned to liquified guano. "We spend half our time hoping he never strikes again and the other half thinking, 'Maybe if he messes up and doesn't actually kill the next one . . .' It's morbid as hell and we hate ourselves for it." With a grimace of hope, she stared at him, opened her mouth, then said nothing.

"I'm sorry," he said again.

She drove him back to his hotel and promised to get him his return flight details soon. She would have him on a flight out in the morning, leaving him one more night in a Seattle that still stubbornly refused to muster so much as a drizzle for him. He did not relish the prospect of another sleepless night, but he had no choice. He threw his things into his bag so that he could be ready to go first thing, then glanced around the room as though the demons that had brought his nightmare could be sought out and bound and forced to stay here. It was a nice thought, but a foolish one.

He slumped into the room's armchair. He was so tired. Exhaustion. Patrick had been right. Between memories keeping him awake and nightmares waking him from hard-fought slumber, he couldn't remember the last time he'd slept eight hours in a row. But he was so tired that maybe tonight he *would* actually sleep.

A knock at the door surprised him; de la Croix would have just called with the flight info, he figured. But he opened the door and a man dressed head-to-toe in black, including a black balaclava, punched him in the face before he could react.

Jasper wasn't much of a fighter. He'd gotten by schoolyard scrapes as a kid based on ferocity and reputation more than anything else. The last time he'd thrown a punch had been at his mother, eight years ago.

His tolerance for pain was pretty high, though. He didn't move quickly enough to block the blow, but it also didn't knock him to the floor. He'd been shot and stabbed multiple times in his life; a punch to the face was manageable.

But he couldn't react in enough time to evade the next punch, which caught him across the jaw and sent him spinning to the floor. The open door fetched up against the side of his head; bells rang; his vision blurred. The man in the doorway stepped inside, drew back his foot, and kicked Jasper in the ribs, just a couple of inches above the knife scar. Pain lanced up his side like a flash of red lightning. He put up his hands to protect his face, but too late   the next kick connected with his temple. His vision went black for an instant, then exploded into something grainy from an old TV set with a busted antenna.

The bad news: The man's foot was drawing back again.

The good news: Jasper passed out before he could feel the next kick.

C H A P T E R

7

WHY DID THEY call it "a ringing in your ears"? It sounded more like a pop song hook playing over and over again, a low and insistent bass line bracketed by a synth beat as annoying as a bored toddler. Jasper couldn't make the sound stop, no matter how much he tried to sink back into the darkness, so he forced his eyes open.

The world slewed at him. Rough hotel carpet abraded his cheek. He blinked his vision clear. The sound assaulted him some more; he recognized it now—the chorus to some idiotic song that Connie had chosen for his ringtone, knowing he would have no idea how to change it. It riled him so much that it forced him to answer his phone, a courtesy he resisted and that she'd been trying to drill into him for years.

His phone lay on the carpet a few feet away. His vision doubled; there were two phones. That was all right, though—apparently he had two right hands with which to reach for them.

Of course, the phone stopped ringing the instant his fingers touched it.

Droplets of pain dripped along his temple, searing hot down to his jawline. He tasted blood, but a quick series of strokes with his tongue confirmed that he hadn't lost any teeth. That was nice. It was a good day when you had all of your teeth, he decided.

A memory flash assailed him: He was a child. Opening his father's nightstand drawer. A half dozen yellow-white human teeth clattered into view.

Like a featherweight too stupid to realize he'd gotten in the ring with a heavyweight, he pushed off the floor and contorted himself into something like a sitting position. The room dipped and spun some more; he closed his eyes against the swirl and felt himself ready to pass out again. When he opened his eyes, the room had stabilized a bit.

Propped up against the room's mini-fridge, he realized he was now holding his phone. His eyes wouldn't cooperate enough to focus on the notifications, but with muscle memory he was able to flip on the selfie cam.

The sight that greeted him was not nearly as bad as he'd feared. No one likes to take a beating, but after almost dying at the hands of his own mother, he had a measured perspective on it. His left eye was black and swelling shut. A small patch of skin had torn away from his temple and hung in a flap; coagulated blood clumped there and tattooed its way along that side of his face. His jawline looked like he'd tried to replace his mandible with an eggplant. All things considered, if you were going to get kicked in the face, the mandible was the place for it. It was the biggest and strongest bone in the face. If the kick had landed on his cheek, he'd probably be looking at broken bones and a decidedly concave mien.

He raised his shirt. From the knife scar up to his armpit, his entire right side was a mass of yellow and black, as though an aggressive rock band had used him as a drum kit replacement. But he could breathe and he knew the feeling of broken ribs from experience—this wasn't it.

It took him another moment to grasp that he might not be alone. Fortunately, the room was small and the bathroom door stood open. From his vantage point, he could tell he'd been left on his own after the beating, with the room door firmly shut. *What a polite attacker*, Howie would no doubt say. *Clearly raised with manners.*

His vision settled on one version of reality, no doubt due to the left eye swelling shut. Two notifications on his screen, along with the time. It was half-past six in the evening, so he'd been unconscious for two hours.

First notification: Voicemail from de la Croix.

Second notification: A text from Connie. be careful

Great idea. Why didn't I think of that?

He played the voicemail.

"Jasper, it's de la Croix." Her voice was excited, electric enough to power a Jumbotron. "Unpack your bags. I'm on my way over. We have something new. He sent us a letter. He sent us a letter!"

Jasper leaned back against the mini fridge and sighed. A static had begun crackling in his ear. He clawed at the side of his head, but it persisted.

After a moment, he realized it wasn't static and it wasn't in his head; it was outside. It had finally started raining.

About damn time, he thought.

C H A P T E R

8

"SHOW ME THE letter," Jasper told de la Croix as an EMT laid careful butterfly bandages along his temple.

Arms folded over her chest, she looked both angry and concerned at once. Someone with a normal childhood might have called it *maternal*.

Jasper wasn't that guy.

"Are you kidding me?" she said. "Are you really kidding me right now?"

"Show me the letter."

"Not a chance. First we have to discuss . . . this."

She gestured to the room in general. Jasper flicked his gaze around. It was a bad time for Seattle-area hotels, he figured. Murders and now an assault. A CSI team had practically dismantled the room, except for the chair on which Jasper sat while the EMT finished up her ministrations. He was covered in bandages, a not-unfamiliar sensation. The one benefit to the pain radiating from three distinct portions of his head was that it made the rain-induced throb of his old bullet wound that much easier to ignore.

"There are a lot of possibilities," Jasper told her.

"Oh?" Arching an eyebrow in a manner both sarcastic and incredulous.

"I don't think it was Bridekiller," Jasper went on, ignoring her pose and her obvious disquiet and her eyebrow. "He wouldn't know I was here and involved. And it's too risky to come after me in person."

"He obviously was petrified of your fighting prowess."

De la Croix's concern was giving way to annoyance.

"You really should let me take you to the hospital," the EMT said. "X-rays on your chest and jaw, MRI to make sure you don't have a concussion."

"I'm fine," he assured her, and flashed his most Billy Dent smile at her, the one he had learned from observing his father, the one that defused situations instantly.

The EMT merely rolled her eyes and shrugged, then packed up her kit. Jasper frowned. His swollen jaw must be throwing off his game. He tried again, but she just blew out an exasperated breath and left the room.

Jasper idly watched the CSI team for a long moment. Fingerprint dust. Luminol sprays. UV lights. A videographer and someone wielding a complicated-looking shoulder rig with an iPhone attached to it. From what he overheard, he understood that this person was shooting spatial video for later use in AR and VR.

"Show me the letter," he tried again without turning back to her, and when de la Croix merely snorted in response: "Why are you pissed at me?"

"Because you just had the shit kicked out of you and you won't let us take care of you."

He looked over at her. Her fuming made her seem younger. With one finger crooked toward the bandages on his head, he managed a lopsided grin. "See? I'm taken care of. Show me the—"

"You heard the EMT. You should be at the hospital."

He shook his head and immediately regretted it as a wave of nausea battered him and then settled into his lower gut. With a deep breath and a pretend hiccup, he managed to cover it.

He thought. De la Croix gazed at him suspiciously.

"I know what a concussion feels like," he assured her. "And I know what broken ribs feel like."

"What about your jaw?"

"I can talk. I can smile. At some point, I'll eat. I'm fine, de la Croix. Seriously. I've been shot, stabbed, and beaten, and it hasn't stopped me yet. Show me the letter."

Uncrossing and recrossing her arms over her chest, she glared at him. "I have no time for your male bravado crap. And I especially don't have the time to deal with my superiors if I turn you back in broken."

He sighed. There was no point arguing with her, so he simply moved on to the next issue.

"Five-eleven, maybe six foot at the most. Big shoulders. A bit of a gut. White. Brown eyes. Eyebrows indicate dark brown hair. And I've just described the majority of males in the region, so . . ." He shrugged. "Did you get all of that?"

De la Croix gestured off to Jasper's left. A Seattle PD uniformed officer stood there, holding out his phone to record everything Jasper had said.

"Great! Show me the letter."

"Excuse me." It was a Seattle detective, wearing jeans and a gray pullover, his badge slung around his neck. "The hotel has cleared another room for you. We'd like to get you out of here and move your things . . ."

Jasper nodded. "Sure."

*　*　*

A few moments later, he was one floor down, in a room identical to the one in which he'd been assaulted, except for a different piece of artwork hanging over the bed. This one was mostly oranges and blues, and it took him longer than he'd've liked to admit to ascertain that it was a whale breeching at sunset. Then again, what was a Tennessee boy supposed to know about whales?

The room offered two chairs—a mesh-backed roller chair at the tiny desk and a faux leather slab with arms that looked like it should recline, but absolutely did not. Jasper chose the not-recliner and sighed into it. De la Croix sat at the desk and said nothing as a uniformed officer brought Jasper's duffel in and left it near the closet. She did not speak until the uniform was gone, the door closed behind him.

"Are you really OK?" she asked, her voice low and laden with concern. "I know you want to seem invincible, but—"

"I swear I'm fine," he told her. And he was. The strange and nigh-toxic brew of adrenaline and sleeplessness had him wired. It was a second wind with a jolt of amphetamine. "I've got a minibar and an ice machine. I'll be OK. Show me the letter."

"No. We need to talk about what just happened."

"It's not a mystery for you to solve," he told her. "Someone spotted me. At the airport. Or here at the hotel, earlier."

Once he'd called de la Croix from his place on the floor, braced against the mini-fridge, it had been less than two minutes before hotel security arrived on the scene. It took four minutes after that for Seattle PD to arrive, another minute for the EMT, and then ten more minutes before de la Croix herself walked through the door. He'd had time to think it through, to piece together how the man in the balaclava had ended up at his door.

"You have it all figured out, don't you?" Her asperity stung.

"No. Not entirely. But there are a lot of people in the world who would like to beat the hell out of me." Someone had slipped him an ice pack during the transit from one room to the other. With a hiss of pain, he placed it against his left eye. Too late to stop the swelling, but after the initial shock and pressure, the cold took away some of the pain.

"A Crow?" she said. Despite herself, she was intrigued, leaning forward, elbows on knees. "Not necessarily Bridekiller, but another one? Looking for revenge for what you did to your parents?"

"Could be. Could also be the family of one of my father's victims."

She clucked her tongue as though that hadn't occurred to her.

"Does that happen a lot? Your dad's victims seek you out for a beating?"

"I've encountered a bunch of them over the years. Always emotional, never violent." He shrugged in a way that lit his side on fire. "First time for everything."

Speaking of his father's victims made him think of World-Vision. And Simon. They were trying to build something, something enduring, something to help those left behind after the depredations of people like his father. The pain and the suffering, he knew, went on forever. It dimmed, but did not fade out. And if the pain went on forever, so too should the help.

It sounded noble and easy. One of those was true.

"I'll be careful," he told her. "I didn't even look through the peephole. It was stupid of me. Billy was out here early on in his career. Killed three. Not much of a stretch to imagine there's a brother or father or uncle or best friend who's still pissed."

Her phone was already out. "I'll have someone pull the files from those murders and we'll start looking up—"

"No." He managed to stand. "Don't get distracted. And now, for real: Show. Me. The letter."

With a nod and a sigh, she rummaged in her purse and produced an iPad, this one smaller than the one she'd shown him before. She fiddled with it for a moment, then handed it over.

The screen showed a scan of a sheet of plain white paper. The text was single-spaced in a sans serif font.

"Nothing special about the paper," de la Croix said before he could ask. "The font is Arial and something about the kerning or the leading or some such nonsense makes our experts think he typed it on a Windows PC as opposed to a Mac. We're narrowing down the exact model of printer, but it's an HP."

Jasper clucked his tongue and started reading the letter.

> Dear police.
>
> You think you can catch me but you can not. I am unstopable. And you should know that by now.

"Improper punctuation," Jasper muttered. "Spelling mistakes. Some weird grammar . . ."

"Chris is looking at it," de la Croix assured him. It took him a moment to remember: Chris, the FBI behaviorist. He'd had to fly back to Quantico, but Jasper supposed you didn't have to be on-scene to analyze a letter.

"Wait until you get to the end," de la Croix said.

He resisted the urge to skip ahead and just kept reading:

> You most likly have "_experts_" telling you what to think about me but they are very **very** _wrong_. I did not kill them because I hated them. I killed them to save them from themselves and to give them the Happy Ending they never would have had otherwise.
>
> These women gave up and settled for lives of **subjagation** and _suffering_. I put an end to that! I did!
>
> There will be only _one more_ and then I am done. I believe.
>
> I see the "media" has named me. It is a _good_ _name_ and I will keep it. . . . .
>
> Yours,
>
> Bridekiller

Jasper woofed out a hard breath and leaned back in the chair. He read the letter again, then one more time. Without looking up, he said, "Talk to me," to de la Croix.

"Are you staying?" she asked. "Your flight is . . ."

He stared at the letter on the screen before him.

There will be only *one more* and then I am done. I believe.

I believe.

He'd told Howie it would just be a couple of days. But that was before this.

"Oh, I'm staying. For sure."

9

THE TASK FORCE office was a madhouse when they arrived, but as soon as Jasper entered, things slowed long enough for whispers and surreptitious glances and some outright gawking. He ignored it. Let them chatter.

"The letter came in yesterday," said de la Croix, "but it wasn't tagged and opened until this afternoon." She shook out her umbrella and hung it on a peg. Jasper had no raincoat or boots, so he just stood there, wet and in a distant sort of pain. His face felt distended and remote from the rest of his body, the throbbing there a unique distraction from his ribs.

"No postmark, no return address, obviously," she went on, ushering him toward an office. "Someone dropped it off at a precinct, addressed to *The Bridekiller Hunters.*"

"And it took a whole day to get to you?" he asked.

De la Croix flung open the office door and growled at the guy sitting behind the desk, who immediately jumped up and vacated, his laptop tucked under one arm, trailing its power cord.

"We get a lot of cranks," she said as they settled into seats. "A day isn't bad."

He allowed it. The office they were in was like the one from the previous day—the smell of stale coffee and armpits hung in the air like smoke after fireworks. Jasper coughed into his hand and gazed at de la Croix expectantly.

She did not disappoint. "No fingerprints, of course. No DNA. Still running down the printer."

"Probably printed it at a public terminal."

"Probably. But if we can find that place, then maybe there's camera footage or an eyewitness."

"Speaking of cameras—"

"Yep." She studied her iPad for a moment, then showed it to him over the desk. "Caught the guy dropping off the letter."

Despite decades of technological advances driven by billions of dollars in investment, the security footage from the police precinct in question was still grainy and so washed out that it might as well have been in black and white. Jasper watched as a figure in a trench coat and a Mariners ball cap walked into the building, paused. It was midday according to the timestamp in the corner and the precinct lobby was nearly empty.

The figure glanced around, then left the envelope on a vacant chair before leaving the building. Jasper noted that he wore gloves.

He. There was that assumption again.

"Do we think this was him," Jasper asked, "or some rando he gave twenty bucks to drop off the letter?"

De la Croix shrugged. "Not sure yet. We have footage from an ATM across the street and we're in the process of getting warrants for some other cameras up and down the block. We'll try to track him back to where he came from or forward to where he went."

He opened his mouth to say something, but just then the door opened and a small blond woman leaned in and said—in a voice too deep and guttural for her form—"Conroy's talking. All hands."

De la Croix hopped up. "Darren Conroy. Special Agent in Charge. He's the one running the task force. Let's hear him out."

Together, they went back out into the main area, which had been quickly and haphazardly rearranged into rows of chairs aimed at a big whiteboard. A man in his fifties, gray at the temples, crow's-feet around his eyes, stood before the whiteboard, impatiently clicking a dry erase marker against the metal edge of the board as people found their seats.

"It's not musical chairs, people!" he bellowed. "Find a seat, don't find a seat, I don't care! Just listen up!"

Jasper and de la Croix made their way to the back of the audience and stood.

"So we got a letter!" Conroy said, his voice hushing the murmur in the assembled law enforcement officers. "Nice of him to forego the Zodiac option and just talk to us in something close to English, right?"

A ripple of laughter. Nervous, but laughter nonetheless.

"He's promised to kill at least one more time. I am goddamn well gonna make him break that promise."

Someone started to applaud, but before it could pick up, Conroy stared daggers and barked, "Knock that shit off! This isn't your kid's Taylor Swift concert."

He turned to the board and started writing numbers.

"There are something like twenty-five thousand weddings a year in the Sea-Tac Metro," he said. "That works out to around four hundred and eighty per week."

"But it's late fall!" someone shouted officiously. "Most weddings are in the summer."

Agent Conroy glared again into the audience. "No shit. I was just getting to that. There's another fifteen thousand per year in the Portland area. We have to hope our guy sticks to his jeopardy surfaces and doesn't range too far from those areas. Between the two metros, we're estimating roughly six hundred weddings per week combined as we head into colder weather."

A groan went up from the audience.

"Shut the fuck up," Conroy said, his tone almost pleasant. "If it was June, we'd be looking at more than a thousand. We have the manpower—"

Someone cleared their throat. Very loudly.

"Fucking hell. We have the *staffing*, OK, to do this. Seattle PD, Portland PD, your job is to hit churches and wedding clerks. Round up lists of weddings scheduled for the next six weeks. Cyber, you're on the registry watch. Narrow down those six hundred as best you can and use facial recognition on engagement photos. We've got a very special, very specific Venn diagram here, people. We're looking for weddings in the next six weeks involving white women between the ages of—" He broke off. "You know the victimology. Match 'em up, overlap 'em. I want to know in thirty-six hours how many weddings we're looking at so that we can be in place."

Another collective groan. Conroy pretended not to hear it.

"What about weddings with two brides?" someone called out.

Conroy nodded as though it was a detail he'd neglected to mention. "If either bride fits the victim profile, it goes on the list. Our guy has only hit straight couples so far, but there's nothing that indicates he won't decide to go after lesbians, too.

"His timing has been inconsistent, so he could strike at any time. It's Tuesday—I want us in position at the proper venues by Friday."

There was a crowd murmur that built in tension and volume until Conroy barked, "What the fuck are you all still sitting around here for?"

A mad scramble ensued as the assembled cops and agents rose from their chairs and made for desks, offices, filing cabinets, coat hooks.

Jasper loitered at the back with de la Croix until the task force was massing at the door. Conroy approached him with an expression of amused disbelief.

"Jasper Dent. Holy fucking hell. Sorry I missed you yesterday—I was briefing the director." He extended his hand. Jasper shook it. "Looks like you've made friends here already."

Jasper gestured to his face. "It's nothing. Really."

Conroy accepted this. "You're here for the duration?"

"I'd like to see this guy caught and figure out if he has any connection to the Crows, yes."

With a nod, Conroy glanced over his shoulder at the whiteboard. "This is only my second serial. How'm I doing?"

Jasper shrugged. "That's two more than me."

"No." Conroy held his gaze. "It's not."

"I think you have the right plan. Makes sense to look for the next victim, since he has such a type. Probably more effective than looking for him. Sure, chase down the letter-drop, but let him come to you."

"Say this letter-drop is a dead end," Conroy mused. "Which it probably is. What next? If I did want to look for him, who would I be looking for? In your estimation."

Jasper took a deep breath. "You have people a lot smarter than me in your Behavior Analysis Unit. They may see more to it. I don't know. It just seems . . . It just seems like he sees himself as the good guy here."

"White Knight Syndrome," Conroy said.

De la Croix took out her iPad and opened a note. He noticed her typing *White Knight???*

"Go on," said Conroy.

"He said he was helping his victims, right? Saving them." Jasper closed his eyes. His pulse had quickened, throbbing along his swollen jawline, his tumid left eye. It was a distraction; he pushed it aside.

"It's someone . . . It's his mother. Older sister, maybe. Maybe an aunt, but I kinda doubt it. A woman with some sort of authority over him, a woman unhappy with her life, with the man in her life. He's her savior. He's rescuing her the only way he knows how. Stopping the misery before it can start."

He opened his eyes to de la Croix nodding excitedly as she took notes on her iPad. Conroy said nothing, but continued gazing at Jasper.

"Something like that, yeah," Jasper said, speaking almost to himself for a moment. "The letter . . . He's of average intelligence, maybe a little lower. But he's cunning. He's observant. He doesn't have the words or the . . ." Jasper stopped. He considered.

"What?" Conroy and de la Croix said at the same time.

"He works in a low-paying field. Or he's unemployed. He doesn't have the words to convince her to leave her husband and he doesn't have the money to help her escape, so he lashes out with violence. It's the only tool available to him."

More note taking. De la Croix nodded. "Yes. This all makes sense."

"You got beat up pretty bad." It was eye-rollingly obvious, but something in Conroy's tone made the observation less annoying than it would have been otherwise. "We think this is connected?"

"It's doubtful," de la Croix said before Jasper could respond. He realized that Conroy had been talking to her, not to him. "No one outside the task force knew he was here."

"Probably a fan of my father's," Jasper said as lightly as he could.

Conroy grunted something like agreement. "It's gonna be a while before we have anything new. BAU will have their profile for us soon enough, but I imagine it's not going to deviate much from yours. Max, show him our coop room and let him get a little sleep."

* * *

Cooping was the time-honored police tradition of sneaking in a nap during a shift. The task force had a couple of rooms set aside with sturdy cots and blankets for those who chose or were voluntold to work around the clock. De la Croix showed Jasper to one such room.

"You really should rest," she told him. "Everyone's out doing what they can. I'll wake you if anything pops up."

He sat on a cot and watched her turn off the light and close the door. It sent a burst of memory through him, of his mother putting him to bed as a small child. He could attach no time or age to the recollection—it was just a momentary blip on the radar of memory and therefore he did not know if it preceded her raping him or not.

Now I'll definitely be able to sleep, he thought mordantly into the dark.

Still, he laid back, hoping that he would be able to rest a little. His face pulsed and complained at him—he chose to focus on his ribs just for variety's sake. They were dull and sore, flaring as he twisted into a more comfortable position on the cot.

One of my father's fans . . .

That made a lot of sense. And both de la Croix and Conroy seemed to buy it.

But he had another suspicion. Another theory. There was no time to test it and Bridekiller was the priority. He tucked his suppositions and his hypotheses into the back of his head, storing them for later.

Unable to sleep, he turned to his phone for distraction. A critical mistake on his part—there was a flurry of texts and emails from Simon. All of them were important, he knew.

WorldVision had been his idea, after all. He understood on a rational, intellectual level that he could help more people through WorldVision than he could by hooking up with the FBI to track down serial killers one at a time. But on an emotional level . . .

On an emotional level, he confessed—to himself only—to a deep sense of satisfaction. He'd been reluctant to come to Seattle, but now that he was here, now that he was in the mix, an almost preternatural calm had come over him. Even being assaulted in his hotel room hadn't really rattled him.

He wondered idly what McCutcheon would make of it. And then he put the man out of his head.

The worst part of the trip was being away. He suffered a tremendous sense of discontinuity when away from the Nod. His routines grounded him. His surroundings were a balm. The regular Scrabble sessions with G. William. Dinners with Howie. Even the meetings with Simon.

He'd met Simon through Howie, actually. Howie had a degree in business administration, a prosaic and—frankly— dull course of study that Jasper did not begrudge him. After the blood and the pain and the body count of their late teens, Howie deserved a boring life. He'd earned it at the point of a knife. He'd earned it at the end of a shotgun.

Howie had been the one constant in Jasper's life, the only person in his life to this day who'd known him before Billy's unmasking and arrest.

When Jasper had first floated the idea of a foundation to assist victims, focusing particularly on victims of serial killers, Howie had immediately put together a business plan and then headhunted Simon from an "abolish cash bail" nonprofit he'd been running.

He flipped away from Simon's messages to Photos. And there was his favorite picture—him, Howie, and Connie at high school graduation. They'd survived. And on that day, they were relentlessly, deliriously happy.

Of the three of them, only Howie had gone to college. Post–high school, Connie spent a year in a performing arts school in Nashville, then one night made the spur-of-the-moment decision to move to New York and try to break in on Broadway. Her father and Jasper had both protested—to varying levels of vociferousness—but Connie had ignored them and left at the end of the semester. To everyone's delight, she'd landed a part in short order. Something off-off-Broadway, but still. It was a tiny part, but it mattered, and now she was climbing the ladder.

Their relationship was open. On her end, at least. Jasper could theoretically date if he chose to, but living in the Nod limited his romantic prospects considerably. He was poison to most, alluring only to the sorts of women he knew it best to avoid: The ones who yearned for the thrill of fucking damaged goods. The ones who thought they could fix him. The ones who liked him broken.

And so he stayed in the Nod, celibate save for those times when Connie came home to visit, times fewer and fewer between as her acting career elevated. He knew she'd been on a few dates in New York, but nothing beyond that. He didn't want to know more. It was her business, and it was her business because he'd assiduously made it so.

She'd last been home over the long July Fourth weekend. Months ago.

She had implored him, early on, to join her in New York. He could sell the house or rent it out or let it sit. But New York held too many memories for Jasper. For Connie, too, truth be told, but she had managed to work past them. Jasper . . . couldn't.

He couldn't work past finding Jennifer Morales in a New York storage unit, dead next to the serial killer Oliver Belsamo, the Dog in the Hat-Dog Killer duo. He couldn't work past being locked in the dark in that same storage unit (83F—he would never *ever* forget it) with the bodies and a bullet in his leg, certain beyond all belief that he would die.

New York was a no-go zone for Jasper. Even with Connie there. And so he'd agreed to her terms—when they were together, they were *together*. But when they were apart . . .

When they were apart, they were still together, but with the risk that it would all end. The knowledge wasn't pleasant, but it was only fair to Connie.

be careful

The last text he'd received from her.

He probed at the tender, bloated flesh of his jawline. In theory, he could keep this from Connie indefinitely. She wasn't due back at the Nod until Christmas, almost a month away. By then, the swelling would be gone or at least inconspicuous enough to be missed or passed off as a recent innocent mishap of some kind.

But he'd done his damnedest not to lie to Connie. To anyone, really. Lying was easy for him—so easy that he rarely even thought of it as lying. One of the lessons he'd learned from his father was that if you could make your life easier with an untruth, you should just go ahead and do it. And sometimes that same untruth made someone else's life easier, too. It wasn't even an ethical issue; everyone benefited.

He'd absorbed that lesson so thoroughly that he was not even consciously aware of it until McCutcheon called him out on it during one early session. It took months of talking through it, but he came to realize that the same skills he used to manipulate those standing in his way were just as pernicious when used to placate and disarm.

In short: Yes, it would make Connie's life less stressful if she never knew of the assault, but lying about it, even by omission, would be one more capitulation to the lessons Billy Dent had imparted to his only child. The path to healing had ditches and thorns.

He did the mental math, figured East Coast Connie was most likely scrounging dinner at a nearby bodega, and called her. They texted frequently, but she preferred hearing him. "I can tell if you're OK by your voice," she claimed.

She picked up on the third ring. He wondered what his voice would tell her now.

"Hey," he said. "How are you? How's the show?"

"One sec . . ." And then he heard her negotiating a purchase with a slightly accented voice in the background. He'd been right. He'd only been in a couple of New York bodegas, and those in Brooklyn, not Manhattan, but when he closed his eyes and listened through his phone, he thought he could see the place: Shelves crammed with chips, crackers, cookies, tampons, toilet paper, bleach, diapers, in no particular order or adherence to logic. A wall of cigarette packs, batteries, charging cables. A rattling refrigerator, its glass door sweating.

"OK," she said, "I'm outside now."

"What's for dinner?" he asked.

"Are you really in Seattle?"

"I asked first."

She blew out a breath. He closed his eyes again and imagined her. Imagined the love of his life. He'd known Howie longer, but Connie had cleaved to him even after learning of his past.

Tall and lithe. A dancer's body. Her hair—once worn long in beaded dreadlocks—was now close-cropped, shorter than his own. It made it easier for her to don whatever wig a part might call for. Purely practical, she claimed.

The up-tilt of her nose. The curve of her lips. The indentation of her waist just above her strong hips.

The scars. Almost invisible, but he knew where to look for them, the ever-so-slightly lighter brown against her black skin.

The scars from the time his own parents had kidnapped her.

"Dinner is a very nice-looking macrobiotic pasta and tempeh thing. Seattle?"

He nodded in the dark. "Yeah. I'm . . . The FBI. They think this guy out here is a Crow."

She said nothing for a moment, then two. "The one killing the brides?"

"Yeah."

He heard her pry open the plastic clamshell containing her dinner. Tonight was a good night—she'd actually left the theater to eat rather than subsisting on a protein bar and a diet Pepsi.

"I saw a thing on Insta about it. You're involved now?"

The worry in her voice ignited the old *screw it* urge in him. He and McCutcheon had walked through it over many months of sessions, this need he had to defy, especially when it involved his own safety.

He bit back every retort his body screamed at him to hurl at her. "I was out of coffee," he said lamely.

"So you went to Seattle? I guess that makes sense."

He laughed along with her. "Connie . . . God, I miss you."

"Tell me about Seattle."

You didn't say you miss me. You didn't say it.

He filled her in on the basics of the case and how he'd become involved. She listened quietly. She was good at that.

"I don't know," he said. "I don't know if I can really help them that much. But you know . . . You know, therapy has helped me. A little bit. But . . ."

She said nothing. He waited, giving her an in, an opportunity. Too much time passed with only her breath and the slight click of a plastic fork on her end as she ate her dinner.

"I don't know," he went on. "Therapy is fine, but I'm thinking maybe catching one of these guys will be like . . . like a nitrous boost."

"You can't shortcut and cheat your way to mental health," she told him.

"Well, maybe not. But has anybody really given it a try?"

She snorted a polite chuckle. "I think a lot of people have tried. But what else is going on? There's something else. Something you haven't told me."

"Nope." He traced a finger along his temple, probing gently at the swelling around his eye.

"Did you meet someone?" she asked. "This FBI agent, maybe?"

He shivered in the dark. He had no attraction to de la Croix at all. No attraction to anyone but Connie, and he wished he could be sure the reverse was true.

"I'm not seeing anyone," he assured her.

"Then what are you avoiding telling me?"

"What makes you think I'm avoiding telling you something?"

"My boyfriend is really good at reading people and taught me some of his tricks."

Boyfriend. It was blatantly manipulative; it was a hook latched firmly in the most tender part of his heart. And it worked because he loved her and he loved being her boyfriend and because—he admitted to himself and then dismissed it— he admired the attempt to influence, to pull his strings. It was familiar, in the original sense of the word, having to do with family.

His family was exceptionally fucked up, but it was still the only family he knew.

"I may have gotten beaten up," he confessed. "Probably one of Billy's fans."

Her voice went hard. "Switch to FaceTime. I want to see."

"I'm fine."

"I want to be sure."

"Con, I swear to God—I'm fine. The FBI already had me looked at. Right now it looks worse than it is. I'll FaceTime tomorrow, when the swelling's gone down."

"Goddamnit, Jazz!" she yelled. "Stop doing this shit! Show me your damned face!"

His phone bleated at him. It was Connie, trying to switch him over to video.

"Connie, please. I'm fine."

"You don't get to do this!" she shouted. "This is the whole reason you're in therapy! To learn that it's not about you protecting me from the world or from yourself or from the truth or from whatever bullshit you've cooked up in your head. And now you've made me that crazy Black lady yelling at her phone outside a bodega at eight o'clock at night when it's freezing out so now I'm really pissed at you."

He sighed and made his way to the wall, flipped on the light. Then he switched over to video and held the phone out at arm's length.

Her face came up on the screen. As always, she took his breath away. It was a cliché, but it was true; every time he saw her anew, he needed a moment to collect himself, to kickstart his lungs. Her eyes were enormous and deep brown, her nose a sculpted jut with the slightest up-tilt. Her bee-stung lips, pursed now in anger, visual memories of the thousand kisses, of the thousand hellos.

Of the last goodbye.

Her ire almost immediately melted into worry and fear.

"Oh, Jazz," she whispered. "Oh, baby . . ."

He caught a glimpse of himself in the postage stamp of video from the selfie cam. He was pleasantly surprised to find that he did, in fact, look a lot worse than he felt.

"It's really not that bad," he said. "The camera adds ten stitches."

It was pure Howie, total cornball, and it worked. For a moment. She hiccupped a laugh, but there were tears gathering in her eyes.

Good resolution on that camera.

"You can't let this happen to you," she said, her voice barely a whisper. He saw now that she had her earbuds in; they picked up every hitch in her voice. "Jazz, please . . ."

"Come on. You know I've been through worse."

"Being shot doesn't mean you get a pass every time you get hurt for the rest of your life. You have to be careful." She wiped fiercely at the corners of her eyes. "Please tell me you'll be careful."

"I'm doing my best. I swear. Right now I'm surrounded by dozens of cops and FBI agents."

Her nose wrinkled. "That doesn't actually sound very safe to me."

"They won't mess with me. I'm white."

"I keep forgetting." And she cracked the tiniest smile.

Good. They were back on firm ground again.

"I miss you," she said, and there it was. There it was. His breathing was suddenly so much easier.

"I have to go," she told him. "I have to go."

"Got a hot date?"

"As a matter of fact . . . no."

Ouch. He figured he deserved that caesura of doubt before the *no*.

"I'm glad."

"You can come visit any time you like. Bring Howie. Bring G. William. I'll leave tickets for you. Good ones."

He wanted to say he would. He wanted to say he would come to New York for a weekend and try it. And maybe he would eventually come for a week at a time. Or a month. Or maybe he would just move there.

He wanted to say it, but the curdle of his stomach, the sudden tension along his lats and down the backs of his calves, told him it would be a lie.

"That's sounds nice," he said instead. And: "We'll see."

* * *

Eventually, his adrenaline high abated and his body screamed for relief. He managed to drift off to sleep almost involuntarily. He wasn't sure how long he slept, only that at some point too soon, there was the soft, insistent pressure of de la Croix's hand on his shoulder, nudging him from sleep.

"There's an update," she said, whispering. "Figured you'd want to hear."

He'd turned the light off again after hanging up with Connie. Now here was de la Croix's face, floating at him in the darkness. They were nothing alike, similar only in the superficiality of their skin, and even there not so similar. But Connie—either deliberately or unintentionally—had put the idea in his head, and so in that groggy moment of waking he considered de la Croix, then rapidly backed off.

He was a one-woman man. Period.

Are you that way out of conviction or fear? McCutcheon's voice asked. *Because you're truly in love or because you think it's safer?*

"What's going on?" he asked.

Moments later, they were out in the main task force area. The place was quieter than he'd gotten used to, less staffed. Agents and cops were out heeding Conroy's orders, narrowing down the field of potential victims before the weekend's weddings.

"Chris emailed from Quantico, came back with a revised profile based on the letter," de la Croix told him, gesturing for him to sit at a nearby desk. "He generally agrees with your assessment—"

"That's nice."

"He did add some details of his own. Our guy is late thirties, early forties."

That made sense. Most serial killers fell into that age range. Jasper's father and mother had both started relatively young, but Billy in particular had really hit his stride in his thirties, and wasn't it monumentally *grotesque* to think of a rapist and murderer "hitting his stride"?

"They also think he's white."

Jasper and de la Croix exchanged a look and then, at the same time, laughed. It was gallows humor, morbid humor, ironically *black* humor. Of course he was white. Most serial killers were. And the fact was, even the ones who weren't wouldn't have been killing white women in the first place— serial killers hunted within their own racial groups, as a general rule. There were exceptions, sure—

(As McCutcheon liked to say: There are exceptions to everything in the world. Even the length of a day changes. No one can live on and in the exceptions, though. Leap seconds cannot sustain survival.)

—but for the most part, serial killers killed people who looked like them. The victims had all been white. For the killer to be anything else would be genuinely shocking.

"They also think he's been married, but now is divorced."

Jasper deliberated on that particular notion. He could see where the FBI Behavior Analysis Unit had landed on the idea of Bridekiller being divorced. Many serial killers had a powerful sense of self-loathing. They felt helpless in the thrall of their fantasies and urges, driving them further and further into the tidal depths of hating themselves. Could Bridekiller be acting out of a personal animus toward not the brides, but himself? His letter made it sound like he had a savior complex, rescuing women from lives under the bootheel of oppressive patriarchy. But maybe he'd missed something. Maybe Bridekiller was doing it to save them from *himself.* He saw himself as a representative of all that was wrong with men. His own wife had escaped him; now he was on a crusade to be certain that no one else would suffer as she had.

"That sounds reasonable," he admitted. "But I have to say—he's sounding less and less like a Crow."

He caught the flicker of concern before she managed to suppress it. "Don't worry, Agent de la Croix—I'm not going anywhere." He gestured to his face. "Like they say in the old action movies: Now this is personal."

* * *

His stomach was contracting in painful hunger, so de la Croix suggested they grab an early dinner courtesy of the Bureau.

There was an Italian restaurant around the corner and down the block. The aroma of marinara and fresh bread wafting outside set Jasper's mouth watering, and he reached for the door of Il Formaggio è Vita without so much as a word to de la Croix, who hung back and studied the façade, worrying at her lower lip.

"Looks expensive," she said.

"Don't think the expense account can handle it? A little above your per diem? That's OK—I'm rich."

"I know. I've seen your tax returns."

He paused at the door and turned back to her. "You what? That's such an invasion of—"

"Settle down, Dent. I'm kidding."

"Oh my God! The fed has a sense of humor!"

She grinned and joined him at the door, which he held open, ushering her in.

The place *was* expensive, the sort of place that didn't exist in the Nod. Smooth, spotless tablecloths, leather-bound menus, and a woman in a tuxedo playing a violin from table to table. Jasper fervently hoped and prayed she would skip them. A frieze decorated an arch to the side of their table, leading into another dining area. It depicted Persephone amid a field of wheat—Hades was frozen eternally in mid-chariot rush, lurching toward her.

"You sure your wallet can handle this?" de la Croix asked from behind her menu.

The prices were . . . breathtaking. Jasper usually dined at Chez Microwave, a very fine and reliable eatery located on his kitchen counter. The finest dining in the Nod or within the surrounding towns would cost half of a meal at Il Formaggio è Vita.

"I think I can swing it." There was no point telling her about the embarrassingly massive option money he'd gotten from a Hollywood studio for the rights to his book. And, he supposed, his life. The deal wouldn't be announced until the new year and he was supposed to keep his mouth shut.

"I don't think I realized the book business paid *that* well."

"It doesn't. But when you hardly spend anything . . ." He shrugged and resisted the urge to offer up his trademark rakish grin. It would probably look ghoulish given his injuries anyway.

They ran out of small talk quickly and as they waited for their food, he decided that the mood of the place was too close, too romantic. The lighting was too muted, the hum of the violin too seductive. He was keenly aware of de la Croix in an uncomfortable way.

Just before the appetizers came, a man in a tuxedo approached the table, bearing a clutch of roses. "Would the gentleman like to buy a rose for the lady?"

De la Croix went ramrod stiff in her chair. "Not a chance!" she sang out, much to the rose-peddler's surprise and consternation.

"Someone's in the doghouse," he muttered to Jasper.

"We're not on a date," Jasper explained. "But how much?"

They negotiated briefly and then Jasper bought a rose.

"I'm engaged," de la Croix said immediately.

He knew she wasn't, but didn't begrudge her the reflexive lie.

"It's not for you," Jasper said. He propped the rose up against his water glass and leaned back, figuring out the best angle for his iPhone's camera. He took three shots, spent some time swiping between them, then texted the best one to Connie.

thinking of u

De la Croix watched the entire process with an amused quirk of her lips. When Jasper was finished, she waited for him to tuck the rose off to the side of the table before saying, "Jasper Dent the romantic. I never would have guessed."

It was said lightly and he wanted to respond in kind, but McCutcheon echoed in his ear: *You use your past to deflect. You use your darkness to deflect. When you're desperate, you use something resembling humor to deflect. You have more deflector shields than an X-wing, Jasper, and look where it's gotten you.*

"I'm trying to be better at being human," he said slowly, rolling his water glass between his palms. "It's not always easy."

The server brought a plate piled artfully with fried calamari for Jasper and a delicately arranged clam toast with pancetta for de la Croix.

"Have you ever been to Italy?" de la Croix asked.

He huffed a laugh. His calamari came with something that was disguised as marinara, but had a peppery kick that made his mouth beg for clemency.

"I've barely been out of the Nod. But speaking of being more human . . . I'm told I talk about myself too much. I come by it honestly—people are usually asking me a lot of questions. But we've been hanging out for a couple of days now and I realize I know nothing about you."

"I'm sure you've sized me up. In your own way."

He hesitated. "As a victim? Yes."

Clearly that wasn't what she expected. Her shoulders went back and her eyes narrowed. "I'm sorry?"

Again, he hesitated. There was openness and honesty and then there was *just too damn much information*. He was still figuring out the line. "It's not personal. It's just how I was raised. It's a reflex."

"Tell me about me as a victim." There was a challenge to her tone, but also a note of curiosity.

He picked up his fork, then put it down again. "I . . . don't think I should do that."

"I'm an FBI agent. Nothing you say will surprise or upset me."

With a chuckle, he moved his butter knife. No reason. Busywork. Keeping his hands moving. "I'm not worried about upsetting you. It's just not good for me, you understand? It's not good for me to give in to that reflex. To let myself assess people that way. People are real. People matter." He cleared his throat. "Sometimes I have to remind myself of that."

When he looked up from his plate, she was gazing at him across the table. Neither of them spoke for a long while, and then she licked her lips, started to speak . . . stopped . . . and then said:

"Well, damn. Your parents really did a number on you, didn't they?"

It was just the right tone; just the right delivery. Jasper snickered, then outright laughed. She joined him, raising her water glass in a salute he matched.

She had not, he noticed, answered in the affirmative when the server had offered drinks or a bottle of wine at the beginning of the meal. He couldn't help assessing her based on that decision—his old reflexes kicking in. Jasper himself declined alcohol on any and all occasions, even when by himself. He had a terror of what he might become when alcohol loosened his superego's grip on his id. His father had drunk very rarely, on social occasions, and the booze never seemed to make him more or less likely to commit horrors, but Jasper didn't feel like testing the possibility. Even McCutcheon agreed.

"For most people, getting a little drunk and doing something regrettable is just a rite of passage. For you? Maybe not so much."

Was there something de la Croix worried about regretting? Was she concerned about the propriety of drinking while baby-sitting the FBI's new toy? Or maybe she was an alcoholic in recovery, for all he knew.

Or maybe it's none of your business, he decided.

"Tell me about yourself," he said. And then: "Jesus, that sounds like a line, doesn't it? I didn't mean it that way."

The server arrived with their main courses—a seafood medley sizzling over linguini with a squid ink sauce for de la Croix and a more prosaic tagliata with asparagus for Jasper. De la Croix waited until their meals were settled before them and the server was gone before replying.

"What do you want to know?"

He shrugged and sampled the asparagus first. It was grilled to a crisp perfection. "How did you end up at the FBI?"

"Do you remember 9/11?" she asked.

"Afraid not," he said. "Before my time."

"I'm a few years older than you," she said slowly, spinning linguini onto her fork. "We lived in Baltimore. I remember my mom bursting into kindergarten and grabbing me and hauling me home without a word. She wasn't the only parent doing that."

He nodded.

"Anyway, the whole . . . The whole *now we are one America* thing didn't last the way some people thought it would, right? Especially for Muslims and Sikhs and anyone else who looked different enough for someone to justify beating on them. But the terror of that day stuck with me for a long, long time. And for a while there, I had a mad crush on anyone in a uniform. Firefighters, EMTs, even cops. Especially cops. Which I know is messed up. But I was just a kid and the pervasive narrative was that the cops would keep us safe. It was BS . . ."

"But you were a kid and you were scared and it stuck . . ."

She studied a seasoned chunk of oyster meat on the end of her fork. "Yep. As I got older, I got a little more woke, but I was still really attracted to the idea of law enforcement. The idea of being a force of order in a chaotic world. And then there was the FBI."

She popped the oyster into her mouth and chewed thoughtfully. "Seemed different in the Bureau. More professional. Less a bunch of good ol' boys getting together to figure out how to thump Black folks and get away with shit. You had to be a lawyer in the Bureau. You wore a suit and tie. It was different. Or seemed different."

"Why serial killers?" he asked.

She smiled with one side of her mouth, as though recalling a secret only she knew. He'd forgotten about his meal and now sliced off a sizable bite of beef.

"I didn't have anything to do with serial killers," she said, patting her lips with her napkin. "I worked Financial Crimes. My major in college was econ. I spend most of my days staring at spreadsheets, figuring out which Russians are oligarchs who need to be frozen out of their accounts."

"Financial Crimes . . . So . . ."

"And then, yeah, you were right—they were looking around for someone close enough to Ms. Conscience Hall to catch your attention. Hoping for a way in."

"So some white girls got killed and suddenly it's all hands on deck."

She looked uncomfortable. "I didn't say that."

"I know the sound of my own voice. But it's true."

Looking away from him, studying the architecture and the frieze, she nodded. Just once. "I like to think that if the Bridekiller was hunting Black brides, the FBI would have jumped into action just as quickly and with the same overwhelming resources."

"But probably not."

"Probably not," she agreed, stirring her pasta on the plate.

They sat in silence for a while, eating. Jasper waited for her to return to the topic, but she didn't.

"It's always white women, isn't it?" he said.

With a flinch, she paused, then set her fork down diagonally along her plate, a signal for the server that she was done. She laced her fingers together and rested her chin on them, staring across the table at him.

"We're not going to talk about this. Just because your girlfriend is Black doesn't mean you get it."

"I didn't claim to *get* anything. But it's always white women, isn't it? They get all the attention, all the resources, all the—"

"Knock it off. You're socially aware. I get it."

"It must piss you off." He studied his plate, about half full. His appetite was gone. "I *know* it pisses you off. Because it pisses me off. My father never killed a Black woman, but he killed a hell of a lot of other people of color, and I can tell you—objectively, factually—that those murders got a lot less attention than the white people he killed."

She looked away, staring off into the distance. "The thing about Financial Crimes . . . The thing about Financial Crimes is that you're dealing with big, broad groups, usually. Corporations and networks. It's a lot of old white men, sure, but greed cuts across race and gender. But it never feels personal because it's all about the money.

"But then you get one of these serials and . . ." She turned back to him. "You get one of these cases and, yeah, you get a nice slap in the face reminding you that it's all about the white girls."

Her tone had gone bleaker and bleaker as she spoke, but rose in something akin to defiance at the end. Her eyes seemed to glow as she stared across the table at him.

The server appeared as though conjured, breaking the spell of her outrage. She smiled up at him and handed him her plate.

Jasper did the same, minus the smile. It hurt too much and besides, he wasn't much for random smiles anyway.

"I probably said too much," de la Croix said once they were alone again.

"Probably not," Jasper told her.

10

B ACK AT THE hotel, he discovered—to his displeasure—that there was an FBI agent stationed at his door.

"This is completely unnecessary," he told the agent, a white man with a buzz cut and blue eyes that reminded Jasper a little too much of his father's.

"I have my orders," the agent said, shifting from one foot to the other, "and I'm following them."

"You might as well hang a sign on my door that says, *Here's Jasper Dent, everyone! Come get your shots in!*"

The agent didn't so much as flinch at the unrelenting power of Jasper's unassailable logic. "You can go in or you can stay out, but I've got my job."

Jasper went inside. The room immediately closed in on him. He'd spent most of the day in small rooms and surrounded by other people. He needed solitude, but also space.

Well, let's see how this works.

He grabbed the room's ice bucket and opened the door. Out in the corridor, the agent gazed at him with suspicion, assessing the bucket like it was a weapon. Which, given Jasper's past, was fair enough.

"Just getting some ice," he said, smiling and holding up the ice bucket.

"I'll go with you," said the agent.

"You really don't have to do that."

"I really do."

And so together they marched halfway down the corridor, where the vending room sat just off the elevator vestibule. The little alcove was too small for both of them, so Jasper went in and filled his bucket while the agent stood outside the door.

It was ridiculous.

Jasper went back to his room, nodding to the agent as he closed the door. Then he sat on the bed and held ice to his face, moving it from his jaw to his eye to the tender stitched area high up at his hairline. There was a lot of territory to cover and only so much ice.

He was too agitated to sit and tend to his wounds, so he decided to unpack his bag. A few shirts, some underwear, another pair of jeans, socks, toiletries . . .

And a slip of paper that fell out when he reached for his toothbrush. Maybe a receipt from somewhere . . . ?

No. It was folded over once. A slip torn from one of the hotel's notepads. Three words in black ink, scrawled:

THIS

ISN'T

OVER

"Oh my," he whispered, staring down at the paper. His eyes darted around the room, as though someone was watching him.

The handwriting was spiky, quick. Probably executed with the pen in Jasper's old room as Jasper himself lay unconscious on the floor. The FBI's handwriting experts would make much of it.

But he wasn't going to show it to them.

Bridekiller was the priority, and his assault had nothing to do with that . . .

He surmised.

He played the percentages, turning the options over in his mind. Even in the event that Bridekiller knew Jasper was in Seattle, he would have no way of knowing he was helping the FBI. It was much more likely that someone had spotted him in the airport or the hotel lobby, someone with a grudge against Billy and no other way to work out the rage.

But even if not . . .

Assume it *had* been Bridekiller, or someone connected with him. In *that* case, that meant there was a leak on the task force.

Either way, he couldn't pass the information along. It would either be a distraction from the case at hand or a heads-up to the leaker.

He would be careful. He would be alert. He wouldn't be caught unawares again. No need to involve de la Croix or the task force.

But he absolutely could not tolerate loitering in his own hotel room. He needed to get out. To breathe.

As a teen, Jasper had managed to unlock the handcuffs chaining him to a hospital bed, then overpowered the cop guarding him and escaped from the hospital into New York City, where he had proceeded to evade the entire NYPD long enough to catch a bus out of town.

Now, in his twenties, that seemed terribly exhausting. He could imagine a scenario in which he lured the FBI agent into his room, rendered the man unconscious, and then slipped out of the hotel, but it was an awful lot of work, and all he wanted was a walk around the block.

Peering out the window, he saw that the rain had let up. Seattle was swaddled in a cold, gray quilt of cloud and mist. He shrugged into his faithful padded flannel jacket and stepped out into the hallway.

"Let's go for a walk," he told the shocked FBI agent.

*   *   *

The task force's offices were in Interbay, but Jasper's hotel was close to Capitol Hill, which he knew only because a pamphlet on his room's desk said so. It was a ten-minute drive in light traffic, fifteen when Seattle's arteries clogged with human plaque. Even at night, Capitol Hill was nicer than what he'd seen of Interbay.

He and the FBI agent stepped out into the cold night air of end-of-November Seattle. The rain had tapered off, but not disappeared entirely. It not so much fell as lingered, a constant wet fog buffeted by the occasional wind. Jasper had no umbrella, but his overshirt had a hood. His FBI guard had no such head cover, so Jasper took pity on him and ducked into the first convenience store he saw and bought the man an umbrella, which led to their first conversation not about Jasper's safety. He learned the man's name was Mike Cortes, he was a Seattle native, worked out of the Seattle field office, and had been with the Bureau for eighteen months.

Hence babysitting duty, Jasper figured, but did not say.

He had the sense of being followed and almost asked Mike if he noticed anything. But that would be giving away too much.

They walked down Federal Avenue, past single-family homes and a park that lay silent and brooding in the dark.

He knew only two cities—New York (mostly Brooklyn) and Nashville. The bulk of his life had been spent within the confines of Lobo's Nod, a town too tired and too old to fight itself any longer. The Nod was the Nod and it was never going to change. Which he appreciated.

At first blush, he'd thought of Seattle as New York, only darker and colder. But three blocks of tidy duplexes in tasteful grays and browns and beiges changed his mind. The city felt more like a town, as though someone had carved a chunk out of New York and dropped a suburb into it. At each four-way intersection, a tree bloomed in the center of the street. A nuisance for drivers, he was sure, but a pleasant interruption of blacktop and concrete.

It would be nice, he thought, to live somewhere nice. A near-tautology that aggravated him not a bit for its simplicity and naiveté. The Nod was familiar, known, and unchanging, and thus he determined it safe. But it was not *pleasant*. It was a small town with all that entailed, good and bad. It was insular, nigh incestuous at times. He did not like it there, but he could not imagine leaving it.

And nothing could force him to leave, he knew. He occupied a rarified air, a rich man in a poor town, camouflaging himself with small-town poverty and a hick's limitations. Unlike his neighbors, though, he was in no danger of losing his house. He didn't worry about healthcare costs. He could live whatever life he wanted, wherever he wanted, and he'd chosen to stay in the Nod when anyone else would have run like hell, given his money.

It was unfair that he suddenly had a life of such privilege that he could, if he so desired, do nothing for the next decade or two, simply subsisting and breathing.

Then again, it was also unfair that he'd been born to two sociopaths in the first place. *Deserve*, McCutcheon often said, was a difficult, complicated word. Very few people actually deserved much of anything, other than basic respect and decency, but as a society we've convinced ourselves that we individually and collectively "deserve" so much.

But if anyone deserved a little break, maybe it was Jasper. Maybe the ravages of his parents and their Crow-kin sufficed to earn him a break.

And maybe not. Hence WorldVision. Hence trying—perhaps a little too desperately—to give something back.

Mike turned up the collar of his suit jacket. The cold fog was like a time-lapse rainstorm, only it came from every angle. The umbrella was a kindness, but useless.

Jasper hoped that wasn't a metaphor for WorldVision, for his involvement in the Bridekiller case, for everything he'd tried to do to atone for his parents.

He glanced around. There were other people out, despite the weather, but none of them seemed focused on him or following.

"Looking for something?" Mike asked.

His tone was not suspicious, but Jasper reminded himself that the guy *was* an FBI agent, no matter how untried.

As they turned at the corner and walked up a block back toward the hotel, the residential area gave way to a cluster of apartment buildings with retail shops at their bases. He noted a sign for Coffee Amore and decided that this sounded great.

"Want a coffee?" he asked Mike. "My treat."

Mike did a double-take. "Coffee? At this time of night?"

Jasper figured a man standing guard might want a little pick-me-up, but kept that thought to himself.

"My sleep's all messed up anyway," he said instead, then gestured to the door of Coffee Amore. Within, through the big windows, he saw that the place was empty save for a single barista, wiping down the counter.

"Nothing for me," Mike said, but followed Jasper in and then stood a post at the door.

Again: It was ridiculous.

With a sigh, Jasper approached the counter. "You still open?" he asked.

The barista looked up. She wore her long blond hair in a single French braid that hung down to the center of her back, two delicate curls dangling at her forehead like crescent moons. Her eyes were slightly narrow, light brown like oaks, the left one set off by a gold ring through the brow. A similar-looking ring adorned her septum, and a cluster of gold studs, rings, and bars ran up from her left ear lobe, around the shell of her ear. With her shirtsleeves rolled up, he could see two full tattoo sleeves, her right arm covered in what appeared to be a medieval tableau of some sort, the left twined with two interlocking snakes forming—he realized, catching a glimpse near her shoulder—a caduceus.

"Who wanted to mess up that face?" she asked in reply, her jaw dropping.

He lightly touched his own jaw, involuntarily. The swelling was still there, but some rest and some time had dulled the pain to the point that he had—for the length of his walk, at least—forgotten about his very visible injuries.

"You probably wouldn't believe me if I said I tripped."

She snorted and leaned forward on the counter. She wore a thin white T-shirt under a blue apron that said—perforce—COFFEE AMORE. He realized, belatedly, that she was beautiful.

"What's the other guy look like?" she asked.

"Wouldn't know. He was wearing a mask."

"Aren't you gonna tell me you fought back and kicked his ass?"

"No, I fell to the floor in a fetal position while he beat the crap out of me."

"Well, that deserves a drink on the house. What's your pleasure?"

"Medium black coffee. No sugar."

She stared at him. "Did you not hear me say it's on the house, big spender?"

"I like black coffee. No sugar."

"You live a wild and dangerous life, don't you?" She poured the coffee with something like disillusionment bending her shoulders.

He thought of Howie. Back in high school, Howie had taken a gleeful pleasure in devising ever more imaginative and unimaginable coffee beverages, some of them bordering on the grotesque. At the Coff-E-Shop in the Nod, he'd been a maestro of caffeinated confections, ever on the prowl to stump Helen Myerson, the waitress-*cum*-barista who, as his amanuensis, indefatigably managed to keep pace with his increasingly fanciful demands.

Helen.

He sighed. The barista, having turned to him with his cup, took note, but said nothing.

"Life's unpredictable enough. I don't need my coffee to surprise me."

She slid the cup of black coffee, no sugar, across the counter to him. "What about your Secret Service guy?" she asked, nodding toward Mike. "He need anything?"

Jasper glanced over his shoulder. Mike stood at the door as though someone had carved him there and forgotten him.

"FBI, not Secret Service," Jasper told her. "And he's fine."

"I should have realized," she said. "He doesn't have that, you know."

With one finger, she gestured around her embellished ear, miming an earpiece.

He sipped. The coffee was amazing and he sighed with pleasure. "Wow. That's good."

She winked at him. "A Shanna special, just for you. I don't make black coffee, no sugar, for just any customer who walks through the door, you know."

A professed introvert and voluntary hermit, he was a novice at most social graces, but he had experience enough to know that when someone worked their name into the conversation, it was polite to return the favor. "Jasper," he said, raising the cup in a salute. "Thanks again."

Out the door, Mike at his side, he thought there was a chance she might be watching him, but when he turned to look, she was attacking the counter with a rag again.

*   *   *

By the time they got back to the hotel, his overshirt was sodden and musty. Seattle hadn't held him in enough disregard to rain on him, just enough to thoroughly wet him down over time. It was almost worse than being caught in a downpour.

Mike took up his position as Jasper carded open his door.

"Need a towel?" Jasper asked him.

Mike nodded.

Jasper ducked into the room, grabbed one of the big towels from the rack in the shower and passed it to Mike, who scrubbed at his face and neck.

"Thanks, man. That was sort of a nice walk."

Jasper shrugged. "Stick with me, Agent Cortes. There'll be more bodies soon enough."

"Yeah?"

"Usually are."

11

SITTING AT THE little hotel desk, he stared down at the slip of paper from his bag. The man who'd beaten him senseless could have continued beating him while Jasper lay defenseless and unconscious on the floor. He could have—easily—killed Jasper.

Instead, he'd taken those precious moments to scribble out a message and drop it into Jasper's duffel.

So he doesn't want me dead. Or he wants me to suffer before he kills me. Either way, I have some time.

Surprisingly, he was not afraid. Being shot by one's own mother had a way of vaccinating fear of more prosaic deaths. Like anyone else, he worried about his own mortality, but in a fashion distinct from the usual illnesses, car crashes, or random violence. When his mind chose to spiral, it spun out lurid impossibilities that poleaxed him with their disquiet.

At the top of this list was his mother, somehow rising from her bed, in a vegetative state no longer, coming for him, to kill him or to make him live. He didn't know which was worse.

That medical science said it was impossible did nothing to assuage the fear that reared up within him unbidden and uncontrolled at the most random of times.

But here and now, his assailant had made one critical mistake—he'd let Jasper know he existed. Now Jasper was on alert. He wouldn't be caught off guard again. And there was no reason to chase the man—he would come to Jasper, given time. And this time, Jasper would be ready.

He slid the paper aside and sighed, then opted for a change of scenery by moving to the bed.

He lay there, thinking now about Bridekiller. He was less and less convinced that the killer was a Crow after all. Charitably, the FBI had leaped to a conclusion. Uncharitably, they had deliberately lied to him in order to get his help.

For whatever his help was worth. Thus far, he didn't think he'd achieved much. Other than developing a profile that their own BAU had come up with independently. And getting himself beaten.

He had a scan of the Bridekiller letter on his phone; he skimmed it again and again. There was something about it that bothered him. Something niggling at him. He couldn't identify precisely what. He tried reading the letter quickly, then reading it slowly, actually mouthing each word as he read it. Then he tried just staring at it, letting his vision double and blur, looking for patterns in the words themselves.

This, he realized after a fruitless period staring at the document, was the problem with assuming a Crow was responsible: Anything could be a clue, but almost everything was not. Crows played games. They built elaborate puzzles out of words and ideas and bodies. They used acrostics and wordplay to communicate with each other in plain sight.

Were the misspellings in the letter intentional? Did they mean something? Probably not, but then again . . . they could. *If* Bridekiller was a Crow.

He sighed and flipped over onto his stomach, still staring at the screen. The misspelled words floated up at him. He saw no pattern there. No revelation. He was a big disappointment to de la Croix and Conroy, he was certain.

Despite the coffee, he was tired. He reached out to flip off the light, then paused, thinking. After a moment, he picked up his phone and called Simon.

"It's after midnight," Simon said without preamble or greeting.

Shit. Time change. He kept forgetting about it. Or kept forgetting to care about it, at least.

"Sorry. But I have a thought and I wanted to tell you right away."

"That's what email is for."

He had no answer to that, so he plunged right on into the issue at hand. "I want us to make sure WorldVision is . . . well, is diverse."

He could almost hear Simon blinking owlishly into the dark at the other end of the line. "You called me at midnight to . . . We have a whole DEI setup that handles this. Our team is small, but I assure you we're diverse. We have—"

"That's not what I meant. I'm botching this badly. I mean that I want to be sure we're paying as much attention to Black victims as white. All victims of color, actually."

"I see."

"I want us to find someone who specializes in this sort of thing. Someone who's really on the ball in terms of the inequity and inequality of resources and media attention paid to Black women victims in particular. And hire that person and let's make this a big part of the org, OK?"

Simon said nothing.

"Simon? You still there?"

"I'm writing this all down." Simon had the mutant ability to twist a simple statement of fact into a rebuke. Jasper fell silent, waiting for Simon to finish his writing.

"If you'd sent this in an email," Simon said without an iota of compassion or kindness or amelioration, "you wouldn't have to wait for me to write it down. And I would still be asleep."

"Noted." Sometimes Jasper wanted to remind Simon who was the boss in this relationship, but mostly he took a perverse enjoyment in having a new person in his life who wasn't intimidated by either the legend or the fact of Jasper Dent.

"This can't just be another bullet point on a presentation slide," he said. "I want this to be a major component of what we do."

"I understand," Simon said. "Are you worried about . . . There may be a backlash. Accusation of white knighting. Of a white savior complex."

"Not if we handle it right. And besides, no one knows I'm involved in WorldVision."

"Yes, I know. I was worried more about *me* being on the receiving end of the backlash."

It was the closest Simon had come to a joke in all the time Jasper had known him, so he rewarded the effort with a forced chuckle.

"Just . . . Please make it happen, Simon. It's important."

"Of course."

Jasper sighed. Now came the part he hated: the apology.

"I know we're just starting to get things off the ground. I know this is a last-minute curveball and I'm sorry. I'm sure you're pissed at me."

"On the contrary. It's great to have you focused on the org and contributing. I think this is an important area for us and I'm glad to have to do the work. This is great news."

"Oh. OK."

"I just wish it had come roughly six hours later or earlier."

*　*　*

It was Jasper's turn to be rudely awakened thanks to the time change. It was barely five in the morning when his phone bleated for his attention, waking him from what had been a blessedly dream-free sleep.

It was Howie. Jasper sat up in bed, holding the phone before him, doing the mental math. It was still morning back in the Nod. Too early for Howie, who couldn't communicate effectively before his third cup of coffee. An icy electric thrill lanced his gut. This had to be bad news.

"What's wrong?" he asked immediately upon answering. It could only be two things. Something with Howie's hemophilia was acting up or . . .

"G. William is in the hospital," Howie told him. "It's not good."

Jasper sank back against the pillows. G. William Tanner, the retired sheriff of Lobo's Nod. The man who had—a lifetime ago—caught Billy Dent and at least temporarily ended his uninterrupted streak of sheer horror and pain. There was a lot of talk in Jasper's tiny circle of friends and trusted confidants that G. William had become a father figure to young Jasper.

Nothing could be further from the truth. G. William had been more important than a father. He'd been the eye of the storm. A center of calm in a life of chaos. A reliable and stead-fast island in an endlessly churning, blood-foamed sea. Trust-worthy and stalwart, stern when necessary, lenient when at all possible.

And hell, Jasper realized, hadn't he just described what a father was supposed to be? He couldn't be sure.

"I'll be on the next plane out of here," Jasper said. He set the phone on speaker so that he could thumb a message to de la Croix while talking to Howie.

"There's no point," Howie said bluntly. "He's either gonna make it through the next six hours or he's not. If he does, you can see him whenever you get home. If he doesn't, you'd still be circling to land in Nashville when he died. No point," he repeated.

No point did not compute for Jasper. Never had. His thumbs paused on the keyboard, a message half written.

"What happened?" he asked.

Howie drew in a deep breath and then began with three hours ago, when G. William had awoken at his customary early hour, only to discover that he couldn't get out of bed. Throwing back the counterpane revealed his legs swollen to almost twice their normal size, the flesh gone taut and bright red. A clearish fluid seeped from his pores. He couldn't reach his phone on the nightstand, but used voice control to call 911. EMTs got him out of bed and to the hospital.

"His kidneys are in bad, bad shape," Howie went on. "That's why he's got all this fluid backed up into his legs. They catheterized him and then they put him on oxygen because his lungs are surrounded by fluid, too. It's called—"

"Pleural effusion."

"Yep. Anyway, he's in and out of consciousness—"

"Where are you?"

Howie's voice took on an aggrieved tone. "Where do you think I am? I'm sitting right next to him. He's asleep. His blood pressure is too low, his pulse is awful, and he's peeing into a bag that I can see from where I'm sitting. A nephrologist and a cardiologist are coming in later. Either he makes it to lunch time or he doesn't, Jazz."

Jazz.

Do people still call you Jazz? de la Croix had asked. And he'd glared at her because the nickname was foolish, childish, something he'd dubbed himself as a kid, trying to distance himself from the name his father had bestowed upon him. But a select few still called him Jazz. Three, to be exact: Connie. Howie.

And G. William.

"What can I do?" he asked.

"Nothing," said Howie. "I'd tell you to pray, but neither of us is into that, so there's no point."

No point. There it was again. Despite his upbringing and his parentage, Jasper did not—could not—subscribe to fatalism.

People were real. People mattered. And as long as that was true, the things we did to keep them close to us mattered, too.

"Tell him I'm thinking of him. Tell him I owe him a Scrabble game."

"I'll tell him when he wakes up."

"Tell him now, Howie. I bet he can hear you."

* * *

Another agent—this one a woman with blond hair so close-cropped that it looked painted on—relieved Mike at some point in the night or early morning hours. She nodded crisply to Jasper when he emerged from the room an hour after his talk with Howie. Sleep had beckoned and seduced him, then left him with the insomniac equivalent of blue balls, tossing and turning fruitlessly in bed until he finally—in frustration—threw off the covers and prepared for the day.

A text from back home told him that G. William had surpassed Howie's six hour deadline. He was too tired and weak for even a phone call, mostly drugged into a stupor, but the big man still lived and breathed, and that fact alone was enough to propel Jasper into the day despite his lack of sleep.

De la Croix met him in the lobby, where the new agent—he didn't ask her name; she didn't offer it—handed him over with the eager air of an exasperated mother dropping off a toddler at daycare.

In the previous sixteen hours, the task force had managed to narrow down the weddings to about a hundred per week that met their specific criteria heading into the holidays. The office space became a madhouse of activity, a wet and angry wasp's nest buzzing with purpose as agents and cops coordinated a hundred different operations. The first wedding was Thursday night and they had to be ready.

"There'll be an agent in whatever catering group is working the reception," de la Croix told him, skimming through her iPad. "And then a couple of cops undercover at the ceremony itself. We're also going to have Tech wire the venues so we can get facial recognition on everyone in attendance."

Jasper shivered. He didn't like the so-called surveillance state, but in this instance, he had to admit it had its uses.

"Well, good luck," he said somewhat lamely. De la Croix blinked at that, as though she'd expected something else from him. It took a moment, but then he realized what it was.

"Nope," he said. "Not happening. Bad idea. Bad, bad idea."

12

"**B**RIDE'S SIDE OR groom's side?" the usher asked.

Conroy and de la Croix had managed to convince him to attend one of the weddings. He'd protested that it was pointless, that the odds of him attending the wedding that Bridekiller was targeting were one in a hundred sixteen, the number of matching weddings that weekend.

"It's even worse than that!" he'd gone on. "We don't even know that the guy is gonna strike this weekend. It could be next weekend or a month from now . . ."

"Look, we're paying you to be here," Conroy said. "This falls under *other duties as assigned*. It's all hands on deck here. We need warm bodies in pews."

He'd forgotten that he was getting paid. The FBI had some sort of consultancy fund and he'd signed some paperwork including his Social Security number back on the plane on the way to Seattle.

So he'd reluctantly agreed to attend one of the weddings. Someone brought him a suit that fit well enough and a car had picked him up from the task force office and driven him to a church in west Seattle on a tree-lined street not far from a school. A cold mist prickled at him as he got out of the car.

His general notoriety ebbed and flowed over the years—he was on an upswing right now thanks to a series of podcasts about his parents and a very annoying viral TikTok account that dramatized excerpts from his memoir. Between his online profile and his facial injuries, he'd been worried he would attract too much attention, but the simple expedient of a face mask—tastefully black, not at all out of place at a large social gathering, even now—took care of that. By sweeping his hair over the line of stitches along his forehead, he was well concealed, and now here was an usher asking him *bride's side or groom's side*.

Jasper froze. Such a stupidly innocent question and it didn't really matter what he said, and yet he couldn't manage to spit out a word, a lie.

The usher watched him. "Did you hear me? Bride's side or—"

"I know both of them," Jasper said sheepishly. "Sorry. You got me going in my head, *Wait, which one* did *I meet first?*"

It was too simple and he felt both thrilled and abashed at the ease of it. The usher laughed a little. "Well, let's put you on the bride's side. A little lighter over there." As he walked Jasper to his seat, he whispered, "Plus, there are some serious honeys over here, know what I mean?"

Jasper smiled under his mask, knowing it would reach his eyes.

He sat alone in a pew, not bothering to check out the *serious honeys*. He was here for business. Glancing around, he tried to spy the FBI's gear, but the church was already wired for sound and video, so they probably had just tapped into the preexisting system. He was pleased to see that he wasn't the only one in a mask, though he was probably the youngest by a wide margin.

The ceremony was longer than he would have appreciated, though short of a full Sunday service. As a child, Jasper had attended church every Sunday, in the company of his father and usually his grandmother. Billy Dent had no religious leanings at all, but knew what was expected in their small Tennessee town. His dismissive attitude toward God bowed to the need to appear human.

The reverend droned on. The usual recitations from Scripture were deployed by the maid of honor and best man, who both stumbled through them, but managed to deliver without serious incident. The bride was mid-twenties, a size eight, black hair in tight curls under her veil, a smile frozen by nerves. Would she end up dead tonight? Would the groom holding her hands, swearing to forsake all others, awaken groggy and drugged in the middle of the night, unable to remember his own name for a moment, confused and bleary-eyed, then shocked into full awareness by the corpse in the bathroom?

Or would they just get married and go on their honeymoon in the morning and become one of millions of other unspectacular married couples in the world?

He tried not to fidget through the ceremony. He followed along in the missal, but did not raise his voice in song. With the mask on no one would be able to tell anyway.

The ceremony concluded without incident. Jasper noticed no one suspicious. They were looking for a white guy, a loner, an outcast, and the only person who fit that bill was Jasper himself.

It's me. Hi, I'm the killer, it's me, he thought mordantly.

As the bride and groom finally kissed—to much applause—Jasper's phone vibrated with a text. It was from de la Croix and it was a map pin for the reception venue.

I have to go to the reception??? he asked.

y, she sent back.

He permitted himself a small groan as the family began to file out.

*　　*　　*

The reception was held three blocks away in a large hall. Despite the chilly fog blanketing the city, he walked. A woman in a very tight red dress walked alongside and tried to engage him in conversation, then became agitated when he only responded with mumbles and monosyllables. He watched her walk ahead of him and admitted that the dress was an excellent choice and that she probably fell into the category of *serious honey*.

Damn. He missed Connie.

At the reception, he lingered in a corner as guests found their seats. There was a seating chart, complete with name cards. Some sort of system with Pokémon characters designating tables. Jasper didn't get it, but the guests seemed to find it charming, amusing, and apropos.

There would be, of course, no seating card for *Jasper Francis Dent*, who was crashing the wedding at the behest of the FBI. So he loitered until everyone seemed to be seated and sought out a chair at a table that had empty spots.

Just his luck—it wasn't exactly the kids' table, but it was populated by teenagers. He would look like a creep.

At least I come by it honestly.

He slid into a vacant seat. The table sat ten, but only six chairs were full, meaning he had his pick, so he chose one between two other empties so as to have plenty of room. The kids barely glanced in his direction—they were busy scrolling their phones and taking selfies. Good.

He was only a few years older than these kids, but the gulf of years seemed uncrossable. At their age, he'd been helping the police . . . then running from the police. He'd seen so many dead bodies. They were eight or nine years younger but he could have been a grandfather to them.

No one seemed suspicious. It was just a wedding reception. He wondered idly which of the servers circulating to pour water and deliver rolls and butter were on the FBI payroll. He hoped no one would ask him his name or how he knew the happy couple or how he planned to eat with that mask on.

The bride and groom arrived after about twenty minutes, to a standing ovation and much applause. So as not to appear *too* much of an outcast, Jasper stood as well and clapped his hands.

Still nothing seemed out of place, out of order, out of sorts. The odds of this being Bridekiller's next target were long, he knew. It was a waste of his time.

He was uncomfortable under the mask and getting hungry. Surreptitiously, he slipped a bread roll into his pocket and then headed to the bathroom, where he inhaled both free air and the roll, sans butter. Stomach and lungs temporarily sated, he slid the mask back into place and returned to the table.

There was an envelope on his plate when he sat down. It hadn't been there before.

It was addressed, simply, to *Jasper*.

13

HE STARED AT the envelope for a long moment. Too long, really. Without touching it, he memorized it—standard #10 white business envelope with privacy watermarks. His name was written in black ink, printed in block letters that could have been from a printer or typewriter . . . or someone with a steady hand and patience.

It wasn't the handwriting from the hotel note. It had to be from Bridekiller.

He took out his phone and took a picture of it. Just in case. Darted his glance around the venue, looking for anyone suspicious.

"Did you see who left this for me?" he asked the table when he spied nothing out of the ordinary. At the same time, he was texting the photo to de la Croix.

The teens at the table gazed at him with bored contempt. He had to remind himself that this was normal, that his own teen years had been the exception, not the rule.

"Come on, guys. Did anyone see who left this here?" He was already standing.

De la Croix: Don't touch it!

"Some dude in a raincoat?" one of the boys said, channeling both uncertainty and disinterest at the same time.

"Raincoat," a girl confirmed.

"I think he went that way?" The boy again, pointing toward the main entrance/exit.

"What color coat?" Jasper asked. His nerves hummed. His brain was vibrating.

His phone rang.

"Gray . . . ?" said the girl.

"No one touch this." He pointed to the envelope. "Someone will be by to get it."

The teens shrugged almost as one. He considered snatching up the envelope, but already a server was headed toward his table with an intent expression and a fixed look in her eye that indicated she was after more than dirty dishes and a tip.

His phone rang again. He answered as he dashed for the door.

"De la Croix! He left the envelope. Gray raincoat. I'm headed outside."

"Stay where you are!" she told him. "I'm getting an agent to retrieve the envelope and we'll have a team there—"

"No time! He'll be gone by then."

Not waiting for a reply, he shoved his phone back in his pocket as he hit the door with his shoulder. His ribs complained, but he shoved through to the outside. A pissy rain spattered along the sidewalk. He looked up and down the street—nothing. No gray raincoat. But there were umbrellas being deployed now as the rain picked up and they blocked his view and—

There! Not up or down the street—across the street! A tall figure in a gray raincoat, hands thrust into pockets, head down against the rain. Wearing a ball cap.

Jasper leapt off the curb, checking left and right as he did so. A car slammed to a halt and bellowed with its horn. He ignored it and plunged ahead, crossing against traffic, dodging behind a car coming the other way in the far lane. Water splashed up along his legs, wetting his borrowed suit pants up to the calves.

Some part of him longed to shout out to the man. Like in the movies. *Hey, you!* Or *Stop!* But that would be ridiculous. He didn't want to give the guy a heads-up and let him start running.

Another car shot by. Jasper leapt back just in time to avoid being swiped. Another horn screamed at him.

The horns caught Gray Raincoat's attention. Jasper thought the man looked back and then quickened his steps.

Shit!

His phone was vibrating in his pocket. No time for it. He charged ahead, ignoring the cars, which beeped and honked at him. One came dangerously close, so close he felt the heat of its engine, but then he was on the other side of the street, hopping up over the curb onto the sidewalk.

Gray Raincoat had definitely picked up the pace.

Jasper ran full out down the sidewalk, dodging umbrellas and their angered wielders. Gray Raincoat, no doubt hearing the cries of annoyance in Jasper's wake, broke into a jog, then an outright run.

Digging down, Jasper looked for more speed, found nothing. His heart pounded. His breath came hard, his lungs hot and tortured, and he couldn't breathe.

Of course not. The mask.

He tore it off and let it go fluttering to the ground as he ran. With his lungs reenergized, his feet and legs quickened. He was gaining on Gray Raincoat now.

The man juked right into an alleyway. Jasper never even considered not following him, even though he knew leaving a public space was a recipe for an ambush.

Up until a few years ago, he'd spent his life taking risks. Might as well fall back into the habit.

The alley was narrow and pockmarked with puddles, lined with trash cans, their lids off, filling with rain. He dodged the puddles, not knowing how deep they were, unwilling to risk a fall or a twisted ankle.

Gray Raincoat was not being so cautious, plashing through the water as he ran straight ahead. The alley opened up in a building-length.

A siren wailed. It sounded close. But no one knew where he was. Hell, *he* didn't know where he was. He didn't know the city. Had no idea of the street name he'd come from or was headed to, the direction he was running . . .

He pumped his arms and eked out a final burst of speed that brought him almost even with Gray Raincoat. With a grunt and a heave, he lunged forward, arms out, just barely able to shove Gray Raincoat in the back.

The man stumbled forward, lost his balance. It was just the split second surcease Jasper needed. He lowered one shoulder and plowed straight into the man from behind, knocking them both down on the cold, rainy asphalt.

His shoulder exploded in pain. But the rest of his body already hurt, so it didn't matter, hardly registered. Gray Raincoat was down on the ground, but up on his elbows, clawing his way into a crouch.

Jasper groaned and grabbed the man's ankles, holding him in place. They struggled like that for a moment, in what must have looked absolutely absurd to a bystander, but which felt utterly deadly and serious in the moment. Rain sluiced down harder, and he blinked it away from his vision, clutching the man's ankles, tugging until the man fell prone again.

With the last of his strength, Jasper brought his hands up higher, gripping the man's calves, then dragged himself over the man's back, holding him down with his own body weight.

"Stop struggling!" he howled in the man's ear, making sure he could be heard over the rain, the ambient street noise. "It's over! Stop fighting me!"

The man craned his neck as best he could. The motion knocked off his hat; rain sparkled anew in tight curls of black and gray. For the first time, Jasper could see the man's face. His skin.

He was Black. His face bore the folds and shadows of a life hard-lived.

The profile flashed through his head in an instant. What could . . . How could . . . This couldn't be—

"Get off me!" the man yelled. "I didn't do anything!"

"The letter," Jasper said, unwilling to budge yet. "You left the letter."

Spluttering through the rain, the man barked, "Is that a crime? Get the hell off me!"

More sirens now. Jasper's instincts warred with his intellect. This man wasn't Bridekiller. Or even the man who'd assaulted him in the hotel. He knew it. But he'd left the envelope. He was connected. Somehow.

He sat up, straddling the man, still holding him down.

"If you didn't do anything wrong, then why did you run?" Jasper asked.

"You were chasing me!"

Well. Good point, there.

From behind: Wheels on wet pavement, the sound of harsh brakes and a siren *whoooooop*ing to a halt.

"Oh, damn," said the man.

"I promise they won't hurt you," Jasper said. "I promise you won't be hurt."

The man snorted laughter. "Yeah. Yeah, I believe that."

Feet pattered behind them. "Dent!" someone shouted. "Dent, you OK?"

Jasper raised his hands, just to be safe. "Don't hurt this guy!" he called over his shoulder. "Do *not* hurt this guy!"

* * *

The cops, for a miracle, managed not to molest the Black man as they hoisted him to his feet, cuffed him, and led him to the squad car parked at the entrance to the alley. Maybe Jasper's presence had them on their best behavior. Or maybe they were that rare breed who took the latter half of *Serve and Protect* seriously.

De la Croix arrived in a siren-screaming police car a few moments later. Jasper, by then, was sitting in the back of an ambulance, his legs dangling over the side, a blanket over his shoulders. She poked her head around the corner of the ambulance. "I know I'll just get something sarcastic and manly in response, but do you need a doctor this time?"

Jasper shrugged and did his best not to show how much that hurt. "I don't think so. Tough to tell what's new pain and what's old pain."

"OK, then let's go. Conroy wants to yell at you."

14

ONROY WAS ALREADY yelling in one of the small offices when Jasper and de la Croix returned to the task force. They could hear his voice and another, raised in anger, in exasperation, through the flimsy door as they approached. Jasper hesitated, but de la Croix flung open the door and ushered him in. Conroy and another man—both of them red-faced and agitated—didn't even acknowledge their entrance. Jasper had a vague memory of meeting the second man when de la Croix had dog-and-ponied him the other day.

"How the hell did he know Dent was at that particular wedding?" Conroy was asking, if *asking* could be defined as *yelling and gesticulating.*

"What if it was—"

"I swear to God, Grenier, if you say it was a coincidence, I'm reassigning you to Birmingham."

Grenier—a broad-shouldered, thick-gutted white man with thinning hair and a pugnacious mien—threw his hands up in the air. "It happens! He brought the note to drop it off and it just turned out Dent was—"

"Alabama!" Conroy shouted, pointing to the door. Grenier rolled his eyes and stomped out of the office, slamming the door behind him.

"I swear," Conroy seethed, "that guy thinks *everything* is a coincidence. Nothing is planned!"

"I mean, it *could* be a coincidence," Jasper said, since clearly no one else would brave Conroy's wrath.

"Not a coincidence," said de la Croix with more authority than he thought the situation called for. At least, he thought that until she held up her iPad, displaying an Instagram post showing Jasper emerging from the FBI sedan at the church, in the moment before he slipped on his mask. Fortunately, the photo had been taken from the left side, so his swollen jaw wasn't in evidence. Unfortunately, without that swollen jaw distorting his features, it was blatantly obvious who he was.

Check it, y'all! Butcher Billy's boy in Seattle! At my cousin's *wedding!*

Just in case *blatantly obvious* wasn't blatant enough. It would only be a matter of time before the "Jazz-o-sphere" collection of digital obsessives added this moment to his personal hellish internet scrapbook of notoriety. Once the movie deal was announced, he knew, it would get even worse. He had no one to blame for that but himself, but the money would be important to WorldVision.

"Wedding's definitely going to go viral now," de la Croix said lightly. As though a man in a mask chasing another man from the reception wouldn't be enough.

Conroy's left eye twitched as he glared at Jasper, arms folded over his chest. "About that . . . When an agent tells you to stand down, you stand down," he said.

"I don't work for you," he reminded Conroy.

"We're paying you. You work for me."

"I caught the guy. Tough to argue with results."

Conroy laughed without the merest hint of mirth. "Shit. You haven't worked for the government, have you?"

"I've never worked anywhere," Jasper admitted.

"It shows."

"Sir," de la Croix ventured, "maybe we should focus on what we have now? The man Jasper caught and the letter?"

Conroy sighed and dropped into a chair. "Fill me in," he told de la Croix.

He was clearly done with Jasper, refocused, so Jasper decided retreat was the better part of valor in this instance. He slipped out of the office and back into the main task force area.

At a desk in the corner, Agent Grenier banged furiously away at a laptop, not Alabama-bound at all. When he noticed Jasper looking at him, he narrowed his eyes, then went back to his computer. It was pretty much what Jasper expected.

Something, though, compelled him to walk over to Grenier's desk. "Hey. Shouldn't you be packing for Birmingham?" he said lightly.

Grenier grunted and didn't even look up from his keyboard. "Conroy has fired me six times so far. Once more and I get a free sub with my next order."

Jasper managed a chuckle at that. "Sorry he got hot in there. For what it's worth, I think we should never discount the possibility of coincidence."

Grenier paused in his typing, but took a moment before looking up. "Yeah?"

"Yeah."

The agent scrubbed at the stubble on his cheek. "I just try to remind people . . . Coincidence *is* a thing. We're not fighting supervillains here. Sometimes they make a mistake or something just happens because it happens."

"If you ascribe motive or intent to *everything*," Jasper chimed in, "then you could end up chasing a lot of rabbits into rabbit holes that lead absolutely nowhere."

"Exactly!" Grenier slapped his desk with an open palm, his eyes excited, as though he'd swiped right and found his soulmate. "Exactly! I'm not saying everything *is* a coincidence—it should just be on the table . . ."

He drifted off, as though realizing to whom he spoke, and then turned back to his keyboard, his manner once again gruff and dismissive. "Anyway."

Anyway.

"Good luck," Jasper said a bit awkwardly, and then ambled away. He found an unobtrusive spot near a dusty corner and studied the task force.

There.

Yes, he was certain.

De la Croix came to him from the office. Jasper nodded minutely in the direction of a uniformed SPD officer who was listening intently as an FBI agent ticked off points on her fingers.

"That uniform," Jasper said. "That guy there. He's the one who brought my stuff down from the old hotel room to the new one, right?"

De la Croix blinked a few times, gazed over at the cop. "I . . . guess. I don't really remember. Why? Did you forget to tip him?"

The lie slipped out before he could even consider it, and he chastised himself internally almost immediately. "No reason. Just trying to keep faces and people straight in my head."

"OK." De la Croix clearly thought it was weird, but just as clearly could not be bothered to say so. "Look, they're ready to interrogate the guy you caught. Want to watch?"

* * *

Through one-way glass, the man Jasper had tackled in the alleyway sat on the far side of a dented metal table. He was not, Jasper noted with grim pleasure, handcuffed or manacled to the table itself. Good. A man in a blue windbreaker with *FBI* stenciled on the back sat across the table, his back to the window.

"Meet Claude Simmons," said de la Croix. "Sixty-two years old."

"Ran like a twenty-year-old," Jasper grumbled.

Conroy, the only other person in the observation room, spoke up. "According to the files we pulled from SPD, Claude's been on and off the streets all his life. Currently lives in a halfway house. Doing OK for himself these days. Got a record for B&E, robbery, a couple of panhandling and nuisance charges, but that's all ten years or more in the past. He's been keeping himself clean and working his way into being a solid citizen."

De la Croix flipped a switch and Claude's voice came through the intercom loud and clear.

". . . a hundred dollars. You know what that kind of money can do for me?"

"I have a general idea," said the FBI agent. "So, a man comes up to you, offers you a hundred bucks to drop off an envelope at a wedding."

Claude shook his head. "I didn't know it was a wedding. He just pointed to the building. Said there'd be a party in there."

Grenier slipped into the room. He and Conroy exchanged a brief glance, but said nothing to each other.

"How did you know what seat to leave it at?" the agent asked Claude.

"Man told me it would be a white guy in a mask. I saw a guy get up and head to the bathroom, so I left it there."

"He didn't specify anything else?"

"No, man. I'm telling you. He just said to drop off the envelope on a table, gave me two fifties, and that was it."

"We found the fifties in his pocket when we searched him," de la Croix said, not looking up from her iPad. "They're at the lab, but we're not expecting to get any prints from them."

"So," the agent in the room went on, "tell me something, Claude. Man paid you in advance. Did he stick around?"

"No. Gave me the money, gave me the envelope, walked away."

"See?" Grenier ventured. "Coincidence. Bumped into Claude here, used him as a messenger. Done and done."

Conroy said nothing.

"So why did you deliver the envelope, then?" the agent asked. "He walked away. You could have just dropped it in the trash and gone about your day, a hundred bucks richer."

Claude's eyes bugged out and his mouth twisted into the grimace of a man who has bitten into rotten fruit. "He *paid* me!"

"Me?" Grenier said. "I'd've taken the money and run."

"Me, too," Conroy admitted.

"Me, three," said de la Croix.

They glanced at Jasper, who shrugged and jerked his chin in Claude's direction. "Maybe this guy should be the cop and we should all be in interrogation."

Conroy snorted laughter. De la Croix shook her head, amused.

In the interrogation room, the agent walked Claude through the scenario for the second time, this time focusing on the particulars of the man who'd approached him. No, Claude did not recognize him. No, he'd never seen him before. No, the man did not give a name or any other sort of identifying information. And no, Claude did not ask *why* the man wanted Claude to deliver the envelope. It seemed harmless enough and it was a hundred dollars.

The man was white. Wearing a mask and a hat, so Claude didn't know anything about his hair color or facial hair. Eyebrows were brown, eyes were brown. Age was difficult to tell. How tall?

"Little shorter than me," Claude said after some thought.

That put the man squarely in the average height range. *Very helpful*, Jasper thought bitterly.

He wore a raincoat that hung below his knees, so Claude couldn't say anything about how he dressed. No, Claude did not notice the man's pants cuffs or shoes—do *you* go around looking at people's pants cuffs and shoes, Officer?

"Agent," the agent corrected him, gently and clearly wearily.

The observation room door opened and a woman poked her head in. "Agent Conroy? Forensics has the letter for you."

Jasper perked up. "When do we read it?"

Conroy headed for the door. "Now."

*   *   *

A forensics expert had steamed open the envelope. Unfortunately, it was self-sealing, so no chance of DNA from the sticker residue, but they took a sample anyway. Then the same expert withdrew the contents with a set of tweezers. It was a single sheet of white paper, folded into thirds lengthwise.

The note read:

Dear police.

Hello how are you? I am good very good. I see you have invitd *Jasper Dent* to your side which I think is a smart move for you,

But not "smart" enough . . . !!

I am not ready to spot but I am also not eager to continue. This is <u>hard work</u> and I do not think you apreciate it!! I have much to do so please tell Jasper to settle in for a long wait! Ha! ha! I will work as fast as I can! Ha!

Yours,

Bridekiller

The letter itself was nothing exceptional. Nothing that offered any further illumination into Bridekiller's bloody cobweb-infested psyche.

But there was a postscript.

Jasper had skimmed the letter quickly and got to the postscript first. He knew when the others were there immediately: de la Croix gasped. Conroy blurted out, "Oh, shit!"

The postscript read:

Ps: Please thank Patrick for the drink!

15

I T TOOK THEM less than twenty minutes to get to Patrick Olefsky's house, even without sirens and lights. If Bridekiller was watching Patrick, they didn't want him to know they were on the way, even though *surely* he would assume that after that letter, the task force would descend on Olefsky's house like paparazzi at a red carpet.

Jasper rode with de la Croix. On the way over, she was in touch with Conroy, who was a block behind them in a Seattle PD SWAT van. They'd agreed that since Jasper had had a small measure of rapport with the man that he would speak to Olefsky and, with de la Croix, break the news to him that Bridekiller had named him.

With all the portents and possibilities that entailed.

Olefsky lived in Montlake, a neighborhood northwest of Jasper's hotel and the task force. The streets were dense clusters of single-family homes, bordered and separated by trees. Patrick's house was gray with white trim, an unassuming two-story shingled domicile in a neoclassical style, with a covered front stoop. Late fall and upper latitudes conspired to ring down night's curtain. It was dark when they arrived, though not yet past five o'clock.

Trees obscured much of the front of the house, but a single light burned in a window. Something hard clotted in Jasper's throat. What if Olefsky was already dead? What if—

He piled out of the car with de la Croix.

"Tac team is one block back," she told him, a hand to her earpiece. "They can roll in five seconds if we give the word. More units coming up on the next block to cover the back of the house."

Jasper nodded. The details of tactics interested him not in the least. He just wanted to know he hadn't failed Patrick Olefsky, that the man was still alive.

The doorbell chimed at de la Croix's touch. Clouds rumpled the sky. The rain had tapered off, but there was still that chill in the air that portended more.

The door opened. Patrick Olefsky glanced at de la Croix, bemused, then turned to Jasper.

"Dear God!" the man exclaimed. "What happened to your face?"

"I tripped," Jasper said. He tried not to lie because lying led to manipulation, but in this case, it was more expedient.

Patrick took a beat, nodded. "I'm sorry. I was trained better than that. I shouldn't have reacted so—"

"It looks worse than it feels."

"I'm glad to hear that. Come in."

He stepped aside and let Jasper and de la Croix enter the house. The first space was a tiny vestibule with a coat rack on which hung a single, solitary black raincoat and a green umbrella. Olefsky backed up, giving them room to enter, and showed them into a well-appointed living room.

On the coffee table was a framed black-and-white photograph of Rebecca Olefsky in her bridal gown. A candle was posed before it, flickering in a glass sheath.

"The wedding photographer gave back the deposit when she delivered the photos," he said, as though an explanation were needed. "She wouldn't let me pay her."

Jasper had nothing to say to that. De la Croix said, "Again, we're so sorry for your loss, Dr. Olefsky."

"Patrick, please. Sit." He gestured to a comfortable gray sofa and sat opposite them in an armchair upholstered in a checked yellow-and-black pattern.

"Have you caught him?" Patrick asked. "I assume that's why you're here."

He vibrated with anticipation. His left leg bounced.

"I'm sorry, but no," de la Croix said. "We're here because . . ."

She drew in a breath.

Patrick's expression became worried, furtive. "Did he do it again? Did he kill someone else?"

"No," Jasper said. He realized that he had no real official capacity or authority here, but he *was* a guest/consultant for the Bureau, so he figured it was all right for him to talk. And he and Patrick *had* bonded during their interview. Somewhat.

"We're here because the killer has sent us a letter, and we have reason to believe you may know him."

Patrick blinked rapidly and sat back. "I'm sorry, what?"

Jasper watched Patrick as de la Croix explained about the letter, about Claude Simmons, about the postscript. Patrick did not go pale at the news, but his Adam's apple bobbed with ferocity as he absorbed it.

"Am I . . . Am I in danger?" he asked.

"It's hard to say," de la Croix told him. "Anything is possible."

"He has a type." Jasper jumped in when de la Croix's comment seemed not to have ameliorated Patrick's concern. "Most serial killers don't deviate from their type."

"Your father did," Patrick said slowly.

It was true and also not true, but Jasper didn't think now was the time to explain Billy's particular psychopathy.

"We think you're safe," de la Croix said, "but we'd like you to be . . . Well, be very aware of your surroundings. There's always the possibility that he might decide you're a loose end to tie up. And, well, we're going to need to go over all of the guests with you again."

"I knew everyone at the wedding," Patrick said. "And I mean *everyone*. There were no strangers. Not even a random plus one I didn't know. None of them are capable of something like this. I say that not just as an acquaintance, but also as a psychiatrist. Trust me."

De la Croix nodded unconvincingly. "I understand. Still, we're going to have to have someone go through the wedding photos and videos with you. I know you did that already, but—"

"It's fine," Patrick said. "If it helps."

While the tac team canvassed the neighborhood, Jasper and de la Croix spent the better part of an hour with Patrick, going over his memories of the night one more time. No one stood out. Nothing special. When they asked him who he had specifically shared a drink with at the reception, he'd laughed and said, without mirth, "It was my *wedding*. I had a drink with *everyone*."

"Did you make small talk with any of the catering staff or venue personnel?" Jasper asked. "Someone you would have shared a drink with? Or bought a drink for?"

Patrick shook his head, very slowly at first, then more rapidly as he became more sure of himself. "No. I mean, I exchanged a few pleasant words . . . The folks who ran the venue were all women. One of the bartenders was a man . . ." He closed his eyes and leaned back, trying to remember. "We had passed *hors d'oeuvres* before the reception . . . Some of the servers were men, but I didn't speak to any of them except to thank them for taking my empties. I certainly didn't share a drink with any of them!"

"Was it an open bar at the reception?" Jasper asked. Maybe the killer meant *thanks for the drink* generally, not specifically.

"Yes," Patrick said somewhat distractedly, then rose—trembling just the slightest bit, Jasper noted—from his chair. "I'm sorry. I need a glass of water."

"Let me help you," Jasper said, rising to touch Patrick's elbow, to steady him. The man seemed to have aged dramatically since the revelation of the postscript.

Patrick seemed steadier by the time they got to the kitchen. It was a cluttered space, with a round four-top table crammed into the corner, counters packed with appliances: a microwave, an air fryer, a very fancy coffeemaker, and an Instant Pot. The sink was piled high with dishes.

"Sorry for the mess," Patrick said, pouring a glass of water from a pitcher. "Can I get you something?"

"No thanks." Jasper glanced around. The floor was a beautiful hardwood, polished and clean, except for one spot, where a plug of a different colored wood—rough and unsanded—glared.

"I can't believe this," Patrick muttered, as though to himself. "I really can't believe this."

"I'm sorry." It was lame and pointless, but there was nothing else to say.

Patrick downed the water, then chuckled without heat or humor and shook his head. The water seemed to have done him some good. He was steadier.

"No, no. Please don't apologize. This is . . . This is death and murder. You know it well."

"I'm not here to talk about me."

"Of course not. Look . . ." Patrick set his water glass down and gazed at Jasper, steady, sure. "Look, I know this will seem . . . forward, but you seem like someone who needs to talk. I'm a good listener and I haven't exercised that part of my brain in a while. Here." He scrounged around for a sheet of scrap paper and wrote his phone number on it, then held it out to Jasper.

"Call, text, whatever. I'm here."

Jasper stared at the paper, not touching it. "I'm not sure if—"

"I don't know anything about serial killer pathology," Patrick admitted, "but I was pretty good at post-traumatic stress and the like. You have all the earmarks."

"Yeah, I know."

"It's like a flashing neon sign: *I'm hurt! Help me!*"

"Good to know." Jasper touched the paper, and it was like a circuit had been completed, power connected.

* * *

They informed Patrick that someone would be watching the house, just in case, and then drove back to the task force.

"Now what?" Jasper asked. The rain had picked up again, dirty spatter on the windshield, the steady *wish-click* of the wipers. "You re-interview everyone from the reception?"

"All the men at least."

It would be a hell of a task, he knew. He leaned back against the head rest. He was glad *he* would have nothing to do with it.

His phone chirped for his attention. It was Howie.

GW is awake. Wants to talk to you. Got a minute?

He was just thumbing back Sure when de la Croix's radio erupted in a panicky burst. An address, a time, followed by words that chilled Jasper to the bone:

". . . husband shot . . ."

16

THE VICTIM WAS Morris Gibson, husband to the third victim and the only Black person in the entire affair so far. De la Croix needed her GPS to get them to the right place, and it took them through a densely wooded park. Jasper was half convinced the satellite had lost its damn mind and sent them off into logging country when suddenly they broke through into civilization again.

When de la Croix pulled up to Gibson's neighborhood, there was already a massive police and FBI presence—multiple squad cars, unmarked sedans with lights flashing. An ambulance had parked half on the curb in front of a Tudor that he assumed belonged to Gibson.

The radio in de la Croix's car had been a chaos of overlapping voices and contradictory commands; she'd snapped it off roughly three seconds before Jasper was going to beg her to do so.

A husband. Was this part of Bridekiller's plan, some new wrinkle they hadn't imagined?

But he should have imagined it, he realized. Bridekiller's letters indicated a loathing not for the women, but for their *mates*. He killed to save the women from what he saw as a life of drudgery, submission, and travail.

It made perfect sense, then, that he would come back for the husbands. First take the wives, to make the men suffer. Then come back and kill the men to avenge the dead wives. He figured he could tell Conroy not to worry about the lesbian weddings, at least.

Perfect sense. Twisted sense. Jasper felt himself slipping into Bridekiller's psyche and was both mollified and horrified to find it fit.

De la Croix flashed her ID to a uniform charged with keeping press and lookie-loos away from the crime scene, then maneuvered her car as close to the action as possible. Jasper was out the door before she killed the engine.

A cluster of uniforms stood by the open front door to the house. Gibson himself lay on a stretcher, attended to by two EMTs. His eyes were closed, his body utterly still, but he wore an oxygen mask with a slight fog scrimming its interior, which at least meant he was alive. The EMTs fussed over him, one tending to a large white bandage on his chest, the other running an IV line into his arm.

"What happened?" de la Croix demanded.

"Is he going to make it?" Jasper asked.

An EMT favored him with a withering look and then shouted, "Move it!" The cops and assembled others parted as the EMTs raced the stretcher down the slope from the front door to the ambo at the curb. He watched them load Gibson in as de la Croix conferred with the cops at the door.

The doors to the ambulance slammed shut. Moments later, the EMTs floored it and screamed their siren through the night as they flew from Gibson's house.

Killing the husbands. Of course. Yes.

He found himself chewing a fingernail and stopped, rubbing the ragged edge against his rough jeans to smooth it out.

Yeah. Perfect sense. Then why didn't I think of it before?

17

T HE HOSPITAL REPORTED back to Conroy, who put out the
word to the task force: Morris Gibson was in stable but
critical condition. No one knew when he would wake up, or if
he would. A bullet at close range had perforated his left lung
and then nicked the aorta before vacating the body without
further damage.

The collapsed lung and blood loss to the heart was plenty,
it turned out.

EMTs in the field had stopped the immediate bleeding and
ran enough saline to keep his volume up and keep him alive on
the way to the hospital, where surgery had repaired the lung
and the aorta. He now had a chest tube and an octopus of IVs
and was blissfully unconscious.

Blissful for him, torture for the task force, who needed an
eyewitness. Badly.

Conroy had uniformed officers on loan from SPD canvass-
ing the neighborhood before Gibson was even in the OR. They
had orders to report in every half hour.

Jasper stood in the middle of the task force's space and
watched the chaos around him. He was the only person who
had nothing to do, no assignment. De la Croix had abandoned

him, shouting into her phone while stalking off toward one of the offices.

He didn't want to steal a desk or a chair from someone who might need one, so he stood. And he watched.

And he thought.

And he blamed.

Should have seen it coming. Why didn't I see it coming? It matches up to his pathology almost perfectly. What's wrong with me? Why didn't I see it?

The cop from the hotel rushed by, offering not so much as a glance in Jasper's direction. But Jasper had caught the surname stenciled on the man's nameplate: McCARTER.

He processed both things at once: Bridekiller's perfectly predictable swerve and the name he now had.

Officer McCarter, did you put that note in my bag?

He could imagine a very simple scenario: Billy Dent in the Seattle area, decades ago, a young serial killer looking to make his mark on the world and on the Crows. Billy called himself Green Jack back then. Murdered three women in the Seattle area, none of them named McCarter. But any of them could have been McCarter's best friend, first kiss, cousin, stepsister, half-sister . . .

Maybe her death prompted him to grow up to be a cop.

And then there's Billy Dent's kid right in front of you. Why wouldn't you pop him in the face? And why wouldn't Bridekiller go after the husbands? And why didn't that occur to you, Jasper Francis Dent? What the hell is wrong with you?

De la Croix emerged from an office, frantic.

Jasper's phone buzzed. He checked it quickly; a text from McCutcheon.

Call me when you can, please. I know GW means a lot to you.

He tucked the phone away. *Consider all the angles. Race? Gibson is the only Black man in the case. One of two people of color. Should we be looking at Robert Huang? Put protection on him?*

Or is it racial at all? He killed the women in one order, but the men in another . . . Starting with Gibson, husband of the third victim . . . Why? Again, race?

It's not always *race.*

Can I find McCarter's first name? Can I get close to him without spooking him? That's starting to sound stalker-y. What would McCutcheon say? Nothing helpful.

He rubbed his temples. The noise around him approached migraine-induction levels. He'd never actually had a migraine, but he imagined this had to be pretty close.

The husbands . . .

He imagined that the task force would assign protection to them, but that would take a while. They were on a manhunt in Gibson's neighborhood, one that would consume all their resources in the short term. It was the first thing resembling an opportunity to catch Bridekiller they'd had, so he understood the impetus to put everything into it.

But the husbands . . .

And what are you going to do about it? he asked himself. *Go babysit them yourself?*

He didn't even know any of them. Not really.

Well, except for Patrick.

Right. And what am I supposed to do if the guy shows up? Throw a batarang at him? Call the Avengers with my signal watch?

We do what we can, McCutcheon had said once in a session. It was the sort of ambiguous compassion that could mean anything, but under the circumstances . . .

He sighed.

*   *   *

In the back seat of the Uber on his way to Patrick's, he thumbed out a quick message to Howie.

hey sorry I got pulled into something. Is g still awake?

It took forever for Howie to respond.

Sorry, man—he's asleep again.

And then:

You OK?

Was he? He couldn't tell. But that was nothing new—he'd been unable to tell if he was OK for years. He had no idea how to define the state of "OK." He had an inkling as to how other people—normal people, adjusted people—defined "being OK," but did not know how to apply the rubric to his own status.

yeah, i'm fine. ping me when he wakes up

Will do.

At that moment, a new text popped up. McCutcheon. Again.

I understand G. William is in bad shape. I'm here if you need to talk.

Jasper *did* need to talk. But so much of his life was already flayed open to McCutcheon. His father and his mother and Connie. G. William had been a topic they'd danced around early on, then abandoned for the more fertile fields of his parents and the woman he loved. Still, McCutcheon knew how important G. William was to him.

And that made it impossible to talk to his therapist about it. McCutcheon would prepare him for G. William's inevitable death, whether by this incident or another. McCutcheon would try to comfort him, reminding him that everyone dies, that there are ways to honor the dead.

But Jasper didn't want to hear any of that. Especially from someone he disliked so much. It was one thing to discuss his parents—he and McCutcheon were united in their loathing of Billy and Janice Dent. And McCutchen liked Connie and spoke well of her, so they were in accord on that front.

But to hear McCutcheon tell him that he had to accept that G. William would die . . . Well, no shit! It was true and he knew it and so he absolutely did not need or want to hear it.

He stabs the wives but shoots the husband. Or should that be stabs the wives AND shoots the husband? Personal vs. impersonal?

What does that mean to him? And did McCarter request running to my hotel when my call came through or was he already close by because he'd just left?

His brain spun.

Patrick's house was as peaceful as it had been the first time he'd laid eyes on it, a mere—he checked his watch—two hours ago.

Two hours.

The same light still burned in the same window.

He clambered out of the Uber and watched it pull away into the darkness. The shadows and the concealment of the trees seemed to augur danger. Bridekiller could lurk anywhere. McCarter could lurk anywhere. If it was McCarter.

A heavy sigh densed a plume of partly frozen breath into the air. Inside, outside. Made no difference. What the hell was he actually doing here? Here, in Seattle. Here, on the task force. Here, on Patrick's front stoop!

The door opened. Patrick cleared his throat.

"You have to actually push the button to make the little ding-dong sound," he said.

Jasper sighed and scrubbed his hands down his face.

"Did something else happen?"

Jasper mounted the steps to the front door. "I can't really talk about that. I just . . . Look, sooner or later, they're going to send some cops to hang out here, but until then, I just think I should sit with you for a little while."

"Oh." Patrick's face fell. "That can't be good."

They stared at each other for a protracted moment.

"Well, come inside. The rain'll probably pick up again soon."

Jasper followed him inside and then back into the kitchen. The dish pile in the sink had shrunk, plates and cups migrating to a drying rack. He looked down at the floor, thinking he'd imagined it before, but no—there was the spot—an almost perfect circle, clearly plugged with a different wood, unpolished and raw.

Bridekiller, McCarter. McCarter, Bridekiller.

He shook his head and made himself focus on the plug, as though to ground himself.

Patrick, filling two drinking glasses from the pitcher, noticed him staring at it. "That's where Rebecca is," he explained.

Jasper nodded slowly. He needed to swallow, but it took him a very long time to do so, his throat constricted.

With an almost jovial air, Patrick tilted his head to one side. "Sorry. I've confused you. Let me explain:

"The Apayao people of the Philippines . . . They bury the dead under the kitchen. Rebecca's wish was to be cremated, but she never expressed a preference for what should be done with the ashes."

He joined Jasper in gazing significantly at the patched hole in the floor.

"Are you Filipino?" Jasper asked. "Was Rebecca?" To his practiced eye, they both presented—as did he—as garden-variety white folks. But anything was possible. And a racial component might be a clue. Morris Gibson lay in a hospital bed from which he might never rise.

"No, not at all. I just borrowed the ritual. I'm sure someone somewhere is outraged at my cultural appropriation, but it's my life. And it's my kitchen."

"Why the kitchen?"

Patrick gestured without drama, listlessly. He offered a glass to Jasper, who accepted it. "Why the kitchen? Something to do with nourishment, I think? In any event, it doesn't matter. I wasn't interested in the efficacy of the ritual, just the fact of it. It could have been anything. In another part of the Philippines, they prop the deceased in a chair in the corner and put a lit cigarette in its mouth."

"Oh." Jasper squirmed. He understood that the world was a big place and he tried not to be the proverbial hick from Tennessee, but some things he just could not accept. The notion of posing dead bodies, to him, reeked of his father and his depredations. As the Artist, Billy had delighted in posing dead bodies in a variety of—to him—sensible tableaux. It was a sign of disrespect, of domination, and Jasper couldn't shake the idea, no matter how hard he tried.

"We don't mourn very well in the West," Patrick said soberly. "We lost the habit of it in the Middle Ages. During the Plague. So many people died that it was impossible to mourn them all in the traditional ways, so people just stopped. The numbers were too great."

"One is a tragedy, a million is a statistic," Jasper said.

Patrick smiled wanly. "Stalin. Yes. I speak from some experience when I say that we've really bungled grief in this country. We privatized it. We made it something to be endured alone by 'rugged individuals'. A solitary pain. And as a consequence, we never face it head-on. I wanted something that would provide comfort. And I found it."

"It really works?" Jasper asked.

Patrick considered the question for long enough that Jasper knew he was taking it seriously. "There's no way to A/B test such a thing, of course, but I think it does. Has. Is."

"I believe you."

Patrick gestured to the small table and they both sat down. "You've suffered your own losses. Your parents aren't dead, but they—"

"They weren't very good as parents," Jasper said abruptly. "I don't miss them."

"Ah, you see, that's the problem." Patrick leaned forward. "You're not letting yourself grieve their loss. It's not about what they did for you or to you, Jasper. It's about mourning the loss of what they *could have been*. They took that from you. We don't just mourn what was. We mourn what never can be. Even bad parents need to be grieved because they never got the chance to be who or what we needed."

Jasper wasn't quite sure he believed that. Or that he wanted to believe it. But something in Patrick's manner made him feel closer to mourning his parents than he'd ever contemplated before. It was a complicated, sticky feeling in his psyche, an old cobweb transferred from finger to finger as he tried to brush it off.

"Why don't you practice anymore?" he asked. "You seem really good at it." He did, too. Direct, no questions—thoughts and ideas, instead. So different from McCutcheon.

Patrick sighed. "Why don't I practice anymore? Rebecca."

"She didn't like your work?"

At that, Patrick smiled his first true, genuine smile, without sadness or wryness. "She loved my work. She was a patient."

Jasper felt like smacking his forehead with the heel of his palm, but knew it would hurt and possibly disturb the line of butterfly stitches. "Oh," he said instead.

"I fell in love with her. And she with me. Ideally, that's not supposed to happen, but it does. A stronger man might have resisted. Might have put it aside and told her to seek out a different doctor. I needed to pawn her off on a colleague, get her out of my life. Ghost her. That's the protocol, if you don't want to lose your license.

"But I was too weak. So I gave it all up. I did the right thing. The ethical thing. I closed my practice, took a teaching position, started a new life . . ." He drifted off. There was an uncomfortable caesura as Patrick raised his glasses, pinched the bridge of his nose.

"Patrick . . ." Jasper stood. "I can go. If you need to be alone—"

"No, no. It's OK. See, this is what I was talking about before." He settled his glasses back on his face and beamed at Jasper. Tears glistened behind the lenses. "We try to lock grief away. Right now, every red-blooded American fiber of my being is telling me not to show you my grief, to hold it in . . ."

He broke out in a sob, then drew in a hard breath.

"And it's really hard to let it show. Almost harder than holding it in."

Jasper felt as though the moment called for something on his behalf, but damned if he knew what. He was an actor in a play, but no one had told him his lines; he had no memory of his cues.

But he knew one thing: He knew in his core that Patrick did not want him to look away. That Patrick wanted to expose this grief, give it to the air shared between them. And so even though he wanted to stand and leave or at least avert his gaze, he forced himself to watch as Patrick wept.

When he was done, Patrick plucked a napkin from a black metal lattice at the edge of the table, wiped his eyes, blew his nose gently. Behind the glasses, his eyes were red-rimmed and swollen.

"It just hits me sometimes," he said, and nothing more.

Jasper nodded. Everything Patrick had told him seemed outlandish at best. But he admitted that his own viewpoint was unalterably Western-centric. Who was he to gainsay the wisdom of a culture just because it wasn't his own? His imagination conjured a brief panorama of Patrick Olefsky, weeping, snot running from his nose, as he knelt on the kitchen floor, carefully pouring his love's ashes through the hole he'd drilled.

"But you're not here to talk about me, are you?"

He wasn't. He wasn't here to talk at all. He was here to . . . wait. To watch. To scream bloody murder if Bridekiller showed up.

But suddenly . . .

Suddenly, yes, he wanted to talk. And not about Patrick.

This was absurd. He couldn't do this.

But Patrick had nailed it. The post-traumatic stress. The pain. The man had only just met him and already understood Jazz better than McCutcheon did or—he surmised—could.

And it happened. Much to Jasper's shock and surprise, without even thinking of it, he opened his mouth and he started talking.

He told him a little bit about G. William. Not much. It wasn't necessary to go into detail; Patrick had read Jasper's memoir and there was plenty about G. William in there, none of it mangled or mutilated by Jasper's cowriter's urging to dramatize.

You get to the deeper truth by exaggerating, Ricardo Sloan had said more than once.

Jasper had retorted that his life was exaggerated enough. No need to convert fact to fiction in some quixotic quest for a *better fact.* A "deeper truth."

"If I were thinking shallowly," Patrick said slowly, "I would say that he's like a father to you—"

"He's not like a father." Jasper bristled. "I don't know what a father is. Or rather . . . I know and I don't like it."

Patrick nodded and waved a hand. "I said *if I was thinking shallowly.* I mean, it's right there, on the surface. They even share the same name. It's almost too convenient.

"But he's not like a father *to you.* To someone else, maybe, we could say that. But to you a father is someone who stands back while you're hurt, right? Someone who pressures you into doing things you know are wrong."

Jasper turned away, uncomfortable. His eyes burned.

Because that was it. That was it exactly. He *wanted* G. William to be a father figure to him. Because he knew what a father figure was supposed to be, knew how the bond between father and son was supposed to be knotted. But he couldn't allow himself to go there, couldn't allow himself to think of G. William that way. The ideal father—the Platonic ideal of it—warred with his own practical, lived experience, and the lived experience won every time.

Every. Single. Time.

"There's a father-shaped hole in the puzzle of your life," Patrick told him. "G. William doesn't fit into that hole. Nothing does and nothing ever will."

Jasper's lips moved without sound. He had so much to say.

Do you think you can save me? he wanted to ask. *Please?*

It was ridiculous. Childish. And yet there were the words, clustered like sugar crystals on the tip of his tongue. He swallowed them down, too sweet, cloying.

"What do I do then?" he asked.

And this, he knew from long hours of therapy, was when Patrick would deftly volley the ball back over the net and onto Jasper's side of the court. He'd witnessed it a thousand times with McCutcheon—begging for answers, for direction, only to be told, essentially, *Well, that's the part you need to figure out.* Or McCutcheon's favorite aphorism: *I can't pick the path; I can only walk it with you.*

"You do what you do with any puzzle missing pieces," Patrick said with an almost savage pragmatism. "You throw it in the trash and you start another one. This one, ideally, with a space the size and shape of G. William."

Jasper said nothing.

"What I mean," Patrick began, "is that—"

"No, no, I understand. I get it. I just . . . didn't expect such a straight answer. That's actually . . . That's actually really helpful."

Patrick smiled and raised his glass to his lips. "Told you I was good at this."

He stayed another hour, and in that hour felt that he'd made more progress than in ten with McCutcheon. Or if not progress, at least comfort. If sessions with McCutcheon were the hard work of laying a new road, then sitting with Patrick had been laying a very short but perfectly even and perfectly smooth stretch of pavement. If he'd been in therapy with Patrick from the beginning, he might not have resisted so much. It was easier than with McCutcheon—it didn't feel adversarial.

Finally, what he wanted, what he needed from therapy. What McCutcheon refused to give him. Answers, not more questions.

Some uniforms showed up at the door (none of them McCarter) and Jasper—with surprising reluctance that he sought to conceal—returned to his hotel.

*   *   *

It took him an hour to poke around online and find Officer Glen McCarter. In a sane world, it probably would have taken longer.

Nothing in the man's Facebook or Instagram accounts generated a clear connection to Billy's victims.

Jasper stared at the photos of Glen McCarter at a barbecue, at a pool party, at a Mariners game. With his girlfriend, his mom, his stepfather, his younger brother.

Nothing seemed off. And while surfaces disguised much, Jasper's gut told him there was nothing to find.

Mike was on duty again. Jasper opened his hotel room door and leaned out into the somewhat stale corridor.

"Hey, Agent Cortes. How well do you know the cops on the task force?"

Mike startled. A jumpy bodyguard did not fill Jasper with confidence.

"The cops? I know a few of them. Why?"

"Glen McCarter?"

"Who?"

Jasper contemplated his options. He could go further, but there was no point in fishing a dead pool. "Never mind."

Back in his room, he regretted saying anything at all to Mike. If Mike said something to McCarter, it would only alert him to Jasper's intentions.

He gnawed at the inside of his cheek, on the side that didn't hurt yet. Might as well even them up.

It was too late to call G. William. It was too late for anything, really. But he was awake and he couldn't sleep until then, suddenly, he could.

18

IN THE MORNING, no one called. No text from de la Croix telling him she was on her way to pick him up. Nothing.

Maybe, he sensed, it was time to let the professional law enforcement people do their jobs. The killer had thrown a hand grenade into the room and now they had to pick through the shrapnel to determine what mattered and what didn't. Jasper hadn't been much help. He hadn't been able to predict Bridekiller targeting husbands, even though it was so obvious a move. He imagined he would soon be packed onto a flight back to Tennessee, perhaps with the perfunctory thanks of the Bureau, but probably not even that.

The good news was that he figured at the very least, the FBI would stop hounding him to help chase serial killers.

In the bathroom mirror, the swelling along his jawline appeared to have abated considerably, but the line weaving under butterfly stitches at his hairline and along his temple looked more gruesome than before, a crusty blackish-red streak Frankensteining his flesh. He gently scrubbed at it with a wet washcloth and improved it not even a little.

No FBI agent at his door. He suspected skulduggery for half an instant before deciding that it was much more likely the task force just couldn't spare the warm body. Not everything was a clue leading to violence.

He emerged from the hotel into a surprisingly sunny day, the sky an almost perfect worn-jeans blue, inlaid with shreds of cloud along the horizon. Without quite intending to, he found himself rambling down Federal Avenue again, the only place he really knew at all in the city. By day, it was a cheerier place than it had been when he and Mike wandered the dark and foggy streets.

He ended up outside Coffee Amore. In daylight, the place was packed with customers. The barista—Shanna—worked double-time behind the counter, her nose piercing glinting in the sunlight every time she smiled at a patron.

It was still morning. Coffee would be good, he convinced himself. People drank coffee. He was people. She served coffee. It was perfectly natural, and he wasn't quite certain why he had to talk himself into it.

Inside, he loitered at the end of the line, watching Shanna work, her motions practiced and reflexive. She grabbed jars and bottles without looking or double-checking, made eye contact with her clientele as she whipped, frothed, sprinkled, and poured.

Finally it was his turn. The place had emptied out a bit, most people taking their drinks to go. A couple of people around his age lingered at tables, pecking away at laptops, lost in their headphones.

Shanna brushed her curls from her forehead with the back of her hand. Obstinately, they boinged right back into place.

"Hello, there, black coffee, no sugar," she said, smiling. He reminded himself that she smiled for everyone. "No bodyguard today?"

He returned the smile, ignoring the slight twinge in his jaw. "I guess I'm more expendable than I thought."

"What brings you to town?" She poured a medium black coffee for him.

"That obvious that I'm not a native?"

"It's the accent."

Better that than recognizing him from news stories or that damn TikTok account or even the very public, very loud APB the NYPD had blasted out for him back during his time in that city. He knew he still had a slight Tennessee twang, a little syrup in his speech that—to Yankee ears—sounded slow and perhaps a bit dull. But he also had a skill she didn't know about.

"What accent?" he asked, mimicking her own PNW cadence to perfection. "I don't know what you're talking about."

He reached for the coffee, but she hovered it just out of his reach, then dumped it in the sink behind her. "I need to make a fresh pot anyway. You don't want the dregs, do you?"

I'm used to the dregs, he almost said.

"OK, thanks." He watched her back as she busied herself at the coffeepot. Another thin white T-shirt under the Coffee Amore apron, and he had a sudden intuition that she was deliberately taking longer than necessary, letting him watch her.

Which should have made him stop.

But didn't.

With a sudden glance over her shoulder, she caught him. Smiled. "Making coffee is that fascinating?" she asked with a slight lilt to her voice.

Clearing his throat, embarrassed, he deflected. "What's with the caduceus?" he asked. "You a doctor in your spare time?"

She turned back to him, held her forefinger and thumb a quarter-inch apart. "Came this close. Burned out. Decided to sling java instead."

"I bet there's more to that story."

"Possibly. What about you?" Her eyes skimmed him from neck to waistline with an air of appreciation he couldn't miss. "Any ink anywhere?"

He laughed at that, surprising her. "Sort of."

"Sort of? How do you *sort of* have a tattoo?"

And so he told her about Howie, about his best friend. Born a type-A hemophiliac, and therefore forbidden by both doctor and mother from getting a tattoo. And a tattoo was what Howie wanted more desperately than anything else in the world.

"So *you* got one for him?" Her eyes widened with surprise and, he thought, admiration.

He pointed to his right shoulder, where—hidden under his shirt—lurked a stylized CP3, for Chris Paul, Howie's favorite basketball player in their youth. Then rolled up that same sleeve so that she could see the string of black Korean characters around his right biceps.

"Asian tats." She rolled her eyes.

"It wasn't my idea," he reminded her.

"What's it say?"

"Howie claims it says 'I am strong and mighty in the wind,' and I'm afraid to have it translated and find out if he's right or not."

She chuckled at that. "Anything else?"

The last two were too embarrassing, he decided. At Howie's insistence he had a thoroughly ridiculous Yosemite Sam tattoo on his back. And as a consequence of his own youthful stupidity, there was the I HUNT KILLERS emblazoned along his chest.

"Nothing that's just yours?" she asked him.

He shrugged, which wasn't the same as lying, he decided then and there.

They were quiet then for too long. She was really, really pretty, he decided in a very juvenile way. And for whatever reason, his beat-to-hell face didn't seem to repel her.

That probably should have been a warning sign. He couldn't let himself see it that way, though.

Connie. Connie, what the hell am I doing?

Shanna plucked a ceramic mug from under the counter and started to fill it. Jasper's phone vibrated for his attention. He looked at it and sighed.

"Better put that in a to-go cup," he told Shanna.

* * *

De la Croix picked him up at the hotel, a little salty that he hadn't been there when she'd texted, as though he were expected to tarry in his room until summoned. They spoke little during the ride to Interbay. Jasper sipped his coffee and thought of Shanna and then made himself think of Connie instead.

Conroy, Grenier, and a few others were clustered together in a makeshift conference room. When Jasper entered, Conroy sarcastically thanked him for making the time, then pointed to a TV screen at the end of the table.

"SPD grabbed the footage from Gibson's video doorbell. We might be about to get our first look at Bridekiller." Without further discussion, he thumbed a remote.

A multi-vocal grumble filled the room when the video began. The quality was terrible. Grainy and too dark in some spots, too bright in others, the highlights all blown out and shining.

"Is this thing from ten years ago?" Grenier asked.

"Eleven," someone said with confidence. "Not even last-gen tech. More like *last* last-gen—"

"Shut up," Conroy advised.

Not that it mattered. Even as the room fell silent, the audio from the screen proved to match the video in quality, as though a harsh wind had been blowing directly into the microphone the whole time.

The video opened *in medias res*, with a man standing at the front door, seen from the right side. The doorbell's quality was poor; its placement was unfortunate. They could see the man only from his shoulders to his waist. From his motion, he seemed to be stamping his feet against the cold as he waited.

A generic trench coat, buttoned over what appeared to be a collared shirt. Colors impossible to determine via the night vision.

"He's white, right?" someone said. "You see his hand there for a minute—"

"Shh!"

As though silence mattered.

A moment passed. And then the man's stance changed. Through the staticky hiss of the doorbell's audio, they heard two voices. Words were impossible, but intent was clear: Anger. On both sides.

"Tech can clean this up, right?" Grenier said.

"Probably," said Conroy, leaning forward, staring at the video.

The man's right hand went into his pocket, emerging a moment later with a pistol. Despite growing up in a town and a county and a state much beloved by the NRA, Jasper had almost no experience with firearms. Billy hadn't been interested in them—too impersonal, too distant—and so his son was not conversant with them. Someone else in the room— maybe everyone else—surely knew what kind of gun it was.

The image flared bright white and the static vanished, swallowed by the enormity of a report. Jasper flinched in his seat.

When the image cleared again, the man was already down the porch steps, running. His back to the camera, a flutter of hair, and then he juked left on the sidewalk and was gone.

The room sighed.

A small murmur of conversation began. Snippets floated to Jasper: *Opened the door . . . So he knew the guy . . . ? Saw him on video and answered . . . ?*

Maybe, maybe not . . . Might not have checked the video first . . . Who knows . . . ?

"No subtlety," someone said. "No stealth. No process or signature . . ."

"Some of us volunteered for this task force because we thought the guy was a Crow," Grenier said loudly. "And it's looking less and less like that every day."

Jasper said nothing, looked down at his hands, felt eyes on him.

"What makes you the expert?" Conroy snapped at Grenier.

Grenier held up a hand, ready to begin ticking off items in proof of his expertise, but Conroy waved him silent and stood up at the head of the table.

"Look, I don't care if this guy is a Crow or not. He's killed four people so far and where I come from, that's four more than we usually allow. Maybe the audio will give us something when it's cleaned up. Maybe not. But we're here until this guy is caught. Got it?"

The room muttered, close to agreement, and people began filing out. Conroy stopped Jasper and held him until everyone but de la Croix had left.

"Mr. Dent, you were brought in on the assumption this was a Crow-related killer. Grenier's an annoying ass, but he's not wrong. This is looking less and less like it's connected to the person described in your father's book." He shrugged. "If you want to go home, I completely understand."

Jasper weighed the options. It would probably be better for him—healthier, in the long run—to go home. But what was waiting for him in the Nod? G. William in a hospital bed, that's what. And he didn't know if he could handle that yet.

Selfishly, he wanted to see this through. Even more selfishly, he wasn't ready to leave Patrick yet. Patrick could help him. Had already helped him.

"I'm going to stay, if that's all right with you, Agent Conroy."

Conroy nodded. His expression—even for someone as attuned to reading people as Jasper—was inscrutable.

* * *

That night, he awoke for no reason he could readily discern, panting softly in the black solitude of his hotel room, his eyes wide, senses alert. Nothing shuffled or breathed in the darkness.

For once, a dream had not awakened him. No lurking, lurid terrors evoked by his gabbling subconscious. But *something* . . .

He had fallen asleep thinking about Patrick. He'd asked if the FBI needed a volunteer to sit with him, but Conroy had assured him that all was well on that front.

It wasn't that, then. What had wakened him?

He rolled out of bed and padded to the door, thinking to check one more time that everything was locked. On his way, though, he felt something crunch underfoot and he froze where he stood.

The light switch was close by. Without moving his feet, he leaned to the right and flipped on the light, then peered down.

A sheet of paper was under his left foot. A whoosh of relieved breath fled him. In that brief caesura of doubt, he'd not known what he might have stepped on or into, but there'd been a half-second of serious concern.

Plucking up the paper, he turned it over to reveal writing on the other side:

YOU
SHOULD
BE
DEAD

The hush of the paper under the door had alerted his sleeping mind, wakened him. Now he fumbled with the locks, threw open the door, and looked down the hallway in both directions.

Nothing. No one.

19

Before he knew it, a week passed in Seattle. Bridekiller must have been on vacation—there were no murders and no further communiques.

Jasper's attention was bifurcated, divided between Bridekiller and the vengeful ghost stalking him. He spent some time imagining different snares he could use to capture or at least tag the mystery man, but no further notes appeared and there was no more contact. He still said nothing to the task force about it—it was his mystery to solve, his past coming back to haunt him.

Bridekiller, after all, didn't leave handwritten notes.

He considered the direct approach: Follow McCarter home. Break in. Threaten him. It would be easy. So easy. He knew how to do it, even with a cop. Cops hadn't frightened Billy and they didn't frighten Jasper. Any human being can be caught off guard and unawares. Any human being can be caught, captured, immobilized. Any human being can be reduced to a target. A victim. A prospect.

It was the quickest, easiest, most expeditious route to either solving the mystery or clearing McCarter's name, and one night Jasper even started the plan, following McCarter home to an apartment in the northern part of the city. He sat outside and watched the cop's windows as they lit and dimmed into the night.

Knock knock . . . Delivery . . . Wrong address? Aren't you Glen McCarter? Opens the door . . . Blitz attack . . .

He could see it. He could feel it. His blood thrummed, feeding his muscles as he sat on the bench across the street and envisioned it.

But no.

No matter his motivation, that would be crossing a bright, hard line he'd drawn for himself. As a kid, he'd crossed the line habitually, convincing himself that the ends justified the means. But now he knew the truth: Justification was too close to self-righteousness, which in turn abutted self-deception. And crossing the borders was dangerous. For him and for others.

As the week maundered by, the mystery deepened for him, and Bridekiller remained at large, out there somewhere. And there was nothing he could do about it. The task force had the resources to pick apart the lousy video from the doorbell, cross-reference time stamps with other doorbell cameras in the area, and more.

There were only a few weddings during the week. The task force had them covered and nothing happened. But Jasper felt the tension ratcheting up as the weekend approached with its total of 174 weddings of brunettes wearing a size eight.

He had become obsessed with size eight brunettes. During his perambulations of the city, he noted them in passing cars, walking the sidewalks. Mannikins in shop windows earned his assessment. There were victims everywhere.

"What if," de la Croix said at one point, "he wasn't thanking Olefsky for a drink *at the wedding*? What if he wasn't at the wedding at all? What if he knew Olefsky some other way and had a drink with him at another time?"

Jasper considered it. It was a decent theory. "We need to get Patrick to go through his history. Male friends he's had drinks with . . . Maybe someone was jealous of him marrying Rebecca?"

"Or maybe Olefsky just doesn't remember," Grenier pointed out. "He was roofied, remember? His memory could still have holes in it, ones he's not aware of."

"So we're back to the killer at the wedding," Conroy said, disgusted. He threw a balled-up sheet of notepaper across the table and watched it land—perfect swish—in a wastebasket. He left no time for acclamation for his feat, continuing right away: "We're running in circles, chasing our tails. It's god-damned ridiculous."

And it was.

At least one good thing came out of it—Patrick.

Unbeknownst to de la Croix or anyone else on the task force, Jasper continued seeing Patrick. Sometimes by phone, sometimes in person, at night, when he'd been cut loose from the task force for the day.

No fool, Patrick had noticed his increased ad hoc security detail—all of the husbands were being watched 24/7 now—and tried to get details out of Jasper, but Jasper refused to spill, always turning the conversation back to himself, a handy eva-sion of what he couldn't discuss, and a solid landing into the territory of what he did, to his surprise, need to discuss.

"I want to help these people," he told Patrick. This partic-ular conversation took place at a rare afternoon meeting. The feds were all locked away in some sort of budget/personnel meeting and Jasper's presence was neither required nor desired. So he'd headed over to Patrick's, using his usual disguise of a ball cap and COVID mask to avoid being recognized by the cops parked one house-length away.

"Well, then you've already failed," Patrick said to him. "They're dead already."

"No, not the victims. The ones they've left behind." He gazed meaningfully at Patrick, who sat on the sofa while Jasper sat in the easy chair. "Closure matters. And maybe I can stop the next victim from dying."

Patrick shrugged. "Maybe you can't. Accept it."

"I just feel like I was better at this when I was younger. I could have done it then."

"Could you have? Were you really better at it? I've read your book. How long did it take you to figure out the Impressionist was copying your father's career? Didn't Helen Myerson die because it took you too long to figure that out? How long did it take you to realize the Hat-Dog Killer was two people, not one? And how many people died before then?

"And how long, Jasper . . . How long did it take you to realize the truth about your own mother?"

Jasper had shrunk into himself as Patrick spoke. He was right. Despite his protestations to de la Croix early on, Jasper had always happily subscribed to the popular notion that he *was* a serial killer whisperer, a wunderkind whose in-born X-ray vision could pierce the fog of madness and bring murderers to justice. But he'd failed as often as he'd succeeded.

McCutcheon would never make him feel this bad, but McCutcheon was wrong.

He followed Patrick into the kitchen, where they waited for the kettle to brew tea. The plug in the floor caught his attention once more.

The ritual seemed so outré to him, but in truth, was it any crazier than burying someone in a graveyard where you would only see them with intention? Was it any more disquieting than placing an urn on the mantel? Was it any less healthy than bottling it all up and pretending the grief didn't exist?

"What you just said back there . . ." Jasper held out his mug as Patrick poured. "You're right. I just keep thinking of all the people I failed. Helen Myerson. Ginny Davis. Jennifer Morales. Melissa Hoover."

"Would you like to tell me about them?"

"Like a grief ritual?"

"If you prefer. Even saying their names can be therapeutic. Sometimes I speak Rebecca's name out loud for no reason at all."

He liked Patrick so much more than McCutcheon.

As though summoned through Jasper's distaste and disdain, McCutcheon chose that moment to text him.

Concerned about you re: G. William. Give me a call.

He slipped the phone back in his pocket. No need to talk to McCutcheon.

"Important call?" Patrick asked.

Jasper shook his head. He had finally managed to speak to G. William a couple of days previous. The old man had sounded weak; it was a shock to Jasper, who'd never heard anything but the booming, powerful tones of the sheriff of the Nod.

Still, G. William was slowly improving. There would be surgery at some point. Serious surgery—replacing valves, rerouting blood vessels. Stuff that made Jasper cold with worry.

G. William, though, took it in stride. "Surgery? Hell, at my age everyone's either about to have surgery, in surgery, or recovering from surgery."

Patrick gazed at him levelly. "What's going on in that head?"

"You've read my book."

"Yes."

"Then you know."

Patrick sat at the table and gestured for Jasper to sit with him. "I know what you put in the book. And I know there's more."

Jasper leaned forward, elbows on the table. "I worry I'm doing more harm than good here," he said. "I worry that whatever insight I had—no matter how good or bad it was—I've lost it."

"Good," Patrick said bluntly. At Jasper's startled expression, he laughed. "I'm not practicing any longer, so I'm not bound by a code of ethics. I can tell you what I actually think. And I think it would be great if you stopped thinking like a serial killer. It would be a sign of health and progress.

"Now what about your dreams? Still having them?"

He shrugged. "There's always bad dreams. The trick is which ones actually bother me. It's been a week or so since I woke up from one. I'm managing."

"That's good. Let me ask you this," Patrick went on. "What's stopping you from getting on a plane and going home right now?"

Jasper goggled. "Don't you want me to catch this guy?"

"No."

It took a long moment for Jasper to collect himself enough to ask the simple question: "What? Are you serious? He killed your—"

Patrick waved him off. "Don't misunderstand. I want him caught. Very badly. But I don't care if you're the one who does it. Quite frankly, I'm not sure you can. And even more frankly, I'm not sure you should. It would be better for you to move on with your life, to put this behind you. I'm confident someone else is up to the task."

Staring down into the depths of his tea, Jasper sighed heavily. He was uncomfortable. But he figured that was a sign that something was right, something was true. His childhood had been a tutorial in twisting the morality and ethics of the world to suit his parents and, by extension, himself. He was beginning to realize that when everything in him cried out to do X, it probably meant X was bad or wrong. And the reverse was true—the more he struggled against Y, the more he probably should acquiesce.

It was like quicksand, he understood. If you thrashed about, you'd just sink deeper. But if you relaxed and went with the flow—like water—you could swim out.

"What are you thinking?" Patrick asked him.

"I feel like you're about to say, *And that's our time for today.*"

Patrick laughed. "No clock. No timer. I have nothing but time, Jasper."

But Patrick did check his watch. "Tomorrow's Friday. The start of the weekend. Are you concerned?"

Weekends meant weddings. Jasper shook his head. "No. We know his type. We're watching."

"Good. Why don't you go back to the hotel and get some sleep? Maybe see if Connie is available back east."

*   *   *

Instead, he found himself at Coffee Amore. He'd been a couple of times during the past week, but Shanna hadn't been on duty. Now she was, and it was late enough in the day that the place was quiet.

"Are you still strong and mighty in the wind?" she asked him as he entered.

He chuckled and leaned against the counter. "Let me surprise you—black coffee, no sugar."

"Medium."

"Let's call it a large today."

"Oh, you *do* live dangerously!" She busied herself with a carafe and a cup. A large porcelain mug shaped like a volcano, growing wider at the bottom. She pushed it over to him and he hoisted it, weighing its contents before taking a sip.

"Any chance you'll tell me what you're doing in town?" she asked.

"You never asked before."

"I'm asking now."

He studied her for a moment. The arch of her eyebrows. The sparkle and glint of the piercings. The way the apron cinched in at her waist and the small cleft of her chin. And the hair, in its French braid as always, down her back, and the two curls defiantly sketched over her forehead.

"I'm here to catch a serial killer."

He expected a laugh or a snort or a dismissive wave. Instead, she leaned back against the sink and nodded thoughtfully.

"This guy killing the women? The ones who get married?"

"Yeah."

"Wow."

"I'm sort of a consultant for—"

"For the FBI. I remember your bodyguard." She considered him, favoring him with a nakedly critical eye, as though assessing his capacity to catch a serial killer. *No, no!* he protested in his thoughts. *For real! I can do it! I've done it before! I have a tattoo and everything!*

"Is that why you got beat up?"

He shook his head. "No. Pretty sure that was something else. And it doesn't really matter."

She clucked her tongue and her eyes traveled the map of his injuries. "I disagree."

"It's OK. It'll heal. I've had worse."

If she asked what he meant, he supposed he would have to tell her about the stabbings. The gunshots. Would he tell her it was his mother who stabbed him? Who'd shot him? That much was in the book, but it was quick, clipped, almost elliptical in its description. Saying it out loud was different. He'd spoken the words to so few people.

But instead, she simply glanced at her wristwatch and volleyed over a non sequitur: "Have you ever seen the Space Needle?"

"It's hard to miss in this town."

"Yeah, but there's a cool angle. Tell you what—I'm closing in ten minutes. I'll take you."

* * *

He never properly agreed to go with her, but he also never declined. He drank his coffee at one of the tables near the window and in almost exactly ten minutes, she emerged from the back of the shop, her apron gone, buttoning up a sleek yet puffy coat the color of lime zest. It set off her eyes brilliantly and made her hair shine.

She tugged a black wool cap over that same hair. "Let's go!"

Together, they walked up Federal Avenue, then cut east around a bend and left the road to climb a set of concrete steps up a hill. A sign nearby introduced him to Volunteer Park, a spread of grass and trees. He didn't know what kind of trees and suddenly felt like he should.

He also felt like he should be holding her hand, but she had both stuffed into her pockets, as though to alleviate his anxiety.

They crossed a narrow road that cut through the park and emerged on the other side near a reservoir. They perambulated the reservoir, its pellucid blue surface a counterpoint to his own internal turbulence. But he could only see it through a chain-link fence. Just like his own elusive peace—within sight, but not within reach.

"Bruce Lee is buried somewhere around here," she told him. "And his son, Brandon."

Father and son. Jasper wondered what it was like to love your father, to cleave to him even in death.

"How does someone become an FBI consultant?" she asked out of nowhere.

"How does someone become a barista?" he countered. Lamely.

She stopped and laced her fingers through the fence, staring off into the water. "I asked first."

He allowed as that was true. "I have some experience. Family experience."

"Holy shit," she said, turning to gaze at him. "You're that guy. You're that kid."

"Holy shit, I'm that guy," he agreed. "I'm that kid."

Shaking her head as though to rearrange the thoughts within, she said, "Someone gave me your book for Christmas two years ago. I haven't read it yet."

She didn't apologize for it, which he liked. And she stared at him unflinchingly, which he liked even more.

"Are you going to catch the guy?" she asked.

Not the question he expected. At all. He'd braced himself for questions about his parents, his upbringing, a series of concentric circles narrowing around a core target, the aim of which was simple, an answer to the unasked and unanswerable question: *Just how fucked up are you?* Unprepared for a question about Bridekiller, he gaped for a moment, then found his footing and responded as honestly as he could.

"I don't know. I hope so. I think so. But I don't know for sure."

With a nod, she turned to go. "I guess it's a good thing none of my friends are engaged."

He followed her the rest of the way around the reservoir. As they rounded to the western side, she pointed out the Seattle Asian Art Museum, a glass-fronted Art Deco construct of heterogeneous white blocks fitted together in an exacting orthogonal pattern. Flanking the entrance were two concrete Bactrian camels. He always associated camels with the Middle East, but of course great swaths of Asia were desert, too.

She led him away from the museum, through a parking lot, to a concrete estrade on which stood a dark granite torus with smooth grooves cut into both sides at irregular intervals, like a bagel carved from onyx, then gouged with furrows and valleys before finally succumbing to a vigorous, scouring polish.

"Black Sun," Shanna announced. "Look through."

She grabbed his arm and pulled him closer. To the sculpture and to her. Their faces nearly abutted as they looked through the hole in the center of the sculpture.

"There's Elliot Bay," she said, "and there's the Olympics. And there's the Space Needle."

At this distance, from this vantage, the Space Needle seemed small, a slender interruption of the sky. The rest of Seattle, the entire skyline, was submerged in greenery, so the Space Needle seemed almost sui generis, standing out of nothing.

"Cool, right?" she asked. It was cold out and her breath frosted the air between them, mingling with his own. He was aware of her. Her closeness, her breath, her heat.

He was aware.

Without pulling away, he turned to look at her. So close he could see the flecks of silver in her eyes. "You weren't really closing in ten minutes, were you?"

"You're very observant. I bet you catch a lot of killers."

He thought. "In fact . . . You don't just work there, do you? You own it."

She did not deny it. She licked her lips against the cold and her septum piercing jittered. "Are you one of those guys who asks permission to kiss a girl? Because that's very sweet and respectful, but I have to tell you that you don't need to ask me."

And he decided to do it. He would kiss her. He would do it right now, before he could change his mind. She was so close it would take more effort not to kiss her, he thought. To escape her gravity would require heroic strength, and to lean the two inches between them and press his lips to hers would take nothing at all.

She would taste like coffee and peppermint, he decided. And he—

His phone rang in his pocket. Her gaze did not waver at the sound, locked on him, expectant.

But he had to answer. It could be de la Croix. It could be news.

He took a step back, held the phone to his ear.

A measured, recorded voice said, "You have a call from an inmate at Wammaket State Penitentiary. Do you accept this call?"

20

THE STATE OF Tennessee counted more than twenty-two thousand prisoners in its various state and municipal correctional facilities, but there were only two that Jasper cared about.

One was Frederick Thurber, whose nom de homicide was the Impressionist. He was the first serial killer Jasper had ever caught and currently resided at Riverbend . . . awaiting execution for his crimes.

The other inmate passed his days in a special medical holding unit at Wammaket State Penitentiary. He was paralyzed from the waist down after suffering a knife blow to his spine.

He was inmate #P094728-1. He was William Cornelius Dent. And he was paralyzed because Jasper himself had driven a knife into his father's back at the thoracolumbar junction, right around T12 and L1, permanently ending Billy's reign of brutality and savagery.

But not ending his phone privileges.

"Hell, no," Jasper said into the phone, and then immediately hit the disconnect button and shoved the phone back into his pocket.

It was cold out, but the cold was not the reason for his shivering. His father reached out on an irregular schedule, sometimes calling several times a day, sometimes waiting months between calls. It was a devious and malicious ploy— even though Jasper had never once accepted a call, Billy was able to keep him on tenterhooks by dint of his random attempts.

There were services to remove his phone number from prison calls, but Jasper had not availed himself of them. It would be an admission to his father that the calls bothered him. Which they did. But he would rather his father hear his voice, hear his rejection, and then nothing. It was a small satisfaction, but better than nothing. Better than the certainty that blocking Billy's calls would just give Billy the gratification of knowing he'd gotten under Jasper's skin.

Shanna's expression combined frustration, concern, and curiosity. He tried a wan smile, but didn't think he'd managed to pull it off. When she asked if he was OK, he knew for sure he'd botched it.

"I think I need to go," he said.

She opened her mouth to speak, but he shook his head. "Thanks for showing me around. But I need to go. I really need to go."

* * *

All the way back to the hotel, alone, he wondered if he'd done the right thing. Yes, the moment had fractured, the intimacy broken, but so what? He could have still kissed her. Could have still made the move.

But it wouldn't have been the same. The inevitability of it had shattered, the consequences became real. Connie could do as she pleased and so could he, but he didn't *want* to. For that moment, yes, he'd wanted to—but no longer. Billy had ruined even that small pleasure for him, one more sin to heap atop

Billy's Everest of them. As though the counting of them even mattered any longer.

If he'd kissed her, it would have been only to prove that he could. And that, he knew, wasn't reason enough.

De la Croix called as he entered his room. Her voice was somber and defeated.

"We got the guy who shot Gibson," she announced with absolute depression leaking from her.

He stood in the middle of the door, gobsmacked. He couldn't believe it. They'd caught him! They'd actually caught him! Almost as surprising was de la Croix's despondency.

"You got him!" Jasper did a little dance into the room. He'd never let anyone see that, but he figured he deserved it. "You got him! Why don't you sound happier?"

"I said we got the guy who shot Gibson," she explained. "I didn't say we got Bridekiller."

He sank onto the bed, staring ahead at the mute, dark TV he'd never even turned on. "What do you mean? Bridekiller *is*—"

"Just . . . get a car to the task force. You'll see."

*   *   *

In the interrogation room was a man in his late fifties, thinning black hair, a resigned expression on his face.

"Meet Gerald Castelano," said Grenier, jerking a thumb at the one-way glass. "He's the father of Maddy Castelano, who was, for about five minutes—"

"Maddy Gibson," Jasper breathed. He stared into the room. "Morris Gibson's father-in-law."

"Again, for like five minutes," Grenier said.

Someone in the room—Conroy or anyone else—should have told Grenier to knock off the gallows humor. It wasn't funny. But no one said a word.

Jasper leaned in close. "This is the guy? *He* shot Gibson?"

"Tech is still working on the audio," said de la Croix, "but we had enough to go on to pick him up. We heard the phrases 'my daughter' and 'my little girl.'"

"He confessed?" Jasper asked.

Conroy and Grenier exchanged a look. "Well, no."

"So, you found the gun that shot Gibson?"

Another look. Conroy said, "Well, no."

Jasper stared into the interrogation room again. "Guys, what if this *is* Bridekiller? What if it was one of the fathers all along?"

Conroy's jaw dropped. "Wait . . ."

"That could . . . That could actually make some kind of sense . . ." Grenier ran a hand through his hair. His expression revealed that it pained him to admit Jasper's idea could be right.

"He fits most of the profile," Jasper said, recalling what he'd read of Maddy Castelano's family. "Divorced. White."

"A little old, though," de la Croix put in.

"So?"

"Do we really think he murdered his own daughter on her wedding day?" Grenier asked.

"Let's ask him," said Conroy.

*   *   *

Grenier brought Jasper into the room, but everyone agreed he would say nothing. He would sit in the corner, arms folded, and simply watch.

Gerald Castelano did not so much sit as attempt to sit, fidgeting, rearranging himself on the chair. There was a common belief that serial killers were cool customers, but Jasper knew from experience that they could be just as anxious as anyone else, especially when pinned in the hot glare of a spotlight.

"Mr. Castelano," said Grenier, sitting across from him. "Gerry. How the hell are ya?"

"I . . . I want to speak to a lawyer," Castelano said, casting his eyes around the room.

"That's a hell of a good idea. I'll get right on that." Grenier stood immediately and headed for the door. Jasper stared at Castelano. He could see it. Barely. A sad, divorced man, filled with self-loathing, ready to protect his own daughter from what he imagined was a fate worse than death . . . and then punish the man responsible for that fate.

Castelano stared back at him. "Wait!" he called to Grenier. "What about him?"

At the door, Grenier paused. "What about him?"

"Who's he? Why is he staying here?"

Jasper assiduously said nothing and instead fixed Castelano with the most Billy stare in his arsenal. It worked—the man was clearly unnerved.

"Who's he?" Grenier barked with laughter. "You don't recognize him? This is Jasper Dent. He hunts killers like you. He can smell your guilt from a mile away. He eats serial killers for breakfast."

In a weird way, it was the nicest thing Grenier had said to Jasper thus far.

"Serial killers?" Castelano's voice jumped an octave. He leaned forward, staring at Jasper. "You think I'm—"

"I can't talk to you. I'm getting your lawyer." Grenier dusted off his hands and stepped out of the room, leaving Jasper alone with Castelano, who pushed his chair back from the table and fidgeted with his hands, gaze darting all over the room.

"*You* can talk to me, right?" Castelano asked.

Jasper settled on a strategy: Silence. He would say nothing. He would simply Billy-eye Gerald Castelano and see what happened.

"I'm not a serial killer," Castelano said. His tone was firm, but wavered at the end, a squiggle of doubt. Not that he wondered if he was, in fact, a serial killer, but rather pondering whether or not anyone would believe him.

Jasper still said nothing, his gaze level and intentional.

"Why would they even think . . . Wait. Wait." A horror lit Castelano's eyes. "Do they think *I* . . . I killed all those girls? My own *daughter*?"

The anguish and shock in his voice were both very real. Jasper knew. He could read people like texts—at a glance, while focused on something else. It was a predator's skill. It was his father's gift to him.

"My own daughter?" Castelano howled it, throwing back his head. Then he slumped forward, burying his head in his folded arms on the table, weeping loudly. It wasn't a put-on. It was real.

"I didn't!" He looked up at Jasper, tears streaming down his face. "I swear to God! I swear! Please! Say something! I didn't kill her. Not any of them!"

Jasper stared. He believed Gerald Castelano. But there was more. More to come.

"I swear." Castelano's voice went low, pleading. "Please. You have to believe me. I would never . . . I could never . . . How would I even do that? How could anyone do that?"

Jasper's left shoulder began to itch. He focused on it mightily, willing it to stop. His body remained immobile, his expression blank and impassive, his gaze fixed and acute.

"I just went to Morris's house . . ." Castelano said, almost whimpering. The man wasn't even looking at Jasper now, eyes downcast, studying his own hands, twisting and grasping at each other on the table before him.

And this was it. This was what Jasper knew was coming.

"He didn't do enough . . . He was supposed to protect her. And I thought . . . There was a part of me that thought maybe he was involved?"

A question, but a dishonest one. Trying to coax Jasper into saying something. Agreeing. *Sure, sure, that's a reasonable thing to think . . . Go on, Gerry . . .*

But Jasper said nothing.

"He was *there*. He was there with her and she died. How could he *not* . . ."

Castelano wiped at his eyes. He drew in a long breath that tortured Jasper with its duration. His shoulder itch had abated on its own, but his body was cramped and sore both from sitting motionless for so long and projecting equal doses of competence and threat.

"I brought my gun. A little pistol I've had for years. We argued. I accused him. He told me I was crazy. I told him that even if he didn't kill her, he still didn't protect her. That was his job. I gave him my little girl and he was supposed to . . ."

He drifted off. He was facing Jasper, but his eyes, unfocused, were witness to something else entirely.

This is how it happened, when they confessed. They started out with one thing. They figured if they copped to *one little thing* then maybe they could get away with the rest of it. And then, eventually, the rest would—

There was a knock at the one-way glass that nearly made Jasper jump out of his skin. He managed to dial back his reaction to a mere flinch. Castelano seemed not to notice.

The knock came again. Without a word, Jasper stood and left the room.

In the adjacent observation room, de la Croix held up a USB stick. Grenier and Conroy were nowhere to be seen.

"What's up? I mean, he pretty much just confessed. I don't know if it'll stand up or not, but—"

"He's not Bridekiller," de la Croix said.

Jasper licked his lips and looked into the interrogation room. Castelano was still staring at a nothing only he could see.

"Maybe, maybe not," Jasper said, a little too quickly. "He shot Gibson. He might not be ready to cop to the rest. Might think he can throw us off—"

"This is the audio from the doorbell." De la Croix waved the USB stick again. "Tech cleaned it up enough for us to listen to the whole thing. It's just like he said. They argued. He accused. They argued some more. It got heated and personal. Bang."

Nothing she said meant Castelano still couldn't be Bridekiller. Jasper shook his head. "No. It's still possible—"

"It's not him, Jasper. He's alibied for the murders. It's not about us. Not this time."

"But, no . . ." he protested, voice weak. "No. No, that's not . . . He's punishing the husbands. That's what he's . . ."

He wanted her to interrupt him. To blurt out, *My God, you're right! You've been right all along!*

Instead, she said nothing. She cleared her throat a few times and then left him alone in the observation room. He stared through the glass at Gerald Castelano and suddenly the man he'd been so certain was Bridekiller stood revealed as just a mad-with-grief middle-aged slob who'd gone and done something ill-advised and spontaneous and galactically stupid.

He stared up, through the ceiling, through the sky.

He'd been so sure! He'd thought he'd found his way into Bridekiller's head, wormed through a back window with a busted lock and taken up residence, squatting there in the fetid darkness, where he would find all the clues they needed to stop the killing.

But he'd broken into the wrong house. He was rifling the wrong drawers, assessing the wrong heirlooms.

What's wrong with me? he asked himself.

When he emerged from the observation room a few minutes later, the first thing he saw was Officer McCarter, standing at a printer across the room. And he decided to hell with it.

He marched up to McCarter and as soon as the man sensed his presence and turned to him, snapped, "You have a problem with me?"

As a species, cops were not used to in-your-face aggression. Their uniforms, badges, and guns tended to keep people around them polite. McCarter recoiled and actually took a step back.

"What?"

"Did my father kill someone close to you?" Jasper demanded.

"What are you talking about?" McCarter glanced around as though looking for the hidden camera. Jasper took a step closer to him.

"Sister? Friend? I can give you the names, if you like. From when he was here back in the aughts."

McCarter took another step back, bumped into the printer. "What are you talking about?" he asked again. "I only moved here three years ago."

Jasper narrowed his eyes. He could tell when people were lying, usually, and McCarter gave off none of the signs. In fact, the man seemed to be on the edge of terror.

He was petrified of Jasper.

"You're sure?" Jasper asked.

"Man, sir, look . . ." McCarter stumbled over his words. He wasn't even sure how to address Jasper—there was no way in the world he'd screwed down the courage to approach him in person and issue a beating.

Was an apology in order? Probably. Most likely. But Jasper was too focused on his own screw-up, his monumental miss. He backed away from McCarter and, without a word to any-one, left the task force.

*　*　*

He wandered. Time passed and he paid it no mind. With relentless steps, he sought to clear his mind, but it didn't work; his mind stubbornly refused to clear. He kept thinking of how much sense it made, how much Bridekiller *had* to be punishing the husbands. How it *had* to be McCarter.

He'd been wrong. About everything. Supremely confident and absolutely wrong.

He needed to break the cycle of his thoughts. He needed an interruption. Where was Billy's phone abuse when he needed it?

Huddled against a wind, he pinged Connie. Nothing. He tried Howie, but similarly nothing. It would be close to eleven back home. Howie would be asleep. Connie would be in another endless rehearsal.

Or on a date.

Or on a sofa.

Or on a bed—

He blocked off that line of thinking. He'd done this to himself, after all. He had no one to blame but Jasper Francis Dent.

He couldn't call G. William—the big man needed his rest. The only other people he even knew well enough to have phone numbers for were McCutcheon and Simon.

Hard pass on McCutcheon. And Simon was business, not personal.

There was Coffee Amore. Shanna. Possibility. Finishing the lean to the kiss. Maybe it wasn't too late. Maybe he could find his way back to that blissful state of gravitational attraction.

No. He couldn't do it. He couldn't go to Shanna. Not like this. Not when he was looking for succor and assurance. It would be human to use her like that, but that wasn't the kind of human he wanted to be.

A cold wind blew at him as he rounded a corner. Had he been of a particularly superstitious bent, he'd have taken it for an ill omen.

But he'd already failed so much. He'd already been beaten senseless in his own hotel room. What else could possibly be coming his way?

He opened his phone and thumbed through for Patrick's number. But the first number that jumped out at him was the last one that had called him. There, in red text, was the phone number for Wammaket.

And it suddenly made all the sense in the world.

21

MORRIS GIBSON'S FATHER-IN-LAW (on a technicality, Grenier insisted on saying) was arrested and charged with assault, discharging a firearm, and slew of other related crimes. If Gibson died, there would be a homicide charge in the man's future, too. No other Bridekiller husbands reported incidents, which was now as expected. The 24/7 guards had been recalled and put back to work at their normal task force functions.

Conroy looked up as Jasper and de la Croix entered his office. "He has something to tell you," de la Croix told her superior.

"Should I get some other folks in here?" Conroy asked.

Jasper hesitated. "Not yet. Not just yet. Let me tell you this first . . ." He frowned, gathered his thoughts, and found that the basket containing them had a wide weave; he couldn't keep the collection in. Talking about his past with Patrick or even McCutcheon was one thing; the hatch to his soul slammed closed when it was anyone else.

Finally, he managed to blurt out, "Look, when I was a kid, my parents teamed up and they manipulated this guy into killing people."

"Thurber," Conroy said.

"Yeah. The Impressionist. It was a message for me. It was specifically designed to get me to do certain things, to manipulate me. And now I'm thinking it might be happening again."

Conroy swallowed. Visibly. "Why?"

"My father called me recently."

Conroy's eyebrows made a very interesting and interested arch over surprised eyes. "Go on."

He explained to Conroy how Billy often called him. How the calls usually came at random. Or what seemed to be at random, but was perhaps dictated by a schedule only Billy's diseased mind could discern.

"But now you think maybe it's not random?"

Jasper sighed. He looked around, but the office was too small for a spare chair. "Maybe not."

Conroy scrubbed his hands down his face. "I don't believe this. Your father calls you in the middle of a hunt for a serial killer and you didn't answer the phone?" His voice rose toward the end, its tenor irritating Jasper into defensiveness.

"I never answer when it's him, OK? There's no reason to."

"Your father has a history of using serial killers to manipulate you."

"He did that with my mother helping him. And she's not in a position to help anyone these days."

"OK." Conroy pointed to de la Croix. "I want recording equipment. Get the warden of Wammaket on the phone. We'll put in a call to Dent, let Jasper talk to him—"

"Uh, I have two things to say to that," Jasper interrupted. "*Hell* and *no*."

Conroy glared at him. "It's entirely possible your pops is behind the whole thing. We need you on the phone with him."

"Not happening." Jasper stood a little straighter. Conroy was giving him what Jasper thought of as "the cop glare." It communicated volumes—*I am in charge. You have to listen to me. I can make your life very difficult if you don't listen.*

But Jasper had endured many a cop glare in his life. He was impervious. "I told Agent de la Croix—I don't talk to my father. That part of my life is over."

"People are dying, Dent." Conroy said it the gentlest tone he'd mustered yet.

It almost worked. Jasper shook his head minutely. He'd lived too long with Billy's voice in his ear. He had just gotten to a point where he could almost forget the honeyed tones, whispering perversions and horrors.

"Did you ever draw a line for yourself, Agent Conroy?" he asked slowly, softly. "Ever cross it? Did you feel better afterward?"

Conroy sighed and strummed his fingers on the desk. "Shit. Let's get someone in the Knoxville or Memphis office to go to Wammaket and play tiddlywinks with Billy Dent and see if anything comes up."

De la Croix immediately turned to the door, phone already out. Jasper wondered if it was a power trip for Conroy that his every whim was instantly accommodated. Or was he just used to it by now?

"And check all his incoming and outgoing calls, as well as his lawyer visits and mail!" Conroy called. She was half out the door, phone to her ear—she waved acknowledgment as she left.

"This could change things," Conroy said once he and Jasper were alone. "Depending on what the local office pulls from Wammaket. First we thought this guy was a Crow."

"Because of what was in Billy's book."

"Right. And then as time went on, things weren't as clear. But now . . ."

"Now it might be deliberate. Billy's twisting this guy and pushing him to fulfill the prophecy of what he wrote years ago. He's either a Crow or he wants to be one badly enough that he'll do Billy's bidding."

Conroy considered. "What about your aunt? Your father has a sister, right?"

Jasper nodded. "Yeah. She's not a part of any of this. Disappeared years ago. Off to live her life anonymously."

"We could probably find her."

"Leave her alone. Please. She grew up with Billy. She deserves a life of peace."

Conroy stood, came around the desk, and leaned out into the main room. "Grenier!" he shouted.

Moments later, Agent Grenier shuffled into the tiny office, wearing an overcoat. "You going somewhere?" Conroy settled behind his desk again. "Got a hot date?"

"Just got back from lunch," Grenier snapped. "Cut me some slack."

"Never forget: Alabama awaits."

Grenier snorted. Jasper did his best not to roll his eyes at their endless sniping.

"Tell him everything you told me," Conroy told Jasper. He grinned over at Grenier. "You're gonna love this."

*　　*　　*

"You know," de la Croix said, "we still have to talk about your assault."

She was driving him back to his hotel. He had no idea where she was staying. The Bureau probably had some sort of rental situation for the task force. Or maybe it was just a not-as-nice hotel. Being a "special consultant" had its perks, he decided.

Or would, if he gave a rat's ass about the quality of his hotel room.

He was only listening to her partially. His focus had broken into pieces, a cracked mirror reflecting different elements at slewed angles: Billy. The agents headed to Wammaket. McCarter's fear, not of discovery, but of the son of the notorious Billy Dent. And Patrick's comment, singing in his ears, that it didn't matter if Jasper was the one to catch Bridekiller or not.

And deep down, Jasper knew this to be true. It was egoism and narcissism and solipsism in the extreme to think that he *had* to be the one to catch the killer. To think that only he could hunt the killer, beard him in his lair, bring him to justice. All that mattered was that no one else died. That no one else suffered as Patrick had suffered.

"Did you hear me?" de la Croix asked.

"Yeah. My attacker . . . It's small potatoes compared to Bridekiller."

She pulled over at the hotel, but before he could disembark, she caught his attention. "When were you going to tell me that your friend came back to visit?" she asked.

He froze, fingers curled around the door handle.

She handed over her phone, cued up to a security camera. He recognized the hallway outside his hotel room. A very familiar figure dressed in black—Jasper felt an immediate twinge of pain in his jaw—walked up to Jasper's door, crouched for a split second to slide something under, then strode briskly out of frame.

"Oh," he said. "That."

"Yeah. That." He voice was tight, the tone dark. "You can't keep things from me. It's my job to keep you safe."

"No, it's your job to catch Russian oligarchs squirreling money away in offshore accounts. They ripped you away from that to babysit me because you're Black and that sucks because I bet you were really good at the financial crimes stuff."

"I'm good at this, too," she snapped. "This isn't about me. It's about you. I saw you with McCarter earlier. You think it's him?"

Her tone told him that she was perfectly OK with rousting and arresting a cop for this, and he loved that about her.

"I don't think it's him."

"Then who?"

"You have to let me handle this," he told her.

"SPD is looking for someone. If you have further evidence . . ."

"SPD has more important things to worry about. Don't worry about me—I'm a big boy. I can take care of myself."

"Your face says otherwise. The swelling's gone down, but those stitches still look nasty and half your face is light purple now."

He chuckled. "Like I told you before: This is nothing."

She slammed her palms against the steering wheel. "Damn it! Stop doing this shit! You're being hunted and you don't even care!"

"I do care," he said very calmly. "But whoever this guy is, he wants to *hurt* me. He's not going to kill me. Not quickly, at least. One thing at a time, Agent. Bridekiller, *then* Jasper-beater."

He could tell she wanted to ask how he could be so sure. How he knew. He was surprised and pleased that she did not.

*   *   *

The weekend passed without incident. Of the weddings of brunette women wearing a size eight, all were present and accounted for the morning after. Jasper experienced a queasy mingling of relief and disappointment in his gut.

On Sunday, Conroy called a meeting to discuss the findings of the agents who'd gone to Wammaket. They were briefed by a man with the familiar neroli accent of home over a speakerphone.

Billy—no surprise—had exercised one of the few rights a prisoner has remaining and had refused to speak to the agents. According to the warden, Billy Dent was behaving inside. Not quite a model prisoner, but nothing to worry about, either.

"Of course, he can't walk," the drawl said from the speakerphone, "so . . ."

Everyone in the room—Grenier, de la Croix, Conroy, a couple of others—looked briefly at Jasper. For a moment, he felt the shock up his right arm as he drove the knife into Billy's back, then the give as the blade found its way between the vertebrae.

He gave no sign of the memory or of noticing the attention directed his way.

According to the Nashville agent, there was incoming mail in great quantities. Billy Dent had a coterie of quite insane fans who wrote to him regularly. Fan mail for a murderer. It boggled Jasper's mind, one of the few things about his father he could not comprehend. Why people rallied to a man who would just as soon saw off their limbs as say hello to them was beyond him, and yet worshippers cleaved to him.

It couldn't be explained by mere charisma. If Jasper believed in the supernatural, he'd've ascribed magical powers to his father. But the truth was so much more disturbing than that.

"Lots of mail coming in, nothing coming out," the Tennessee agent was saying. "Billy Dent hasn't so much as licked a postage stamp since he got here."

"He might get someone else to send mail for him," Jasper said. "Please check any inmates or even corrections officers he has regular contact with."

Silence on the other end of the phone. The agent realizing who had spoken.

"We'll do that," came the reply after a moment.

"What about phone calls?" Conroy asked.

A throat clearing over the speakerphone. "Yeah, well, this is the weird part."

Everyone in the room straightened in their chairs. Jasper's back speckled with cold finger-traces down either side of his spine.

"He's made about two dozen calls in the past six months. Several of them to his son's cell phone or the old family landline in Lobo's Nod. But there have also been several calls to, well, to us."

No one spoke. Everyone looked around the room, as though someone else had answers. All eyes eventually found Jasper, who merely shook his head.

"What do you mean *us?*" Conroy asked.

"The Bureau, sir," the agent replied. "He's called four . . . no, five different field offices in the past six months. Baltimore, Newark, Memphis, Houston, and, well, Seattle."

The small spots of cold on Jasper's back grew.

"Let me get this straight," Conroy said, leaning into the speakerphone. "Billy *fucking* Dent has been calling FBI field offices—including this one—for *months* and no one reported this? No one filed a single piece of paper on it?"

Distressed silence filled the room like noisome steam. The anxious quiet from the speakerphone lingered. Jasper's knowledge of the FBI hierarchy was limited, but he had the sense that Conroy was high enough up that someone would be copyediting a résumé soon.

"Sir," the speakerphone finally said, "we're in contact with the field offices and doing a complete search of—"

"I want a full report in half an hour," Conroy said. "I want to know who he talked to and what it was about. Everything's recorded, right?"

"Well . . ."

He'd heard enough. Jasper stood and slipped out of the room. He didn't need to eavesdrop on FBI business. And besides, he thought he might throw up.

He leaned against the wall outside the office and sipped his breaths. His stomach settled. Fresh air. He needed fresh air.

Ignoring the looks of those around him, he staggered to the door and past the curious gaze of the security guard stationed at the task force entrance. Outside, he paced the length and breadth of the parking lot. Billy. Billy was involved. Somehow.

The task force was made up of local cops and feds, but also FBI agents from other field offices. Possibly those Billy had called.

Was Bridekiller a fed? Someone on the task force?

He crouched down, breathing slowly and carefully.

Grenier? The man was full of bluster and apparently was highly regarded, but also hadn't contributed much. Could he be deliberately scuttling the investigation from within?

Or . . . Conroy himself? Someone that high up in the bureaucracy?

Anything was possible. His mind spun with the possibilities.

He called Patrick.

"I was just thinking about you," Patrick said. "I found a really nice lemon-spice tea at the store today and figured we'd try it the next time you're here. Decaf, of course."

He pictured Patrick in the kitchen, unpacking groceries. What would it be like to have a normal life? Even with your wife dead, a normal life.

"Yeah, that's great. Look, can I tell you something?"

"Of course."

He briefly explained that his father had been calling FBI offices. "Which means," he went on, "that it's probably a Crow after all. Or a wannabe, letting Billy pull his strings. I mean, at first I thought it was a Crow, then I didn't, and now I'm sure it's—"

"You want to know what I think?" Patrick's voice had lost all casual jollity. "I think you're nuts. You're nuts to be involved in this crap. Get the hell away from here. This is going to destroy you."

"I don't think you understand. If it's Billy, I have to stay."

"Why? Who appointed you the janitor of your father's messes?"

It was a good question. An excellent goddamn question, actually. Jasper had spent most of his life answering it.

"Because I could have stopped him. I could have done something. And I didn't."

"Jesus Christ!" Patrick exploded in a way McCutcheon never could or would. "You were a *child*, Jasper! An abused, controlled child with little to no agency. And then, if I recall correctly, you later put a knife in his back, so you *did* do something."

Truth. And meaningless. As long as Billy breathed, Jasper felt responsible for him. A twisted inversion of parent-child culpability.

"And can you even be certain it's him? Maybe he called the FBI to gloat about something. Why would your father go through all of this trouble, setting up Bridekiller and such? Just to get your attention?"

"Possibly. It might also just be to amuse himself. A way to pass the time in prison."

"That's . . . grotesque."

Jasper exhaled and stared up into the clear Seattle sky. "That's Billy."

They sat in silence on their phones for a minute or two, and then Patrick said, "Come over. Let's talk for real. This is important."

Jasper shook his head, even though Patrick couldn't see. "No. I need to think about this."

"You called me for a reason."

"I know. And now I need to think."

He found a curb that didn't look dirty or damp and sat at the edge of the parking lot. Billy's involvement changed everything. The Impressionist had pretended to be a victim's relative in order to get close to Jasper. None of the husbands were pretending, obviously, and they all had foolproof alibis in the form of positive Rohypnol tests.

Someone on the task force, though . . .

Serial killers often tried to insinuate themselves into the investigation, but it was a poor and false conjecture to assume that the killer had managed to do so without further evidence. A lifetime of movies and TVs and thrillers had trained the world to presume that the killer was someone they knew, someone right around the corner, someone familiar. But it was just as likely that the killer was known to none of the investigators.

Still.

He would have to keep his eyes peeled. Conroy's bluster could be a cover. Grenier's, too. And they both knew which wedding Jasper was attending, which would have made giving directions to Claude Simmons easy.

His heart was pounding wildly. He forced himself to take deep breaths. *Box breaths*, Connie called them, some yoga thing.

Get the hell away from here, Patrick had said. *This is going to destroy you.*

And the other day: *What's stopping you from getting on a plane and going home right now?*

What *was* stopping him?

He could be in the Nod by nightfall. He'd have a late dinner with Howie, drop by Simon's office in the morning . . . then head over to the hospital to spend the day with G. William. He'd bring the Scrabble board—the little travel-size one—and play all day. He'd even let G. William get away with some of those proper nouns he always tried to sneak in.

And then . . . And then maybe . . . Maybe another plane? To New York.

Maybe.

Two weeks ago, he never would have even considered it. But Patrick was right—he was no longer the serial killer prodigy. Like all kids with a talent, he'd grown up and was now just another adult with a peculiar interest, albeit in something very dark and very disturbing. But there was nothing forcing him to adhere to his old patterns. He could forget about Billy. Block the number.

Go away.

He could give it up.

Couldn't he?

"There you are!"

It was de la Croix, running up to him from the door. Her air was frantic, her energy amped and agitated. They'd heard back from the field offices, maybe. They knew what Billy was up to.

She gained him and he stood. Before he could say anything, she said, "He struck again."

It hit him like . . . Well, like being kicked in the jaw by a masked man.

"What?" he said stupidly, even though he'd heard her.

She clenched her fists and had nothing to punch. "He. Struck. Again."

"No he didn't," Jasper said, stubborn and aggravated. He'd read the weekend summaries this very morning, emailed over by someone Conroy had assigned paperwork to. All potential victims accounted for in the mornings after their weddings. No more dead size eight brunettes. Friday brides alive Saturday morning. Saturday brides alive Sunday morning.

De la Croix's expression had gone hard and angry as she spoke. Now it crumbled . . . *melted* . . . into sheer helplessness.

Jasper's throat worked with difficulty. What? What had they missed?

What had *he* missed?

C H A P T E R

22

Her name was Carolina O'Doul—she was keeping her birth name—and she would never be older than twenty-seven. Jasper looked down at her in the bathtub of the hotel room, her eyes glazed and staring up forever. Her wedding dress was a sleek, modern affair with a plunging décolletage, the impact ruined by the stab wound through her breastbone.

Blood congealed around her in the tub.

Jasper sighed wearily. They'd warned him. They'd told him.

She was a redhead.

23

"A REDHEAD . . . He broke the pattern."

Hours later. A conference room at the task force. Once again Grenier, de la Croix, Conroy, Jasper, a few others. Jasper's mind raced.

A redhead. A *redhead*.

He couldn't help it—he swiftly, mentally cataloged the redheads Billy had killed over his decades-long career.

"Did he really break it, though?" Conroy asked. "I hate to be indelicate, but did the carpet match the drapes?"

"Medical examiner says yes," someone anonymous to Jasper chimed in.

"Maybe she dyed her pubes," Grenier offered.

Everyone glared at him.

"Jesus Christ! People do that!" Grenier protested. "I'm not making this shit up!"

"Have someone check," Conroy said wearily.

"What if it's not him?" de la Croix asked, and then said what they'd all been thinking, but no one wanted to speak aloud: "What if it's a copycat?"

"Anything is possible," said Conroy. "But it's unlikely."

Unlikely because the murder was too perfect, Jasper knew. The cops always held back certain details so as to weed out crank informants and copycats. In the Bridekiller case, they'd never told the press about the roofies. As far as anyone in the media or the general public knew, the husbands were drunk off their asses and slept through the murders through the auspices of Jameson, not pharmacology.

But the ME's preliminary bloodwork on Carolina O'Doul's husband showed Rohypnol in his blood. They were still working out the concentration and the derivation, but its presence was a point against a copycat. If it matched the same batch as the other husbands', it would eliminate the copycat possibility entirely.

"He knew Jasper was at the one wedding," Conroy said. "So he figured we were staking out the weddings that matched his victim profile and switched things up."

A murmur of agreement around the table.

"It's not that simple," Jasper said. "Even for a highly organized killer like Bridekiller, switching up the signature or the victim profile isn't just something they do. It's a compulsion; they can't control it. Plus, this isn't something he can turn on a dime. It's hasn't been all that long since he saw me at the wedding. Trust me: This guy's been stalking his victims and prepping his crimes for *months*. He didn't just pick O'Doul out of a hat a couple of days ago."

An annoyed silence filled the room. Jasper was quite familiar with the sentiment. He had a knack for puncturing theories and desperately held beliefs. He was an explosion of glass at a display of balloon animals.

Someone's cell phone chirped. At the other end of the table, a young agent with a blond crewcut checked his phone and then announced, beaming, "ME says no pubic hair dye!" with a little more verve than the news called for.

"Are we throwing away the whole fucking profile?" Conroy asked. "Someone get BAU on the phone. I want Chris's assessment five minutes ago."

Even though no one looked at him, Jasper couldn't help feeling guilty. Yes, BAU had confirmed the particulars of his own profile, but still—he was the only one in the room who'd drawn up a profile in the first place.

Muttering something unintelligible, he excused himself. Eyes like arrows pierced his back as he left the room. Making his way to the restroom, he first ascertained that he was alone and then leaned against the wall. A scrim of sweat had collected at the back of his neck and he wiped it away.

Just be better, he told himself. *Shake off the cobwebs and* think. *Do a better job. Figure it out.*

His phone buzzed.

It was G. William.

A spike of fear thrilled through him, a lightning bolt cleaving him from clavicle to gut, electrifying his heart into a too-harsh rhythm. If something had happened . . . Howie might use G. William's phone . . .

But no. It was just the man himself calling. Jasper's pulse and heart rate—ramped—hit the brakes and began to slow at the sound of G. William's voice.

"Got another one, did he?" the big man said, his voice both gravelly and breath-starved. His lungs were still recuperating from the excess fluid that had swamped them.

No preliminaries. No pleasantries. It was like old times. Jasper flashed to his own past: He was seventeen years old, standing in G. William's office, sneaking a look at the paperwork on the first Impressionist killing . . .

"Yeah, he did," he said. "I'm doing a bang-up job out here."

G. William cleared his throat. Or maybe it was a cough. Hard to tell. "Save beating yourself up for another time. Changed his signature?"

"At least his victim type. First redhead."

"What do you think it means?"

Jasper blew out a breath. "Well, hell, G. William—I thought you were calling to tell *me*."

The big man laughed, then coughed, then held the phone away for a moment. Jasper closed his eyes and tried to picture it. Tried to imagine G. William in a hospital bed, plugged into the machines that beeped and booped his likelihood of surviving the next days, hours, minutes. Charts and graphs of his very life force, etched in pixels, cold and remote from the man himself.

"I'm just being your sounding board," G. William said. "Figured it might help."

"You have more important things to do."

"I have—literally—nothing to do. My Scrabble partner lit out for parts west and I'm connected to so many goddamn wires and tubes that I can't scratch my balls without an alarm going off."

Jasper didn't laugh. The image wasn't funny to him.

"I'm worried about you, big man."

"That's mighty nice of you, Jazz. But let's you and me focus on what we can fix. The doctors will take care of me. Is this a farewell? He said one more, and then he killed a redhead. Is this his way of . . . punctuating his career?"

"Like adding an exclamation point at the end of a sentence?" It was an interesting idea, Jasper thought. Far more palatable than what had first occurred to him, the thought he'd been afraid to voice.

That Bridekiller had lied. He wasn't finished after "one more."

He was just moving on to a new kind of victim.

Like Billy had.

"When the profile doesn't fit," Jasper said slowly, "sometimes it's because we screwed up. But sometimes it's because we just don't see the victims the way he does. That there's an element beyond the obvious that we just aren't seeing."

"You should probably be tellin' those fancy FBI folks this instead of me," G. William offered.

"Yeah, probably."

* * *

Jasper asked to go back to the crime scene. The FBI had video, photos, and spatial video of the whole thing, but he wanted to be there in person. To see what the killer had seen, hear what he'd heard, smell what he'd smelled. His first trip had been short and he'd been distracted by the hue of Carolina O'Doul's hair. (Confirmed by both the ME and O'Doul's perplexed mother to be naturally red. Had she ever dyed it brown or black? they asked Mrs. O'Doul. No, she responded.)

The hotel manager unlocked the door. Two Seattle cops flanked it and allowed Jasper to duck under the crime scene tape. De la Croix followed him. He was beginning to feel bad that she had been assigned to perpetual babysitting duty.

They each slipped on latex gloves, then puffy booties over their shoes.

"He changed things up," Jasper muttered as he paced the length and width of the room. "Why?"

Fingerprint dust lay thick on every surface. The bed was an unmade tangle. CSI had swept through the room in record time, but it would be a long time before the room was released back to the hotel. Conroy wanted to preserve it as-is for the time being. Just in case.

Is this a message for me, Billy? Are you trying to poke into my head and look around? Or maybe you just want a Father's Day card for once.

Jasper peered into the bathroom. It was a large space with a shower and a separate, small-ish tub with jets. A decent enough bridal suite, he thought, as though his opinion mattered one whit.

"Why a redhead?" de la Croix asked from behind him. "Do you think he's making a point about . . ." She trailed off.

Jasper turned away from the bathroom. The mental image of Carolina O'Doul's body sprawled in the bathtub flickered like a strobe light. "A point about what?"

"I don't know. I was going to say . . ." She chewed at her lower lip. "Maybe he knows we know he's into brunettes and this is his way of flipping us off at the very end? Sort of like . . . *You don't know me!*"

He grunted and nodded.

"But then," she said, her tone self-recriminating, "I think about those letters. All the errors and glitches. I'm not sure he's smart enough to . . . He's really organized, right, but I'm not sure he's *smart*. You know?"

Jasper nodded again. "I've been thinking about those letters, too. About the misspellings and stuff."

He idly flicked the light switch. The bathroom light came on, along with a fan. In any decent, sensible mystery, he thought a bit acidly, that would be a clue.

"What about the letters?" she prompted.

He flipped the light and the fan off and sighed. "I don't know. Don't most systems have autocorrect? I feel like most of those errors would have been caught."

Her eyes lit up. "So . . . He made them deliberately?"

"Yeah."

"But why?"

"Maybe to throw us off. Maybe to make us assume a certain level of intellect or education."

De la Croix's eyes widened with excitement. "But that's . . . That's big! You haven't said anything about that to Conroy or Grenier. You should—"

Jasper shook his head and walked past her toward the messy bed. "I should nothing. Maybe it's intentional. Or maybe he just has autocorrect turned off. Or maybe Billy just told him to do it. Who knows?"

Standing by the bed, he opened both arms, spreading out his hands to encompass the chaos of sheets and blankets. "There are ten thousand bits of data in this room alone. The twist of the blankets and the positioning of the pillows. The slight smell of nail polish and lip gloss. The trick is figuring out what matters and why. We could spend *days* trying to decode the importance of the typos in his letters. And what if it *is* intentional? So what? His next letter could be in perfectly grammatical English. Or French."

"Next letter? You think he'll write to us again?"

Jasper stared down at the bed. Connor Belmont, Carolina O'Doul's instant widower, had admitted that they'd "fooled around a little," but were both "so tired." In Belmont's case, that was Rohypnol talking.

The latest instant widower, Belmont matched the others in terms of his reaction to the Rohypnol, his general confusion upon awakening. The task force had a team at his hospital room, where they'd conducted a swift preliminary interview. Doctors weren't letting them talk to him again until he'd had more time to recover from both the drug and the shock.

Another dead woman. Another ruined man.

Had O'Doul fallen asleep before or after her husband? Had she been dragged from her bed half-awake and puzzled or had Bridekiller blitz-attacked her while she watched her new husband doze?

There was, he supposed, an answer in the bends and folds of the linens. And maybe the FBI had a bedclothes expert who could tell them.

But again—did it matter? Would it lead them anywhere other than down another rabbit hole?

"I think he wants to write to us," Jasper said. "But I don't know if he will or not. He might—"

His phone buzzed for his attention. Thinking it might be Howie or G. William with another update, he checked the screen.

The text was from Patrick.

When you have a moment, can we speak?

* * *

It was oddly formal and oblique for Patrick. It immediately piqued Jasper's curiosity. They had spoken on the phone not long ago, but the text seemed to demand a face-to-face meeting.

He didn't want de la Croix to know that he was seeing Patrick, so he made a lame excuse and got her to drop him off at the hotel. He wandered into the lobby, watched from a corner window as she pulled away, then immediately hailed an Uber. He was at Patrick's less than thirty minutes later.

Patrick met him at the front door, his usually placid expression troubled. He kept taking off his glasses and cleaning them with his shirttail as he gestured Jasper into the living room.

Jasper sat. Patrick paced, not looking over, stroking his chin, clicking his tongue. Jasper had the sudden and bizarre sense that he had become the therapist, Patrick the patient.

"Patrick?"

Patrick shushed him with a wave of one hand and kept pacing. Finally, he spoke, and while he did not cease his back-and-forth, he did slow down a bit.

"I'm in an ethical tight spot here," Patrick said. "I hope you'll bear with me."

"I'm not a cop," Jasper said. "And I don't work for the AMA or whoever would be judging you."

"I've already surrendered my license—there's no one left to judge me." He drew in a deep breath and finally stopped, turning to face Jasper. "Except for myself."

"Take as long as you need."

Patrick nodded, stroked his chin for another moment, then stared off at a spot just above Jasper's left shoulder.

"Let's speak . . . hypothetically. Would that be OK?"

"Sure."

"So. Hypothetically. Hypothetically, let's say that someone who once was in a position to listen to privileged personal information had thoughts about the possibility of someone having a reason to go around killing women on their wedding nights."

Jasper swallowed. "Sure. Go on."

Patrick sighed and steepled his fingers. "Let's further say— hypothetically—that this person hadn't really thought about the other person—"

"The possible killer."

"Right. Hadn't really thought about the possible killer in a while, but recently realized, oh my . . . There's a chance . . ."

"Patrick." Jasper spoke the word with all the firmness he could conjure, then waited, gazing steadily through the distance between them. "If you know something . . ."

"But I don't!" Patrick shouted. His anger was sudden, intense, and brief—in an instant, he flung himself on the sofa and buried his face in his hands. "I don't *know* anything. But I *might* . . .

"I was going through some of Rebecca's things. She'd moved in about a month before the wedding and there were still things in boxes. I found a picture . . . I'd forgotten . . ."

He felt around to his left. A side table. Slid open a drawer and withdrew a photograph. Held it out.

Jasper stood and approached. It was a woman—size eight, dark brown hair—in a wedding dress. He knew nothing of fashion and so couldn't determine if the dress was a particularly impressive or overwrought example of the genre. To him, it was just white and lacy and too much.

It took him a moment to realize. This wasn't a photo of Rebecca. It was someone else.

The tips of his fingers went cold and nerveless as he took the photo from Patrick.

"Patrick. Who is this?"

Patrick shook his head and reburied his face in his hands. "If I'm wrong . . ."

"You have to tell me. What's going on here?"

It was just a picture of a woman in wedding gown. But she was none of the victims to date. He felt a cold trickle, like a melting icicle dragged down his spine from the base of his neck to his waist.

"Who is it?" he demanded. "Why are you showing this to me? Is it his wife, Patrick?"

The BAU assessment: married or divorced. Right?

"Patrick!" He shouted, comfort and politeness be damned. The icicle was inching back up his spine now. "Patrick! Is this his wife? Do you know who he is?"

Patrick shook his head, softly, then violently. Then he looked up, his face red and flushed, his expression stricken. "Not his wife," he whispered. "His mother."

Jasper's fingers, already numb, went clumsy and spasmed open. The photo drifted to the floor.

He was back in his hotel room. In bed. Dreaming as he had his first night in Seattle. His mother in a wedding gown, climbing atop him in bed. Connie dead in that same bed.

He took a step back. Patrick watched him with something like fascination mixed with fear. Jasper tried to remember where the bathroom was, but his mental map of the house failed him.

With a muted cry, he bolted for the kitchen instead and just barely made it to the sink before vomiting up everything in him.

24

PATRICK BREWED HIM a cup of tea while he rinsed his mouth in the bathroom. When he emerged, the mug was on the kitchen table, next to a spoon, a small dish of sugar, and a jar of honey.

"I didn't know which you'd prefer," Patrick said.

Jasper sat at the table. His knees were weak. His breath shook. He stirred honey into his tea and the spoon clattered against the edge of the mug.

"Do you want to talk about it?" Patrick asked, gazing at Jasper over the tops of his glasses.

Jasper wrapped his hands around the mug, felt its warmth. "Not until you're ready to talk," he retorted.

Seeing Jasper in such distress had seemingly jolted Patrick from his own misery. He was collected and cool once more. He sat at the table and pushed the photo, which he'd retrieved, across to Jasper.

Who did not look at it.

His mother. His mother. Why does it have to be his mother?

"Grant Whitford," Patrick said quietly.

Grant Whitford.

He turned the name over and over.

Grant Whitford. Grant Whitford. Grant Whitford. The name buzzed in his skull like a wet wasp.

He sipped at his tea, still avoiding the picture. "Tell me more."

Patrick sighed. "I was unpacking the boxes. I didn't realize . . . or I'd forgotten. I don't know which. But there were some old office things in one of them, too. I saw this picture and I remembered . . ."

"He's a patient of yours."

"*Was*," Patrick clarified.

"Was." Another sip. His throat, raw from the force of projectile vomiting, welcomed the honey.

"I'd forgotten about him. Honestly. But Grant had . . . He'd brought me that picture—"

"What did his mother do to him?"

And there it was. The question Jasper did not want to ask. But he'd managed it. He'd forged it in the heart of his soul and forced it out. And he could withstand the response.

He thought.

He hoped.

Another raped little boy. Another mother who—

"His mother did nothing to him," Patrick said, his tone reproving, though gently so. "It was his father. He was a terror, I gather. Abusive. Violent. Grant said this picture"—he tapped the photo, drawing Jasper's attention to it—"was taken ten years after their wedding."

Patrick leaned back and studied Jasper as Jasper stared at the photo. For the first time, he realized that there was something plastic and alien about the woman's smile.

"His father insisted she be able to fit into her bridal gown. That she not have changed since their wedding." He paused and wiped his glasses for the millionth time. "He made her put it on every year for their anniversary and if it didn't fit . . ."

Jasper didn't ask him to finish the sentence. There was no need.

It fit.

Not the gown. Although to his unpracticed eye, it seemed as though Mrs. Whitford had probably avoided a beating on her tenth anniversary. The gown fit, yes, but more importantly *the idea* fit.

Patrick had no idea of what was in the letters. Bridekiller's nascent savior complex. His urge to protect married women by killing them.

It. Fit.

It all fit.

"Why did he give you this?" Jasper put his hand over the photo so that Mrs. Whitford would stop looking at him.

"This was years ago. And I don't have my notes any longer. But I think he was just trying to . . . I think he was trying to humanize his mother for me."

Jasper nodded. "Thank you, Patrick."

Patrick sighed heavily, slumping in his chair. He passed a hand over his forehead. "Did I do the right thing?"

"Yes. Absolutely." Jasper pulled the photo close to him, still covered by his downturned palm. "You did the right thing."

*   *   *

"You went and talked to a witness on your own?" Conroy demanded.

"I'm here to help," Jasper said. "You're welcome."

They were in Conroy's office. Conroy and Jasper and de la Croix. Conroy was angry, but much more calm than Jasper would have imagined him being at the news.

"I wasn't thanking you."

"I know. You should have been, though."

Conroy glanced over at de la Croix, as though to say, *This guy isn't worth it.* De la Croix's return glance seemed to say, *Don't look at me—I'm just the babysitter.*

Jasper realized suddenly that he had no idea *who* had specifically asked for him to come into the task force. De la Croix had recruited him, yes, but she'd only ever referenced "the Bureau." Did Conroy even want him here? Or had he been imposed from further up the food chain?

"Is there a connection to your father?" de la Croix asked.

"I have no idea. First order of business is getting this guy off the streets."

"I'll decide the first order of business," Conroy said.

"I have a name and some particulars," Jasper said. "Do you want details on a possible suspect, or would you prefer standing around waiting for another murder?"

Conroy bristled, but managed to suppress what no doubt would have been a vigorously profane retort. He frowned at the photo. "Was she ever a redhead?"

"I still haven't figured that part out."

"Do we have Olefsky's file on the guy?"

"No. When he surrendered his license and closed his practice, he handed all files over to the licensing board for redistribution to whomever took over the individual cases. But he still had the guy's name, age, and an old email address that may or may not function." Jasper held up a slip of paper.

Conroy plucked it from Jasper's fingers. "Grant Whitford," he read. "Well, Grant Whitford, you're about to have a really shitty day."

* * *

Jasper insisted on going with the agents who went to confront Grant Whitford.

Conroy grudgingly acquiesced, but only after Jasper not-so-subtly threatened to abandon the task force and return to Lobo's Nod.

If Conroy *didn't* want Jasper here in Seattle, then he was certainly being pressured from above. Because Jasper had given him a golden opportunity to rid himself of the pest from Tennessee and Conroy hadn't taken it.

Then again, maybe Billy was calling the shots and had ordered Conroy to keep Jasper in Seattle.

He couldn't get a decent read on Conroy. The man was too swaddled in his own bluster and perpetual outrage for Jasper to figure him out. Since he'd been put in charge of the Bridekiller task force, Conroy had to boast a history of competence and success.

Then again, it was equally possible that the man had stumbled into a sinecure or been promoted—Peter Principle–wise—to the upper reaches of his own incompetence. Maybe no one actually expected him to solve the case.

In any event, Jasper couldn't figure out if Conroy had asked for him or not.

But if not the man on the ground, then who?

Who wanted him here?

On the way to Grant Whitford's last known address, he asked de la Croix—point-blank—who had requested his presence on the task force.

She paid particular attention to the road ahead and said only, "Look, I get orders, I follow orders."

He couldn't get anything more out of her for the duration of the drive.

25

They had a' no-knock warrant and a tactical battering ram. Grant Whitford's front door could resist neither.

With Whitford's name, age, and old email address, the FBI had managed to track down an LKA—last known address. It was on the northern edge of a neighborhood called Bitter Lake, and Jasper thought that might be a good name for it. The city's hip and vibrant air gave way to crumbling grays and browns.

It reminded him too much of the Nod. The houses gone worn, almost weary, as though they just wanted to stop standing up. A chain-link fence surrounded the meager property of Whitford's LKA. The house was two stories, maybe two and half with an attic, he thought, but it slumped like an old man and seemed smaller.

Seattle PD closed off the block on both ends with two patrol cars parked at angles to prevent vehicular escape. A tactical team had taken up position one block over, beyond the scrub-brush backyard.

As Jasper watched, three cops shouldered the battering ram into position.

It took them only two hits and the door swung open.

"Landlord says Whitford has paid his rent on time." Grenier's voice, from somewhere behind him. "As far as he knows, no one else lives there with him."

"Inside," Conroy said. His voice, crisp. Not a hint of rage or rodomontade.

Four cops went first, shields up, guns drawn. Three FBI agents followed. Someone handed Jasper a blue windbreaker with *FBI* stenciled on the back in yellow. He shrugged into it. His palms were damp. He was up on his tip-toes. He wanted to be inside this building *very* badly.

Conroy and Grenier flanked the open front door, waiting. Jasper never could have imagined the cool patience floating off the two of them in those prolonged moments.

Through shoulder mics and a radio from a nearby car, he heard the crackle of "Living room! Clear!" and "Kitchen! Clear!"

The voices continued. Jasper stood back from the front door, peering forward, but there was only the sliver of an entryway and then darkness.

An infinity of moments passed and then: "All clear! Repeat: All clear!"

Grenier slid easily into the house. Jasper stepped forward, but Conroy stopped him with a hand on his chest.

"You know what to do and what not to do, right?" Conroy asked him.

Jasper bit back a retort. He'd been keeping crime scenes clean since the age of eight, courtesy of his father's own twisted notions for "Take Your Child to Work Day." He could ghost anywhere, any time.

"I'm not a child," Jasper said with more than a little asperity. *And even if I were, I'd know better than you how to handle a crime scene.*

Conroy nodded and stepped aside. Jasper and de la Croix entered, followed by Conroy, who immediately split off to the left, following Grenier through what looked like a living room.

The house had a stale smell to it. Not an unlived-in smell of disuse and disregard, but rather the smell of a place that has been used, but not aired out. He wondered when Grant Whitford had last opened a window.

The entryway was floored in old, chipped tile. The hallway it led into was—at first glance—hardwood, but when Jasper stepped on it, he realized it was a wood veneer. Some kind of cheap linoleum. Like the kitchen floor in his own house.

On the left, the living room was cramped but tidy. A small sofa and matching love seat perpendicular to each, facing a fireplace filled with dust and ash. A grandfather clock stood in one corner, its hands positioned to some time in the future or the past, but definitely not the present.

"I want to see his bedroom," Jasper said.

Together, he and de la Croix made their way to a wooden staircase carpeted with what had once been a mauve runner, but which now was best described as a muddy purple. Conroy and Grenier followed them up and headed down a hallway, following a cop with a flashlight.

Another cop emerged from a doorway to the right. "Bedroom," he said, jerking his thumb in the direction whence he'd come.

Jasper stopped in the open doorway, gazing inside.

"Did you guys touch anything?" he asked over his shoulder.

The cop snorted, insulted. "Just the floor. *Sir.*"

The FBI was one thing, but cops were rarely members of the Jasper Dent Fan Club. Partly because of the number of their NYPD brethren he'd ended up getting fired and/or prosecuted when he'd hunted the Hat-Dog Killer in Brooklyn. And partly because of his very public appearance at several Black Lives Matter rallies with Connie.

In the bedroom, the drawers to a dresser hung open. Socks and underwear dangled from the fronts. The closet door stood open and a jangle of hangers cluttered the entry.

Someone had packed. In a hurry.

Did he know? Did he know we were on to him?

"He moved fast," de la Croix said, whistling. "You think he knew?"

He shrugged. "Just what I was wondering. I don't know how."

She regarded him coolly for a moment. "You know what I'm wondering? How did Olefsky get in touch with you, anyway? How did he have your phone number? I gave him mine, but—"

Her radio spat static just then, rescuing him from an awkward conversation. "De la Croix?" came Grenier's voice. "Is Dent with you?"

She narrowed her eyes at Jasper, as though aware of precisely what bullet he'd just dodged. "Yes, go on."

"Bring him up to the attic. Conroy wants him to see this."

The entry to the attic was at the end of the upstairs hallway, opposite the stairs coming up from the ground floor. They walked the creaking floor in the semi-dark until they reached the ladder pulled down from the ceiling.

Jasper had a brief flashback to his own childhood home, long since bulldozed by the wealthy parents of one of his father's victims. Billy had closed off a closet on the ground floor, then built a ladder like this, concealed in the basement, leading into his trophy room. Jasper had spent many an hour in that trophy room, organizing his father's trophies, dusting them, attending to them. Always wearing gloves, of course.

The ladder in Whitford's house was only superficially similar, but when his feet first touched the lowest wooden step, something in its shallow, riserless tread sent a shiver up through his body and he paused for a moment.

"You all right?" de la Croix asked.

He had the absolutely impossible, absolutely ridiculous, and absolutely *real* sense that he was about to mount these steps and end up in Billy's trophy room.

"I'm fine. I don't like heights," he lied. A small lie. He chastised himself anyway. Even small, necessary lies were dangerous for him. A quick nip to an alcoholic.

He emerged into the attic and stooped to help de la Croix up the last few steps. Then he turned to take the space in.

It was a large, open room, running the length and width of the house, its size blunted by the slant of the roofing timbers. A rough plywood floor made it possible to walk without being wary of the spaces between joists.

There were small windows at either end of the attic, but no other source of natural light. Two naked light bulbs hung overhead, each of them roughly one-third the distance from opposite ends of the house. Harsh shadows purled and twisted in and among the ceiling beams. The air was frigid; Jasper could see his breath if he looked just right.

At the far end of the attic, Conroy and Grenier stood at a very boring Ikea-bought desk, a piece of dull pressboard furniture that seemed very out of place by virtue of its prosiness.

The desk would need to be studied, but for now what truly drew his attention was the wall behind the desk. There a corkboard had been mounted and on the corkboard, the photos.

There were a dozen of them, with a space for a thirteenth between the fifth and sixth. Jasper knew that if he held up the photo Patrick had given him—the one currently in the possession of the FBI—that it would fit there. It belonged there.

Because the woman in all twelve photos was the same. It was Grant Whitford's mother, unchanging from year to year on her anniversary, wearing her wedding gown. Her eyes simultaneously begging for help and beseeching her husband to approve.

In one of the photos—the ninth—her hair was dyed red.

*　　*　　*

The numbers didn't match up—Carolina O'Doul was the fifth victim, not the ninth—but Jasper was certain that Whitford wasn't playing this out literally. It was all symbolic to him. Somewhere in his mind, it made perfect sense. If Billy *was* pulling Whitford's strings—and they still weren't certain of that—then he was masterfully manipulating the man's preexisting traumas and psychoses.

"Are the parents still alive?" Jasper asked.

Conroy blinked. "I'll get someone on that. You think he killed them?"

"I think there's an excellent chance Dad killed Mom at some point. Or Mom went into hiding. Or they killed each other. Or maybe they're living in a retirement community somewhere."

"That's a lot of possibilities."

"Fortunately, you don't have to rely on my guesswork. You have the ability to find out."

Grumbling, Conroy stepped away and began barking into his phone. Jasper came closer to the desk. He leaned in to stare at the photos for another moment, then studied the desk itself.

Pressboard or something like it. It was a dark brown, with some scuffs and scratches at the edges, but otherwise in decent shape.

"What do you see?" De la Croix had sidled up to him and was studying him studying the desk.

He cleared his throat and asked, "What do *you* see?"

She ran a finger along the back edge of the desk, bumping against a small, nickel-wide circle of raised rubber with grooves cut into it. "This is one of those things to keep your cables from falling behind the desk. So, I'm guessing he had a laptop here."

"Yeah."

"Sat here, stared at Mom, plotted and schemed. Looked up weddings online, made his plans."

"That's what I'm thinking."

"Why the attic if he had the whole house to himself?"

"Good question."

"And why leave the photos behind?"

"Another good question."

"What's the answer?" she asked.

He broke her hope. "Hell if I know."

He was beginning to think that Patrick was right. That he wasn't as good at this as he'd spent a lifetime thinking he was. And for the first time, that thought liberated him. Elated him. Maybe he wasn't condemned to spend his life mucking out the stalls of psychotic souls.

"I'll tell you what's weird, though," Jasper said, craning his neck to look under the desk. "There's no outlet here. The closest one is . . ."

He peered around the attic. She spotted it first. "There."

The outlet was mounted on an exposed stud on a perpendicular wall. It was a ways from the desk. Nothing a reasonable and cheap extension cord couldn't fix, but still . . .

"It's weird," he said, almost to himself.

"Whole thing is weird," she agreed. "Why not just put the desk over where the outlet is?"

"Maybe he didn't realize. Maybe he didn't care." Jasper pinched the bridge of his nose. "Maybe it doesn't matter. Or maybe it's the biggest clue in the case."

He whuffed out a hard, cloudy breath, and de la Croix leaned in. "Are you OK? Should we leave?"

Before he could answer, Conroy called out from the other side of the attic. "Just got off with Seattle PD. Dad was Marcus Whitford. Died of lung cancer in 2015. Mom's Deborah Whitford. She falls off the grid in 2020, at the height of the pandemic."

"What does *falls of the grid* even mean?" de la Croix demanded, saving Jasper from having to ask the question. "She's just gone?"

Conroy shrugged as he came back over to the two of them. Grenier joined them all, too. "Stopped Zooming in to work in

July 2020," said Conroy. "Didn't pay taxes in 2021 or since. Had an apartment not far from Whitford's place, but when the landlord evicted her, there was just some furniture and kitchen stuff. No personal effects."

"What do we think happened to her?" de la Croix asked.

"Her husband was already dead," Jasper pointed out. "Her terrorizer. She didn't have to run from him."

"But maybe she ran from her son?" Conroy offered.

"Or *with* her son," Grenier said. "What if it was a sexual thing between mom and Grant?"

Jasper's blood thickened as a cold wind blew through him.

"Anything's possible," Conroy allowed.

"Trauma bonding," de la Croix added. "It happens."

Conroy considered this. "What do you think, Dent?"

But Jasper barely heard him. He was back in the dream. And he was back in an abandoned house in Lobo's Nod just a few months shy of his eighteenth birthday as his mother patiently explained how she'd taken his virginity at age six, how she'd used him as a toy and planned to kill him. Until Billy intervened with the notion that twisting the boy would be better than killing him.

"Dent? I said, what do you think?" Conroy nudged him.

They don't know, Jasper reminded himself. *They don't know. We didn't put that in the book. I never told Sloan, so it never went in the book. They don't know.*

"Jesus Christ, Dent," said Grenier. "You in there?"

He couldn't move.

I gave you your name, your identity. I took your virginity and I made you mine.

De la Croix leaned in, her concerned face hovering into view. "Jasper? You OK?"

You are the flesh of my flesh, the blood of my blood. You are mine. And I am yours.

"Someone reboot him," Grenier said.

Jasper managed a shiver and a wan smile. "Sorry. It's cold as hell up here."

They weren't buying it. Too close to honesty. He cranked up the smile, throwing in a little sheepish, a little puppy-dog eyes, a self-effacing chuckle. Manipulation. As natural and reflexive to him as breathing. According to McCutcheon, he manipulated for two reasons: One was to rearrange the outside world to his own liking, for his convenience. The other was to prevent the outside from coming in, to keep people out.

Neither was a healthy response to the world, to trauma. Since manipulation was second nature to him (*maybe even first nature*, a voice sometimes whispered to him, a voice like his father's), it had taken months and months of intensive therapy to recognize it for what it was as it was happening. In the past, he'd seen it after the fact, sometimes even regretted it in retrospect. But now he knew how to discern it as it was happening, or even beforehand. It was a crucial step in stopping it altogether.

Not today, though. Not when the specter of his mother's incestuous violations hung in the air like the cobwebs oscillating in the near-imperceptible breeze in Grant Whitford's attic. Almost invisible, almost intangible.

Almost.

So screw McCutcheon and screw his own mental health. What he needed right now was to *get out*, so he slipped oh so comfortably back into the old pattern, back into the smooth-talking, easygoing Jasper Dent who had seduced to his side teachers, social workers, cops, and victims alike.

"Guys, for real, if you want my nuts to drop off, by all means, let's stay up here. Come on."

Conroy grunted and stepped aside, letting Jasper down the ladder. He had a few moments alone in the hallway as the others came down. By the time they'd all gathered again, the tension, the spell, the worry had been broken. Sometimes all you needed was a quick break, an opportune diversion, to recast the scenario.

"What about the rest of the house?" Jasper asked before anyone else could start peppering him with questions. "Any evidence Mom is staying here with him? Or was?"

Grenier shook his head. "Place is a ghost town. There's some cereal boxes and canned food in the kitchen. The fridge is practically empty. One other bedroom, but it's empty."

"So he was living alone," Jasper said. "And Mom's been in the wind for years."

The next part was easy because it was honest. So it was almost as easy as lying.

"He thinks he's rescuing them," Jasper said. "Like she needed to be rescued. But he couldn't do it then because he was a kid."

"But that was *years* ago," de la Croix protested. "His dad's been dead since—"

"Doesn't matter to him. He's in the grip of the memories and the trauma. He relives it every day, I bet." And that was a little too honest, too. A little too close to home.

"Does he understand they're not his mother?" Conroy asked. "I mean, is he completely delusional?"

Jasper stuttered on the answer. "I don't . . . I don't know. I'm not sure. He seems so highly organized, but . . ." He shook his head. "I don't know if it's possible for him to be delusional and so organized at the same time. He's living in the real world. His delusions have to be with himself, not with reality. He thinks he's a knight."

"Not literally, though, right?" Grenier's voice was laden with exasperation.

"No," Jasper said with a sigh. "Not literally." So much for metaphors.

* * *

It would take a crime scene team hours to go over the house. Jasper let de la Croix drop him off at the hotel once more, then ambled down the street to the coffee shop. He rarely craved the company of other people, but Coffee Amore wasn't packed. And he realized that after walking through Grant Whitford's home and mind, he wanted to be around someone normal.

Shanna was pulling an espresso behind the counter for a kid who looked barely old enough to drive and yet was insisting on observing and approving every step of the process. At the jingle of the doorbell, she glanced up, saw Jasper, and blinked twice, as though to clear away something caught in a contact lens.

"Is that enough?" the kid was asking. "Did you measure in ounces or milliliters?"

"It's exactly forty milliliters," Shanna said. She handed over the espresso and slipped a cover on it.

"I didn't ask for it to go," the kid said dolefully.

"And yet you're going," Shanna told him.

Jasper did a poor job concealing a grin as the kid slunk out the door and into the cold. He took in the environs. It was just him and Shanna. Made sense—most people in the area were heading home.

"About the park . . ." he began. He had no phone number for her. No email. Nothing at all. They hadn't been in touch since the not-kiss, the call from Billy.

Since he'd fled.

She shook her head to stop him. "I'm guessing that phone call wasn't about the thing here in town. I'm guessing it was something old, right?"

He opened his mouth to speak, but she cut him off again.

"I don't want to know. You don't owe me anything. And I can probably find out for myself if I actually read your book, right?"

After a moment of weighing the thought, of wondering if he actually wanted Shanna to read the book or not, he shrugged. "You'd get the gist of it, for sure."

"Fair enough." She managed a smile. "On to more important things: How black do you want your coffee today and how much sugar can I not put in it for you?"

He chuckled at himself as he sidled up to the counter. "I'll shock you and try something different today," he said, eying the menu. "What's a latte?"

Shanna barked in derision. "What's a latte? Oh my God. Have you been living under a rock for the past century?"

"Worse. Tennessee."

"I know they have lattes in Tennessee, yokel." She started rummaging around. "You trust me?"

"With my life." He meant it as a joke, but it came out far too serious.

She poked her head around the steamer to gaze at him. "It's just coffee, man."

The grin she flashed poleaxed him.

There was no music playing today, so the shop was quiet but for the sound of Shanna's ministrations behind the counter. He watched her measure and pour, mix, stir. It was soothing in its own way, and when Shanna began whistling—softly, to herself, as though unaware she was actually doing it—he found himself even more charmed.

Down, boy, he thought. *That's not why you're here.*

But it could be. There was nothing stopping him.

Nothing but Connie.

Not her words or her actions. Those gave him the all-clear.

It was her existence.

Shanna finished, combining all her ingredients and hard work into an oversize mug that seemed more appropriate for soup than coffee. She poured a large dollop of foam atop the steaming liquid, then a spritz of whipped cream, followed by a few careful squirts of chocolate syrup to sketch out an amazingly accurate goofy-face emoji.

"For monsieur," she said, carefully sliding it across to him.

He gawked at the emoji. "That's really good! You could make a living at that."

"I *do* make a living at that," she chided him gently. "And it's nothing any reasonably competent barista can't do. Go ahead." She leaned on the counter with both elbows, face cupped in her hands. "Try it."

He stared down, then looked back up at her. Her nose ring tilted up to the left when she smiled, as she did now.

"What's in it?"

"You trust me with your life, but not your palate?" she asked in mock indignation.

He chuckled and picked up the mug. The handle was comically small, so out of all proportion to the enormous mug. He felt like he should stick out his pinky, but he needed the extra stabilization.

The emoji wobbled at him and began to dissolve. Before he could become sad about that, he took a quick sip, then a longer one.

It was . . .

Wow. Yes. It was.

He grinned at her over the mug.

"Not bad?" she asked, arching an eyebrow. And when that eyebrow piercing shifted, it caught the light just right, and he forgot his own name for a moment.

"Not bad," he agreed.

"Better than black coffee, no sugar?" she asked. He figured she'd forgiven him for the park. He had another chance. Did he even want it?

"Let's not go too crazy," he said with a flirtatious grin of his own. His heart thrummed. He drank some more.

"He drinks more!" Shanna shouted, raising her fists to the sky in triumph. It made her body do wondrous things under her apron and he told himself to stop. "He drinks more! Success! I can now retire at the top of my game."

"Don't do that—it would be a shame for the world of barista-hood to lose such a talent."

She clucked her tongue at him and pulled another espresso, which she downed almost as soon as it hit the cup. "So. Catch any serial killers today?"

He shook his head and sipped at whatever concoction she'd conjured for him. It had notes of chocolate and caramel, as well as a silky texture that he suspected had to be more than just milk, but what? It was nothing on the menu, that much he was sure of.

"Not today."

"Well," she said, shrugging, "there's always tomorrow."

He laughed. "Sure."

She set down her empty cup and leaned toward him. He was frozen, unable to react as she came closer to him, so close that he could see the individual, fine hairs of her brows, so close that he felt her breath.

With a steady, questing finger, she stroked his jaw. It was still tender, but not nearly as bad as it had been; he managed not to flinch.

"Looks a lot better today," she said softly.

He almost said, *Am I becoming handsome?* but it felt a step too far. Or, more accurately, a step just far enough. Which in this case was too far. For him. Now.

Or was it?

He was in his twenties. His girlfriend was three thousand miles away and had no qualms about dating. Had given him permission to do the same . . .

No. Had *insisted* he do the same.

So what was stopping him?

He cleared his throat and turned slightly from her. She ran her fingertips up the side of his face to his forehead, where the butterfly stitches stood stark against his skin.

"Does this hurt?" she asked.

"Not much."

"So brave." He'd expected it to be sarcastic, mocking. It wasn't.

"Who wanted to mess up this face?" The same question she'd asked before. But then, it had been saucy and flirty. Now it was melancholy. Resigned.

"Someone I pissed off," he said. And it was the truth.

"A serial killer?" Absolutely serious.

He shook his head, the motion causing her to break the delicious contact of her fingers. "No. Someone else." Not McCarter, he was certain. And compared to Billy, to Bridekiller . . . "It doesn't matter. Not really. It probably won't be the last time someone beats the hell out of me."

She sighed and dropped her hand to the counter. Her eyes—cloudy hazel—held his own. "You don't make it easy, do you?"

It could be his motto.

"I don't know how to make it anything but difficult."

Just then, the bell rang. A couple—late thirties, Asian—came in, laughing. Jasper nodded to them and took his drink to a table as Shanna smiled and asked what she could delight them with today.

26

Where was Grant Whitford? The man had fled his home for some reason. He couldn't possibly know that the law was onto him, so why had he decamped so suddenly?

These were the questions that kept Jasper awake. Those and no doubt the enormous volume of caffeine in the liquid confection Shanna had evoked for him.

He unlocked his phone and stared at Grant Whitford, the image taken from the man's driver's license file. The photo showed a white man in his early thirties with a scrub of brown beard, his hair close-cropped. His eyes were a vibrant blue, an ocular hue against which Jasper held an irrational, unshakable prejudice. His father's eyes were blue, and he couldn't look into azure orbs without a shiver of recognition and revulsion, no matter to whom they belonged.

Whitford had a look about him. Like maybe he'd earned that revulsion. It was nothing specific or pointed. It was a reaction to a gestalt.

Where are you? Where are *you?*

His phone vibrated in his hand as a mail notification slid into place. It was from Simon, so Jasper decided he could not in good conscience ignore it, especially since the subject line read "Candidates for you."

Jasper,

Attached please find dossiers on six potential candidates I'd like to hand off to the headhunter. This is for the diversity position we discussed. All have experience with nonprofits and/or NGOs. All are women. Four are women of color. I'm sure the recruiters will have other suggestions, but I've vetted these personally and feel strongly that any of them would be an asset to the org, especially in the position you describe.

Please get back to me ASAP so I can proceed.

Simon

There were six PDFs attached, each one efficiently named with the last name and first initial of the candidate. The very last thing Jasper wanted to do right now was divert his attention from Grant Whitford, but . . .

. . . he was highly caffeinated and sleep had offered him not much as a coquettish wink,

. . . he was at an impasse with Whitford for now, and

. . . he'd been dodging WorldVision work for weeks, even before the trip to Seattle, and

. . . the new hire had been his idea. No, his *insistence.*

He thought of de la Croix, sitting across from him at dinner. He'd made a decision then and there, and part of being in charge was—had to be—following through.

He opened the first file and read through it. It taxed the same part of him that analyzed crime scenes and suspect dossiers. There were clues embedded in each CV, in each biography. Clues that would lead not to a particular pathology or danger, but rather to a sense of whether he could work with this person. Whether she would be the one who could comprehend his vision, execute on it.

He fought against his own prejudice and gave the two white women the same careful consideration he'd given to the women of color. White women above a certain age inevitably made him think of his mother.

The more he read, the more he bumped up against a wall that had loomed in the distance ever since he'd taken the first tentative steps toward founding WorldVision: He knew nothing about business.

Or nonprofits.

He hadn't even gone to college.

What was he *doing*?

He had to trust Simon. And Howie. And maybe, someday, himself.

He wrote back to Simon, thanking him for his diligence and hard work, ending with agreement that all six women seemed well-suited to the position and giving his blessing for Simon to begin the recruitment process. He would be only nominally involved at this point—no one was to know of Jasper's involvement in WorldVision, so Simon would conduct the interviews (recorded for Jasper's edification), and so far as anyone knew, they were working for an organization funded by a secretive, anonymous "wealthy eccentric."

Which, he supposed, was the truth.

He'd hoped reading the potential hire files would bore him to within spitting distance of sleep, but his brain still revved at the stoplight of night. It was late, but he called Patrick anyway and was both pleased and surprised that the man picked up on the first ring.

"Is it him?" Patrick asked immediately. "Did you get him?"

"I can't tell you," Jasper said. "I really shouldn't—I really can't talk to you about that."

"Oh." The disappointment oozed into Jasper's ear over the phone, palpable and greasy with discouragement. "I think I got a little caught up in it, honestly. Once I actually told you. I hate to admit this, but it is sort of exciting."

"I'm sorry I can't say more."

"No. No, believe me—I understand the need for discretion. For confidentiality. Why did you call, then?"

The question itself—and not the manner of its asking, which was polite and noncommittal, not judgmental or critical in the least—ashamed Jasper. He hadn't thought he'd needed a reason. He'd just—pathetically, he decided—needed to hear a friendly voice and maybe complain about his inability to sleep, a minor failure, to be sure, but one more on a teetering stack of them.

His presumption rankled and almost by gut reflex, he said, "Well, I'm wondering if there's anything else you could tell me about Whitford."

"Oh." That note of disillusionment again. Same syllable. Same intonation. "So you *haven't* caught him."

Neatly and blatantly skirting the obvious, Jasper said, "I'm just wondering if there's anything else you remember. Did he grow up around here, for example? Is there a childhood home or a—"

"I think he grew up around here," Patrick said. "I'm not sure, though. We talked about his childhood, but it was all about his parents, not really . . . Who, not where, you know?"

Jasper *mm-hmm*ed encouragingly.

"But wait . . ." Patrick went silent. Jasper obeyed and waited. "I think . . ."

Jasper waited again.

"He *did* once say something about a boat trip on Puget Sound. And I think that was when he was younger. So . . . So, yes, I think he grew up here." Another pause, this one laden with curiosity and wonder. "Is that important?"

Jasper wasn't sure. He didn't think so—surely someone on the task force had already pulled every conceivable public record on Grant Whitford and quite a few private ones as well. Conroy knew where Whitford had been born, where he'd gone to school, and probably when he'd been potty trained. Jasper had just managed to kill time with Patrick and there was nothing gained from murdering those minutes.

"It might help," he said equably. "Is there anything you can remember? That Puget Sound thing . . . Did they own a boat? Was there a place they stored it?"

He hailed from a landlocked state and a poor town therein. He had no idea what people did with boats, but maybe there was a shed somewhere or something . . . ?

"I really don't remember anything like that." A note of irritation had crept into Patrick's voice. Whether at the incessant questioning or at his own inability to answer firmly, Jasper wasn't quite sure. Still, he decided it was time to put an end to it.

"OK, well, thanks."

"How are you?" Patrick finally got around to asking.

The question he'd been waiting for . . . and now regretted drawing. No closer to sleep, he felt a lingering fog creep through his thoughts anyway. The idea of talking about himself was suddenly exhausting.

He told Patrick he felt fine, then rang off. Wide awake, he hurled himself up off his bed and paced his room. It took not long.

Peering through peeled-back curtains, he could make out Volunteer Park in the distance, through a toothy two blocks of houses and trees.

His friends would ask, *What was Seattle like?* And he would respond, *Well, I saw the hotel. And a cramped, smelly task force office. And a few murder scenes.*

And a cute barista showed me the Space Needle.

Who was he kidding—he didn't have any friends. Other than Howie. And Howie knew well enough not to ask about sightseeing.

He sighed and leaned his forehead against the window as the city sparkled beneath and beyond him. Out there, at least a hundred women were preparing for their weddings this weekend. And they would all be in danger.

Because he'd failed.

Again.

Turning away from the window, something caught his eye on the desk. He leaned in close, careful not to touch.

It was a color printout. A photograph of Jasper himself, taken while he sat in Coffee Amore. The size of the mug indicated it had been taken this very evening.

Someone had drawn a targeting bull's-eye over his face and written **END YOUR WORTHLESS LIFE**. In red.

He stared at the photo.

And then he laughed.

It made sense.

He understood.

And, strangely, with understanding came sleep.

*　　*　　*

He awoke at dawn, a grayish half-light boiling the clouds outside his window. The photo was still on his desk, untouched. He would maybe give it to de la Croix at some point, but he no longer thought that would be necessary. It didn't involve Bridekiller. He was sure of it. And equally sure it didn't even involve Billy.

Thinking of Billy made a new thought expose itself, thoroughly unsought and unbidden:

If he grew up here, his dad is probably buried here.

Fathers and sons. He knew something of the dynamic. When it was twisted.

It popped into his head without precursor or forethought. He'd learned to value such insights, bottled messages hurled over the high wall that bifurcated conscious thought from the subconscious, so he didn't dismiss it immediately.

Is Billy in touch with Grant Whitford somehow? Is this all about fathers and sons, my father, his father?

It made him recall Bruce and Brandon Lee, father and son, both buried not far from his room.

Grant Whitford's father wasn't Bruce Lee, but neither was he Billy Dent. He wasn't a killer, so far as they could tell. It would be convenient and easy to suppose that Whitford *père* had been an earlier Bridekiller, passing down his depredations and his predilections like eye color. (For Jasper was certain that a photo of the deceased father would reveal startlingly blue eyes, like the son. Like Billy.) But all evidence pointed to Whitford's father keeping his rage and his misogynistic violence in the family. Nothing on his record more serious than a few speeding tickets and a single incident in a bar on the night the Sonics either won or lost whatever passed for an important game in . . . whatever sport they played. He couldn't remember.

Grant Whitford had not learned to hate women from his father. He'd learned to hate men. And he'd learned a deep and wretched enough pessimism that death seemed preferable to marriage, a decision that Jasper acknowledged might be true more often than not . . . but not a decision Whitford was empowered to make for the women he'd murdered.

But it was still about fathers and sons, in the end. Whitford was molded by his father, in the negative spaces, if nothing else. So desperate was he not to be his father that he'd surpassed the man's evil in almost every way.

Fathers and sons.

"Oh, hell, I'm going to the grave, aren't I?" Jasper said aloud, still lying in bed.

* * *

On his way out, he taped a note to his own room door. **I KNOW WHO YOU ARE**, it read.

27

THE NEEDLE FOG bit frigidly at him as he stepped out of an Uber at the cemetery. It had been trivially easy to find where Marcus Whitford was buried. Such information was publicly available in any number of databases. So Jasper stood in the cold outside the cemetery and waved weakly to the Uber as it pulled away.

The day was the gray of an old man's beard. The fog—failed rain clinging to the ground—stabbed at him, a frosty pointillism. Denuded trees cracked the gray-paint sky, scraping against rank and file of ragged, uneven headstones, slabs jutting from the soil like the edges of so many serrated knives.

A flurry of his internalized voices hurled advice, questions, deprecations:

Wait, why *are you doing this again?* Connie.

Another graveyard? Really? Howie.

This can't be good for you, and it ain't gonna accomplish any-thing. G. William.

Why not just tell the police to do this? Patrick.

McCutcheon, at least, was blessedly silent.

He sighed. At himself. At the voices.

Mostly at himself. His breath made a hard white cloud.

The cemetery website did not give an exact location for Marcus Whitford's final resting place, but there was a photo of the headstone, so Jasper knew what he was looking for. As he passed through the wrought-iron gate to the cemetery proper, he took in a deep breath at the size of the place.

This was going to take a while.

He maundered through the cemetery, beginning with the first row, hoping unrealistically (and, as it happened, fruitlessly) that he would encounter Marcus Whitford's headstone right at the outset. No such luck.

Second row. He moved quickly, not allowing himself to linger or dawdle, not permitting himself the brief mental math that would tell him if someone had died after a long, bountiful life or after a meager week of breathing or somewhere in between. He had spent the past several years learning to live up to his old childhood mantra of *People are real. People matter.* But there was no profit in humanizing these dead souls. No gain at all. It would only slow him down.

Halfway through the cemetery, the fog finally burned off. The clouds lightened, but never parted, although the day did grow just warm enough that he shucked his jacket and slung it over his shoulder as he paced the rows. He no longer needed to consult his phone for the picture of Whitford's headstone; it was as firmly planted in his memory as in the ground. A reddish granite segmental arch flecked with white and black, his name engraved in simple sans serif along with his birth and death dates. Nothing else. No "beloved husband and father." Not even the simple nouns without a cloying, lying adjective. Might as well have engraved "Burn in hell."

He wondered idly what he would put on Billy's grave, when the time came. Or his mother's.

Cremate them and pour them under the kitchen, Patrick advised. *It works a treat. Trust me.*

He shook his head and backtracked to check the graves he'd daydreamed past. Still not Marcus Whitford.

The cemetery was a web of grasses pocked with headstones, the lawn well-trodden but well-maintained. The only actual path was a car-wide gravel lane that cut through the property from east to west. He'd crossed it many times in his meandering that morning, but for the first time, as he looked up, he saw someone else on that path, ambling from the far side of the cemetery toward the gate. And two things occurred to Jasper.

First, he realized that he should have started at the far end and worked his way toward the entrance.

And second, he realized that the man crunching along the dew-damp gravel was Grant Whitford.

28

HE STOOD THERE, frozen. Nothing had prepared him for this. He had come here because he couldn't stop thinking about fathers and sons, because he'd somehow imagined that standing over Marcus Whitford's grave might kickstart some impulse or engine of insights. He hadn't expected to see Bridekiller his own damn self strolling down the path, hands jammed into the pockets of his brown, waled jacket, head tucked down against the breeze.

A welter of thoughts and instincts and reflexes upchucked from down deep. *Tackle him! Chase him! Hang back! Call the cops! Run him down! Grab him! Run away!*

Fight and flight and freeze warred with each other.

Patrick rescued him. *Not your job. This is for the police and the FBI.*

He watched Bridekiller get smaller and smaller as he headed to the exit. With a deep breath, he stepped onto the path and followed at a casual distance. Whitford never once looked back.

i found whitford, he texted de la Croix. And then used the map on his phone to send his location.

Neither he nor Whitford had made it much closer to the gate when Jasper's phone vibrated with a series of exclamation points and:

do not engage! on our way!

no sirens, he sent back. He didn't want Whitford spooked by the sound of the cops.

By now they'd gained the cemetery gate. Jasper hung back enough to watch which way Whitford turned. How long would it take the task force to get here? *Should* he tackle Whitford? Keep him in place until they arrived?

Yeah, that's a good idea. Get into a fight with the guy who's an expert at murdering people.

Except . . . he murdered them when they were unconscious. And also, not to be sexist about it, but they were women.

As he vacillated, Whitford stamped his feet against the cold and turned right. Jasper watched him through the iron bars of the cemetery fence and then, with a sigh, hung a right himself and followed.

He was not particularly skilled at the art and craft of tailing someone. Stalking? Yes. Absolutely. He was a masterful stalker. His father had inculcated in him from a young age the fine art of stalking prospects (read: victims, usually women). But following someone? That was a related and subtly distinct skillset, the difference between sourdough and yeast. The end result was the same, but you got there with a series of different steps, and one took much, much longer to come to fruition.

He'd always been better at skulking around a house or a business while the subject was stationary or moving through a known series of locales and daily routines. Actually trailing someone at a safe but visible distance while remaining unnoticed was difficult and anxiety-making.

But Bridekiller made it easy. Grant Whitford never once turned around. Not so much as an over-the-shoulder glance did he throw In Jasper's direction.

This tailing stuff was turning out to be easy.

Or . . . wait. Did the fact that Whitford was making it easy mean that he knew Jasper was following him? Was he luring Jasper somewhere? Something from an old *Star Wars* movie floated to the top of Jasper's mind, someone saying, *It's the only possible reason for the ease of our escape.* Something like that. The bad guys let the good guys go so that they could follow them . . .

But that was what Jasper was doing, right? Letting Whitford go so that he could follow him . . .

Unless the prey was actually the predator. Bridekiller's subliterate communiqués aside, the man was wily, smart, and dangerous.

we're almost there

Jasper texted back to de la Croix: he's left the cemetery. i'm following him. not sure of the street name

A moment and then: that's ok. i'm tracking your phone

Jasper indulged in a moment of offended ire, but then texted back: that's probably fair

sorry, not sorry

He suppressed a chuckle and turned his attention back to Whitford. While slowing down to text with de la Croix, he'd allowed Bridekiller to get a little further away. Jasper realized now that the man was headed to a streetcar stop at the corner. He'd seen the streetcars on some of his perambulations of the city, but had paid them not much mind. Public transportation back home was limited to the occasional, inconvenient bus service, so he'd never really adapted to the idea of getting somewhere without a car. Connie, on the other hand, had taken to New York's subway system as though evolved for it.

A bell rang in the distance. A streetcar trundled over the hill. Jasper figured he had two choices: Let Bridekiller go and hope the feds could stop or track the streetcar—

Yeah. Right. Like he was going to do that.

He broke into a light jog, hoping he wouldn't draw Whitford's attention. Running for a streetcar wasn't unusual, but also not unusual was turning around at the sound of running feet.

The streetcar wheezed and whined to a stop, lurching forward into its halt. Whitford did not look around; he climbed aboard. Jasper broke into a full run, hoping that Whitford wouldn't just exit through the door on the opposite side.

He managed to gain the streetcar before it stuttered back into motion, bounding up the steps as the engine coughed and sputtered to life. He fumbled for some cash and handed it over, less concerned with the change than with scanning the interior for Whitford.

It was early morning; the streetcar was packed with commuters. Every seat was taken and clusters of people stood in the aisle. Jasper grabbed a handhold as the streetcar tilted and rolled. His heart thudded and descended, then sparked and skipped a beat when he spied Whitford at the far end of the car, standing and leaning against the wall, gazing sullenly out the window as Seattle cranked by.

on the streetcar thing now

ok we're tracking. we'll get him at the next stop.

Jasper nodded as though the gesture meant anything at all. The next stop. He had no idea when that was, where that was. He trusted that someone on the task force was conversant with the Seattle public transit system.

The car trundled along, grinding its path. He kept an eye on Whitford. The streetcar moved about as quickly as a school bus; not so speedy that someone couldn't or wouldn't risk jumping off while in motion. That, Jasper realized with a sudden pang, was what *he* would do in this situation. Being followed, he'd get on the streetcar and then hop off in the middle of the trip to lose his tail.

Bridekiller continued moping at the window.

When the car came to a stop, it so shocked Jasper out of his staring fugue that he actually gasped out loud, prompting a mingled chuckle from a young Korean couple in the seat closest to him. He was in a denser, more urban area—there were skyscrapers at the corners and people in business attire milling about.

Whitford came pushing through the aisle toward Jasper, who had no choice but to disembark. He lingered by the open door and the steps, glancing around. Whitford came down the steps . . .

. . . just as three police cars and two unmarked sedans pulled up to the curb and surrounded the streetcar, blocking it in.

Whitford was no more than a foot from Jasper; his sudden intake of breath was audible. Jasper could see the flare of Bridekiller's nostrils.

And then Whitford took off running, shoving past Jasper and racing through the gap between the streetcar and one of the patrol cars before anyone had even had a chance to open a car door.

"Freeze!" someone bellowed through a roof-mounted PA system. "Freeze now!"

Whitford wasn't listening. He cleared the car and ran down the open street.

Jasper didn't think—he took off after Bridekiller. It would take precious seconds for anyone to get out of the cars and they couldn't afford to sacrifice even that meager span.

His breath clouded the air before him as he ran. A streetlight ahead was red, so nothing was moving, and Bridekiller wove in and out of traffic like a champion motorcyclist late for his wife's delivery date. Jasper pounded after him, desperate not to lose sight of him, hoping that the task force had left cars back at the ends of the block . . .

He heard footsteps all around him, wondering at the strange acoustics of the open street, but then realized de la

Croix was just a few paces behind him, pumping her arms. She blew past him like an Olympian at an elementary school field day, her breath so even and so controlled that he felt like a four-pack-a-day man struggling to get upstairs.

She jumped the curb and ran pell-mell down the sidewalk, drawing parallel to Bridekiller, who was still Froggering his way through the stopped cars. Once he reached the end of the block and the stoplight—if he did so before the light turned green—he'd have open space and a chance to bolt down a side street.

He never got the chance. De la Croix juked left and rolled over the hood of a Tesla, coming up right behind Whitford. He threw a look over his shoulder—panicked—and she tackled him right there in the middle of the street, slamming him against the rear bumper of a Ford pickup.

By the time Jasper caught up, she'd already dragged Whitford out of the honking, complaining path of traffic and was in the process of slapping shut his second handcuff.

"Well, damn!" Jasper said, breathing hard.

De la Croix's lungs seemed no worse for wear. "Second place, women's hundred-meter relay in college. First place, hurdles." She shrugged as she hoisted Whitford up to his knees, his wrists bound behind him. "Almost went out for the Olympics, but life got in the way."

He grinned at her. She grinned back.

*   *   *

Chris, the FBI behavioral specialist, was now inbound on a commercial jet from BWI to SEA, hustling back from Quantico with an on-ground time estimated to be two hours away. On-site time at the task force office was another hour past that. So they waited.

Jasper had watched Whitford carefully when de la Croix and two uniformed officers, mindful of his own observation the first time he'd set foot inside the task force's demesne: *Nice sense of purpose going here. Get a suspect in here and he'll be terrified.*

Whitford's terror, if it existed, was cloaked under a heavy coating of bafflement and curiosity. He'd glared around at everything and everyone as they led him through the outer office area, but evinced no fear that Jasper could detect. While they waited for Chris to land, Grant Whitford sat in the interrogation room, hands chained to the table.

"What are we thinking?" Grenier asked.

"I'm thinking we're waiting for Chris's plane to land," Conroy snapped.

"C'mon. Doesn't anyone have a theory?" He jerked a thumb toward the interrogation room. "Why this guy? Why these girls?"

"Women," de la Croix said a moment before Jasper planned to.

"Why these *ladies*?" Grenier drew out the word, sing-song. "Well, why?"

"He only mentioned Olefsky specifically," said de la Croix. "It can't be a coincidence."

"So he killed Rebecca Sizemore to piss off his old therapist?"

"This is the part that makes no sense," de la Croix mused. "Why point us right to his therapist? We had no leads in that direction."

Compulsion, Jasper thought, but did not say. Bobby Joe Long.

"He's compelled to do it," Grenier said with an authority that rankled. "There's no logic behind it."

"But why her?"

"I don't know!" Grenier flung his hands in the air. "Maybe he was pissed because she took his therapist away."

De la Croix wasn't buying it. "Then what, he actually only wanted to kill Rebecca Sizemore and the rest were to distract us? Make us think it's a serial killer?"

Jasper glanced over at Conroy, who had checked out of the conversation, fiddling with his phone.

"It *is* a serial killer," Grenier insisted. "Motivation doesn't matter."

"OK, so, sure on a technicality. But Rebecca was the second of five victims," de la Croix pointed out. "So this guy kills another woman before getting to his real target? Then three more after the fact? That's ice-cold."

"He has no conscience. No remorse." Grenier cleared his throat to catch Jasper's attention. "What about you, Wonder Boy? You have to have a theory."

Jasper didn't let the *Wonder Boy* crack or Grenier's tone faze him. "You're forgetting the Billy Dent angle."

"I'm sure as hell trying to," Grenier said, his expression miserable. "That nest of pit vipers and brown recluse spiders your old man calls a brain is not a place I want to experience."

"Still working the field office angle," de la Croix said. Specifically to Jasper: "You think your father picked the victims, not him?"

"I don't know. I'm sure your behavioral team will figure it out."

Conroy looked up from his consultation with the oracle of his phone, sighed heavily, and looked over at Jasper. "Maybe, maybe not. If your father *is* involved, though . . . How about you take a crack at him right now?"

Jasper startled. He hadn't expected this. Not at all. Through the one-way glass, Whitford had put his head down on the table, burying his face in the angles of his elbows. It was impossible to tell if he was awake and alert.

Also impossible to tell was if the notion of him speaking to Whitford was Conroy's idea or someone else's. Again, Jasper wondered who exactly had decided that Jasper Francis Dent would help out on the Bridekiller case. Whoever it was— Conroy or someone else—must have been something close to thrilled. Yes, it was pure luck and coincidence that Bridekiller walked past Jasper at the cemetery . . . but then again, no one else possessed the particular and precise agglomeration of pure fucked-up characteristics that had led him that graveyard in the first place.

Me and the killer, visiting the grave. Two peas in a pod.

He took a little too long responding to Conroy. Grenier, arms crossed over his chest, snorted an amused, knowing eructation, as though to say, *I knew the kid didn't have it in him.*

"I'll go in, sure," Jasper said, his tone calm, light. Not warm, but not frosty. A pitch-perfect, I-have-nothing-else-to-do-and-since-you-asked-so-nicely . . . timbre.

Grenier snorted again, this time a little less amused, a little more concerned. Jasper did his best to ignore it.

"You want someone in there with you?" Conroy asked.

Jasper was rolling up his sleeves, as though upon entering the interrogation room he would pick up a shovel and pickaxe and begin mining for gold. "No, I'll be OK."

"We'll be watching." De la Croix's intonation held nothing but surety. No worry or warning. Just assurance.

"OK," he said, and walked into the interrogation room.

Grant Whitford was sleeping. A slight, nasal buzz emanated from the shadows of his crooked elbows and his back rose and fell with gentle regularity.

It was something of a cop truism that guilty people didn't sleep well and so tended to fall asleep when left to their own devices for long stretches of time in interrogation rooms. Jasper wasn't sure how much stock he placed in this old bit of received blue wisdom, but he knew for certain that he couldn't question a man in dreamland.

Someone playing bad cop—Grenier, for example—would have slammed the door. Kicked over a chair. Smacked a heavy book on the table by the man's ear. Something to startle Whitford awake. But Jasper wanted the man collected, not panicky.

So he very calmly sat across the table from Whitford. Waited a moment. And then said—softly—"Grant. Grant, wake up."

Bridekiller snored.

He thought of Grenier and Conroy and de la Croix watching him through the glass. He thought of the cameras capturing these moments for posterity and jurisprudence.

And he thought of his father. In a prison infirmary for the rest of his life, but still reaching out beyond the penitentiary walls.

He resisted the urge to shout. Instead, he pushed the table forward, just enough to jostle Whitford, who grumbled and then sat up, found the limit of his handcuffs, and leaned forward on the table.

"Can I have some water?" he asked.

"We can arrange that," Jasper said. "But first, I'd like to talk to you. Are you willing to talk to me?"

Whitford blinked rapidly several times, clearing his eyes. He leaned forward a bit more, peering at Jasper as though through fogged-over goggles. "Who are you? Why am I here?"

"You ran from the police. Remember?"

Whitford became agitated at the mention of the police. He tugged against the chain hitching his handcuffs to the table, and even though he found no play there, he kept tugging in smaller and smaller motions.

Jasper flashed back—quite involuntarily—to the one time he'd visited his father in prison. Wammaket State Penitentiary in Tennessee, not far from Lobo's Nod. Jasper had been seventeen and Billy had been four years in to multiple life sentences, but had sauntered into the visitation room as though he could saunter right out whenever he wanted. He'd sat across a table like this one, manacled like Bridekiller.

And then had proceeded to spelunk the depths of Jasper's teen mind and soul, as though all Jasper's hard-earned defenses were tissue paper.

Now, almost a decade later, he assured himself there was no such worry with Bridekiller. They had no history. Jasper would be the spelunker this time.

"What do you know about the Crows?" he began.

"Can I have some water?" Whitford asked, his voice querulous. Jasper ground his teeth together. This man had murdered five women in cold blood and now whined like a petulant child. The temptation to reach across the desk and grab Whitford by the hair and smash his face into the table was overwhelming.

"In a minute," Jasper told him. "Crows."

Whitford stared dully across the table. His blue eyes seemed almost gray, sparkless, lifeless. "Caw?" he asked.

"What do you know about the Crows?" Jasper tried again.

"As the crow flies?"

"Something like that. Do you know the Crow King?"

Grant blinked at him peevishly and licked his dry lips.

"What about Jack Dawes? Name ring a bell?"

"I just want some water."

This was going nowhere. He felt eyes lasering into the back of his head through the mirror. Time to move on.

"Tell me about the women, Grant. The brides. Why did you pick them?"

"Pick them?"

Grinding his teeth together, Jasper gripped the edge of the table to tamp down his temper. "Yes. Why did you pick them? Or did someone assign them to you? Did you receive instructions?"

Grant sighed and slumped in his chair, staring forward at his own manacled hands. "Nothing prettier than a bride. Right? That's what they say. They say she glows." He frowned. "Or is that pregnant women? I can never remember. But they glow. Some of them. Sometimes."

"What's the deal, Grant? Was Rebecca your real target?"

"No, no, I shop at Walmart. Better prices, and I like the old lady who says hi to me when I come in."

The man was either doing an excellent job faking nonchalance or de la Croix had slammed him too damn hard into the rear of that Ford. Either way, Jasper saw some native cunning, but not nearly enough skill and organization to get away with five murders.

He had help. He was being manipulated for sure.

Billy. Oh, Billy. Here we go again . . .

"Did you kill them because they reminded you of your mother?" he asked, and Grant's eyelids twitched, his gaze flicking up, his eyes brightening.

Yes.

Yes, this was it.

"Let's talk about your mother," Jasper said, and Grant Whitford absolutely *lost it*.

Bridekiller rose up from his chair with a guttural sound that was half-growl, half-roar. His chair flew back, clattered to the floor, and in the same instant, he grabbed the edge of the table and heaved.

The task force was in a temporary facility. No one had thought to bolt the table to the floor. It flipped up toward Jasper, who shoved himself back and tipped his chair over. His head smacked against the floor and the room flashed red then black then red again before his vision cleared. The table was coming down at him, and so was Grant Whitford, heaving the table over and also carried along by it on the tether of his chain.

Jasper tried to roll to one side, but the table crashed into him, catching him just above his right hip. Not far from where his mother had stabbed him years ago. He sucked in a breath at the blast of pain. And then Whitford himself stumbled over the table, flipping headfirst to crash bodily on top of Jasper.

They flailed against each other, tangled in Whitford's chain, hemmed in by the hard rectangle of the table, its mass shifting with each movement from Bridekiller, its edge pressing into him.

"Don't talk about my mother!" Whitford shouted. "Don't talk about my mother!"

Crushed under the weight of the table, Jasper could not say, as he so badly wished to, *Fine! I'll shut up about your mother!*

It had been only a few seconds, he knew, but still—when the door to the interrogation room flew open, his first thought was an ungenerous, thoroughly emphatic *Finally!*

Whitford lay atop him, his face near Jasper's own, his eyes wide, his slavering mouth open and howling. Jasper couldn't move his hands—one was trapped under his own body, the other pressed to his side by Whitford—so he craned his neck as far as possible, terrified that Whitford would try to bite him.

And then de la Croix had Whitford in a choke hold, pulling him back as Conroy and Grenier worked to wrestle the table up and off. Once a scintilla of space had opened up, Jasper freed his hands and clawed at the floor, pulling himself out from under Bridekiller and into a safe corner of the room.

It took them a few minutes to wrestle Whitford into submission, the man still screaming about his mother the whole time. De la Croix helped Jasper out of the interrogation room as more agents and cops went in. Jasper figured Whitford was in for a beating and he was OK with that for the time being.

"You all right?" de la Croix asked once they were out of the room.

"I'm done," he said. He'd meant it to be strong, final, staunch. Uncompromising. Instead, it drifted out on a whisper.

"I don't blame you," she said. "I really don't."

"I'm done." A little stronger this time. A little more meat on the bone. He felt so weak. He felt beaten and whipped. A part of him worried he might start crying.

"I'm just going to pack up and go home," he told her. "You guys can take it from here. If it's Billy, I hope you fry him good. I really do. I'm done. Lose my number, Agent. I'm done with all of it."

She bit her lip and nodded slowly. He thought there might be some species of apology incoming, but she did not embarrass herself with the attempt. There was no reason for an apology in any event—he was an adult. He'd agreed to come here. And as Patrick had predicted, he'd failed except for the times he'd gotten lucky.

Straightening his shirt, patting down his body to make sure he had his phone, his wallet, he nodded back to her and turned to the door.

CHAPTER

29

The note was still on his hotel room door, with an addendum.

NO YOU DON'T, it read.

He ignored it. This was one problem that wouldn't follow him home from Seattle, he figured. He could deal with it later from the safety of the Nod.

Crumpling the note, he tossed it in his trash can once he was in the room, then filled the bathroom sink with cold water and dunked his face in it long enough for it to begin burning, especially around the stitches. The shock of it calmed him, settled him.

He couldn't do it anymore. He just couldn't. If it was his father at the wheel, then fine—a point to Billy Dent. But Jasper still breathed free air. Game, set, and match.

Once he was home, he would make a couple of phone calls. One to McCutcheon, to officially fire him. The other to Patrick, to see if they could work out a virtual arrangement. Sure, he wasn't licensed, but he was good and Jasper wanted to keep talking to him.

The decisions felt right.

He packed his bag, checked the time to his flight, and decided he had enough time and composure for a last cup of coffee before he left.

Hauling his duffel down the street and around the block, he saw with pleasure that Coffee Amore was packed. The tables were crowded, the counter two-deep with customers. He smiled as he entered, the cold air of outside at his back, the humid and fragrant coffee shop air before him. He lingered for a moment, enjoying the contrasts.

"You're letting the heat out!" Shanna called from behind the counter.

He closed the door and took up a spot at the counter. There was a second barista working today—a young Latino guy with a neat van Dyke and a tattoo of a swan on his neck—and he and Shanna scurried back and forth, pouring, mixing, blending, steaming, frothing. They communicated wordlessly and with apparent telepathy, handing off cups and carafes, stepping aside at the steamer, dunking used metal cups into the small, soap-filled sink.

The bearded dude got to him first, but Shanna called over her shoulder, without even looking, "I've got him, Jorge."

Jorge shrugged—no skin off his nose—and pointed to the next person in line, who ordered something that sounded like pure liquid diabetes.

A moment later, Shanna came over to him and slid a medium cup with a lid across the counter. "Black coffee," she said. "No sugar. Did I get it right?"

There was a note of pique to her voice, but also a playful note. He supposed the two worked together, in this instance.

"You know me too well," he teased.

She nodded to his duffel. "Leaving town?"

"Yes." A part of him wanted to add *sorry*, but that felt presumptuous.

She considered briefly, then reached into her apron pocket and handed over a folded-once piece of paper. He opened it automatically, expecting to see her name and number, or maybe her Tinder handle. Instead, he read: *half cup brewed coffee, half cup cream . . .*

He blinked.

"If it's too complicated for you," she said, her voice again tight and light at the same time, "I'm sure you can find someone back in Kentucky to put this together for you."

"Tennessee."

"Is there a difference?"

"Probably not as much of one as I think."

With a wan smile, she offered her hand. He shook it.

"It was nice meeting you, Jasper Dent."

He realized he didn't know her last name.

"Nice meeting you, too."

He might have stood there for an hour, holding her hand, if not for the throng around him, the hard, just-civilized urgency of caffeine addicts in their version of an opium den.

There was nothing more to say. He let go of her hand and waved weakly to her. Tucking the recipe into his pocket, he returned to the cold air.

She was already on to the next customer. She did not look up as he left.

*   *   *

In the car on the way to the airport, his side began to throb. Maybe the adrenaline rush from his encounter with Bridekiller had finally subsided. Or maybe he was just relaxed enough to notice.

He had his driver pull over at the nearest pharmacy and wandered the aisles, looking for painkillers. There were three different ones and they each advertised themselves as good at one thing or another, but he didn't know which would be optimal for his particular injury, so he took a bottle of each over to the pharmacy counter and plunked them down.

"Which one is best?" he asked. It was the kind of thing parents would teach a child, he realized. He was constantly tripped up in the real world by knowledge he lacked that his parents should have imparted in the course of parenting.

Look at it this way—you don't know which painkiller is best for a table landing on your guts, but you know everything there is to know about transferring bodies from location to location without leaving DNA behind. Yay, me.

"Depends," the pharmacist said, arranging them with the labels facing out at Jasper. "This one's good for headaches. This one for muscle pains. This one—"

"I had a crazy dude trap me under a table and hit me right in the spot where I was stabbed repeatedly a few years ago."

The pharmacist pursed his lips and contemplated this for too long. Questions flickered in his eyes and in the set of his jaw, but finally he said, "Well, I'd use this one," and slid one bottle forward.

"Thanks." Jasper dug into his pocket for cash, paid, then twisted open the bottle.

"Oh, one thing!" the pharmacist called out. Jasper had already begun to walk away from the counter, but now turned back, the cap in one hand, the bottle in the other.

"The dosage guidelines say take one to two tablets every six hours," the pharmacist said, "but with the pain you're describing . . . at your height and weight . . . I'd say you're OK to take three. Try that first and see how you feel."

"You sure?" Jasper asked doubtfully. He generally didn't take medicine and was suspicious of it. A lingering lesson from his crazed grandmother, whose dementia made her untrusting of anything that wasn't boxed, canned, or otherwise packaged before 1990.

"Yeah. Dosage guidelines are for the average case. Your case isn't average."

That made sense. Jasper nodded his thanks and walked out the door, palming three tablets, and settled back into the car. There were courtesy bottles of water in the back seat and he'd already downed three pills when it hit him:

Dosage.

"Shit," he said, and told the driver that they weren't going to the airport after all.

He needed to talk to Patrick.

CHAPTER

30

Patrick was waiting for him, the front door open, standing just inside. He wore a cardigan and a worried expression.

"Come in, come in!" he called as Jasper slid out of the car. "It's freezing out."

It was. Jasper hurried to the front door and let Patrick usher him in.

"I put the kettle on," Patrick said. "It's so goddamn cold."

Shanna's hot coffee had been drunk on the way over. He followed Patrick into the kitchen. Two mugs of tea on the table. "Pick your poison," Patrick said, and after only the slightest hesitation, Jasper took one of them. The tea smelled like hibiscus and roses. He added a goodly dollop of honey and stirred. When he drank, it was strong and sweet.

"You caught him," Patrick said, sipping from his own mug. "I'm proud of you."

Jasper didn't want the compliment to affect him . . . but it did. Of course it did. A drizzle of emotion bedewed him and he couldn't speak for a moment. He covered by drinking the tea.

"I'm not here to talk about that," Jasper said.

"I'm surprised you're here at all." Patrick's tone was wounded. "Agent de la Croix called to say they had Grant in custody and that you were leaving. I didn't think I'd see you again."

"I'm not very good at goodbyes," Jasper said. It was a confession, and one he hadn't intended to make. He felt artless suddenly, especially given the circumstances. "I tend to leave people in the lurch. It's easier that way."

Hell, why had he said that? He was way too comfortable with Patrick.

Patrick sat across from him as he had so many other times. "You don't like connections, do you?" he asked. "You have a core group of people in your life and they're the only ones you trust."

"Trusting people gets you hurt." It was another truth blurted out. Jasper felt almost giddy at saying it. And alarmed at his giddiness.

"I need to ask you some questions," he said, trying to get back on track. The word *questions* had some trouble coming out. Why hadn't he ever noticed how unutterably *weird* the letter *q* was? And how weird was it that you *had* to have a *u* after a *q*? Who came up with that rule? Like, really, what was the point of *q*? Why not just, just *k* or *kw* instead? Was anyone in charge of this stuff? Was anyone keeping track?

"Oh, crap." Jasper's voice sounded thick and distant. It was muffled in his own ears as it vibrated up his jawbone. He looked down at his mostly empty mug. "You roofied me, didn't you?"

Patrick tilted his head to one side and offered a small, almost apologetic smile. "Afraid so."

"But . . . I picked the mug."

Patrick shrugged. "I dosed the honey. And the sugar, too, just in case you switched it up."

Jasper laughed. Well, *this* wasn't good! Not at all. He'd planned on catching Patrick off guard, easing into an interrogation, but now . . .

Now he couldn't stop laughing. This drug . . . He'd never been roofied before, but it really was like being drunk, he decided. A warmth suffused his body, a pleasant numbness that filled his limbs and core. Patrick chuckled and Jasper didn't know what was so funny, but it didn't matter. He laughed along with Patrick and looked at his mug and really wanted to drink the last of the tea and what the hell, right, he was already drugged, so might as well, right?

He tipped the mug to his lips and drank the last of the tea and then his vision doubled as he tried to put the mug back on the table and he heard a clunk and thought that maybe

31

His throat was raw and sandpaper-gritty, his eyelids unwilling to lift. His eyes flitted and jittered in their own dark. Light patterns swirled. Phosphenes. The word floated to him from some high school biology class. Photons emitted from the eyes themselves, self-generated images animated on the screen of the inside of the eyelids.

A gust of nausea blew through his stomach and then rode its way out on a horrific tasting belch.

His arms stretched back behind him. Sharp pain at his wrists.

Zip ties.

Where? Why?

He groaned. His dry lips protested the effort. His throat clenched.

Forcing his eyes open, he recoiled at a bright light. The chair on which he sat—to which he was *bound*—creaked like a haunted house.

It was not the first time in his life he'd awoken to discover himself bound. He decided that it would be the last.

One way or the other.

With several painful blinks, he lubricated his eyes enough to perceive a shadowy figure at the edge of the bright light.

Patrick stepped into the aureole and hunkered down before Jasper. "Awake?" he asked. "For real?"

With the bright light partially eclipsed by Patrick's body, the pain in Jasper's eyes abated enough for him to peer around. He recognized the space immediately: Grant Whitford's attic. Was this a team-up scenario? Had he misjudged things that badly? He knew he'd missed all the big signs that pointed to Patrick's involvement, but he hadn't thought they'd been working together. Maybe this was his blind spot—serial killer duets. It had taken him too long to deduce that Brooklyn's Hat-Dog Killer was simultaneously bifurcated and conjoined—the Hat Killer and the Dog Killer. He'd lived the first seventeen years of his life dreading his murderous father and venerating his absent mother, only to suffer a gunshot and repeated stab wounds at the hands of the Crow King, his maternal monster. Far from at odds with each other, his parents functioned like two gears with perfectly meshed teeth.

As his head cleared the smallest bit, he realized: No. This was *not* Grant Whitford's attic. It couldn't be. The FBI had commandeered that space and when last Jasper had seen it, it had been covered in fingerprint dust, lit by large workshop lights, cluttered with the accoutrements of a crime scene investigation in progress.

This attic was similar in the way unfinished attics are, but smaller. And there was a table, the same as in Whitford's attic, a single lightbulb . . . but not much else.

It was *Patrick's* attic, he realized. He *hoped*. He couldn't imagine that Patrick would have risked guiding even a drug-compliant hostage anywhere else.

He tried to speak. His throat rebelled. He was so thirsty that he would drink piss if it were offered.

"How did you know?" he finally managed to whisper, the effort grinding his throat.

"That you had figured it out? You were leaving town and then you suddenly came back. I'm not an idiot, Jasper. I can add two and two and get four."

It was true—Patrick was not an idiot. He was, in fact, one of Jasper's nightmare scenarios: a highly educated, impeccably trained student of the human psyche who had turned serial killer.

"Why?" Jasper asked. "Was it *your* mother? Not Grant's?"

Patrick stepped back a few paces and pulled over a chair from the shadows. He sat down and leaned back and worried at his lower lip. Trying to decide how much to reveal. Deciding it didn't matter any longer. He was in control.

And he was dying to tell, Jasper realized. He wanted someone to know how he'd pulled it all off. How and why.

"It had nothing to do with mothers," Patrick said. "Well, except for yours."

Jasper startled. His mother. Janice Dent. The Crow King. Was Patrick a Crow after all?

His stomach lurched and wailed at him. His nerves were alight with fire. His mother. His *mother*. Was she even still at Kettle-Herrara? Had it been a ruse all along? Were the doctors there in on it? Was she awake and coming for him?

Sweat beaded along his hairline. Dripped down the back of his neck. He strained against the zip ties. His *mother*. The Crow King was coming for him.

"You know, this is the third time you've woken up," Patrick told him with air of calm annoyance. "The third time we've tried to have this conversation. I think this one will stick. I hope so. I'm tired of repeating myself."

"What about my mother?" Jasper demanded.

"No, no." Patrick waggled a finger, a parent out of patience with an obdurate child. "First, tell me what made you realize it was me. And don't make me say *quid pro quo*. We're not cosplaying old movies here. What clued you in? Tell me."

He had to know. Had to know about his mother. Whatever it took.

Even the truth.

"Dosages," Jasper said. His throat burned at speaking, but he did anyway. He'd hoped for a startled or distressed expression from Patrick, but Bridekiller merely gazed at him thoughtfully.

"Dosages," Jasper said again. "You recovered faster than the other men. Because you were more careful with your dosage. You knew your exact weight. You didn't for the others, so you overcompensated."

With a sigh, Patrick slapped his palms on his thighs. "You're right. I never even considered that. Well done. You're as good at this as I worried you were."

"That's why you were working so hard to undermine my confidence." The memories of their ersatz sessions together flashed through Jasper's mind. What he'd thought of as blunt-spoken compassion, a desire to ease Jasper toward a better, healthier life, was really nothing more than manipulation. Negging him like a pickup artist in a bar.

And it had worked. Jasper had doubted himself, doubted his skills, his abilities, his knowledge.

"I didn't have to do much," Patrick said. "You were already in a precarious state. Every patient has to be broken down before you can build him back up. Your McCutcheon had broken you down pretty well. I only needed to give you a little push in the wrong direction."

"But why . . . Why pull me closer? The envelope . . ."

Patrick sighed. "We're not going to waste time going over every little detail, OK? I had the letter written already. It was ready to be delivered. And then I saw online that you were at one of the weddings and, I don't know, it just seemed too delicious not to do it. Add a postscript and a name and everything worked beautifully."

"You said something about my mother . . ." He managed to make the words strong.

Patrick shrugged and made a show of bending to one side to retrieve a bottle of water from the floor, twisting open the cap, and pulling a long swallow.

Jasper cleared his throat. The rasp filed away at his breath. "Can I have some water?"

"No," Patrick said flatly.

"Well, damn."

"Grant's mother ran off in 2020," Patrick said. "A lot of people used the pandemic as an excuse to reset their lives. He was a grown-up and she was tired of dealing with Grant's issues and I can't blame her. I only dealt with them because I was being paid. And because I realized he was useful. Mind you, there was nothing wrong with him a competent therapist couldn't help, but I found it more fruitful to go in another direction."

He quaffed more water. In a panic, Jasper realized he was about to pass out and struggled against it. He had to stay awake. He had to know.

With a tsk, Patrick went on. "Poor Grant and his mommy issues . . . like you. Oh, you do a good job not talking about it. But your memoir so studiously avoids the topic of Janice Dent that it's like the hound of the Baskervilles. The dog that didn't bark. I knew that I could poke you in all the most interesting, most productive places if I made this about mommy." He leaned forward, staring at Jasper. "Are you still awake? Are we going to have to do this all over again when you wake up?"

"'m OK." Thick and sludgy syllables in his mouth. The taste of morning breath and alleviation. It wasn't his mother. Not Janice. Maybe Billy, still. Pulling the strings. But not Janice. At least it wasn't her. He sagged against the chair in relief.

"I mean, I guess it's my fault," Patrick went on. "Your condition, that is. It's funny—you forget how powerful these drugs are. When I woke up in my hotel room, I actually forgot for a moment. Can you believe it? I'd killed her . . . then dosed myself to make it look good . . . and when I woke up, for a moment, I couldn't remember! I actually couldn't remember! And then of course it all came back to me." He grinned. "And I knew I'd gotten away with it, too. Until you came."

"Sorry, not sorry."

"I was petrified. You were the legend. The hunter of hunters. I had to think of a way to throw you off my scent. So even though I thought I was done, I realized I had to do something. But it would do no good to push you away."

"So you drew me in closer." Jasper coughed, a rough hot wind in his throat. Words were difficult. "To worm your way into my brain. Point me in the wrong direction."

"Worm my way? *Worm?* I think I deserve a better verb that that. I scalpeled my way in. I carved a delicate slit in your psyche and slid right in and you never even noticed."

"Your professors would be so proud."

Patrick snorted with derision. "Wrote letters to the FBI to sow confusion. And then you literally walked through my door. Presented yourself to me. And I realized that you were so broken that I could put you back together in any configuration I pleased."

Rebecca was the real target. The only target. Patrick had murdered four other women in cold blood just to make it look like a serial killer. Just to cover his tracks.

And then . . .

He cleared his throat, decided it had felt better cluttered.

"Whitford. Was he even involved at all?"

Patrick burst out laughing. "You've met him! What do you think?"

Mind racing, Jasper struggled to assemble the puzzle pieces. He'd already done much of this in the car on the way to Patrick's, but the Rohypnol had knocked over the table and scattered the pieces again.

"Former patient, right? Paranoid delusions? Schizoid?" He groaned lightly, his voice rough and challenged by the drugs, the dehydration. But he had to say it. Say it all. "Something made him malleable for you . . ."

"It's a species of histrionic personality disorder." Patrick's tone became quite serious, almost professorial. "Combined with a derivative of scopolamine, it made him quite pliant for my purposes." He stroked his chin. "Also really wrecked his brain, possibly for good, but given the fates of the brides, I'd say he got off lucky, wouldn't you?"

"All to distract us?"

"Don't gainsay it—it worked. Had him running from his own home so that I could stage it for you." He gestured around them. "A desk and some photos, just like my own attic. That's all it took. Grant was just . . ." He tapped his chin, thinking. "Chum in the waters. Raw, bloody meat to distract the sharks from the swimmers. And once the swimmers have escaped and the sharks realize they've been had, suckered in by some doctored photos of a bridal gown model and a man with a hopelessly demolished psyche . . ." A diffident shrug. "Well, by then the task force has already been dissolved. The freelance expert is already back in Tennessee . . ."

He could see it now. Patrick deftly handed just enough over to make the task force think the crimes were solved, the killer caught. None of it would stand up to in-depth scrutiny, but by the time someone realized they'd been had, it would be too late. Time was always on the criminal's side. Justice delayed and justice denied and all that. If they couldn't catch him in the heat of the moment, with the crimes fresh, how would they do it months or years later, when they realized they had to start all over again?

"I've had an exfiltration plan in place since the beginning. I had all kinds of time to plan. You never start something without knowing how it will end. Your father said something like that in your book, right? '*Never go after a prospect without knowing how you'll get away.*' I took it to heart. Fake IDs, used cars, all kinds of stuff.

"But I had to delay a bit because I really thought it would take you a few more weeks to find him," Patrick mused. "And I would have more time to play inside that devastated brain of yours. But then you got lucky. How *did* you find him?"

It was a mark of the power of the drugs in his system that it took Jasper a moment to remember exactly how he'd found Whitford. He licked his lips—dry flesh on dry flesh—and told Patrick how he'd gone to see Marcus Whitford's grave and had run into Grant by pure coincidence. Patrick shook his head and said something about Grant being such a daddy's boy.

"You think you're this brilliant deductive genius," Patrick said, "but at the end of the day, it was just pure luck."

"No. I went there because I knew fathers and sons mattered. I didn't know the particulars, but my instincts were dead on."

Patrick harrumphed and waved off the comment like a bad stink. Jasper tried a different tack.

"We thought you were losing confidence," Jasper said. "The timing between kills made no sense. But it's because—"

"I was choosing them based on my convenience, not any sort of urge or schedule," Patrick admitted. "Why not make it easy on myself?"

He had Patrick relaxed now. In a comfort zone. Murder was easy for him to discuss. More relevant—he *wanted* to discuss it. He'd kept it so close and hidden for so long.

But there was one topic they hadn't broached. And that Patrick had avoided it made Jasper think it might—just might—be a weak spot he could probe.

He drew in a deep breath. He forced himself to focus. He was on fire and his vision was still touch and go. But he had to bear down and get through it, push through the drugs and the pain.

The zip ties were no looser. The chair was sturdy, but he thought with enough force, he might be able to break it against a wall or the floor. At least cause enough damage that he could get his arms free. But he needed Patrick distracted. So.

He summoned as much strength as he could find for his voice. Eyes locked on Patrick, his tone pitched low, he said, "You must have hated her so much. Why did you even marry her?"

This seemed to catch Patrick off guard. He rose from his chair and paced the width of the attic, chin down, thinking. Just as in Whitford's attic—as in most attics, he figured— there was a small window just beyond Patrick and through it Jasper could see black sky when Bridekiller stepped just to the left. Then Patrick. Then black sky. Then Patrick.

He craned his neck. There was another window at the other end of the attic. Nothing but black sky again.

"It was nothing I hadn't done with other patients," Patrick said slowly. "Over the years. A man has needs. And the pretty, insecure ones are so easy . . ."

He stopped and approached Jasper, then knelt before him so their eyes leveled.

"But unlike the others, she threatened to report me. God-damn #MeToo and all of a sudden women decided they didn't have to just lie there and take it anymore. So I had no choice. I really had no choice." He seemed to truly want Jasper to understand this. To empathize, if not sympathize. "I had to tell her I loved her, that I would surrender my license volun-tarily . . . I couldn't let it get out, you see? If it went public, then the others might come squirming out of their hidey-holes and tell what I'd done to them. You sleep with one patient, you lose your license. Sleep with a dozen and you're going to jail."

He took Jasper's face in his hands. "I couldn't let that happen. I had to stall."

"And then you planned."

Patrick smiled, releasing Jasper. "Yes. I planned. I insisted on a big wedding after a year's engagement, to give me the time I needed to set the plan in motion. I . . . I've spent my life treating people with various mental illnesses. I could see it happening to me, in real time. I could feel my old self, shedding."

"And you felt powerless to stop it."

"No," Patrick said after a moment's thought. "No, not the case. I made the conscious decision to go with it. It just felt *right*.

"So I just browsed the usual wedding sites, found women who looked like Rebecca . . . And I invented a serial killer. Tell me, and please be honest: As an expert, as a connoisseur . . . how did I do?"

"Five out of ten," Jasper said.

Patrick frowned.

"I think you're letting your present condition color your judgement. I plotted it all meticulously, right down to setting up Grant to take the fall. It's so convenient that weddings are announced publicly. In advance. Gave me plenty of time to figure out where they were staying, how to get into the rooms . . .

"I did one, and I did Rebecca, and I did a few more, just to throw off any doubts." He smiled genially, an avuncular acquaintance recounting a humorous anecdote over drinks. "And you know what I did after Rebecca was finally dead? I burned her to ash and drilled a hole in the floor and I poured that bitch down there with the spiders and the mice and the sewer pipes." Standing, he dusted his hands together, and Jasper had a flash of Patrick doing the same as he stood after funneling his bride under the kitchen floor. Proud of a job well done. Proud to have accomplished his goals.

"And I would have been finished, then, if not for you."

The chair squeaked a bit. Jasper managed to move from side to side without looking suspicious—he hoped. Patrick was in a different zone. Not entirely paying attention.

Jasper pushed him a little further.

"You're a sociopath."

Patrick roared with laughter. "Leave the diagnoses to the experts, please, Mr. Dent!" He removed his glasses and wiped amused tears from his eyes. "You say that word with such disdain. And—dare I say—a touch of self-loathing. But let me tell you this: Someday, it'll be just another protected, neurodivergent class. They'll call it sociopathy spectrum disorder." He grinned wickedly. "You'll be on the list, too, Jasper Francis Dent. Trust me."

"Can I *please* have some water?" Jasper asked. He had progressed beyond parched. And he wanted Patrick to turn around and rummage through his things. Just for a moment. To test the chair again.

"Not a chance," Patrick said pleasantly. He turned and strode over to the table against the wall. Same design as the one in Whitford's attic, the one, Jasper now realized, Patrick himself had set up. Hence its distance from the outlet. It had never been used for actual work—it was a set. A background to a play that Patrick had been directing all along.

He thought of Connie. He would see her again. He had to.

Back and forth. Left to right. Just for a moment. While Patrick's back was turned.

The chair was dismally sturdy. Given time, he could break it.

Time he was certain he did not have.

From the table, Patrick picked up a small black satchel, then returned to Jasper's side. "I'm going to give you a good dose," he said, down on one knee as though to propose, rummaging in the satchel. "Enough to keep you out until we get across the border."

"Mexico?" He didn't relish being drugged for that long.

"No. Canada. Don't worry—I want you alive long enough to figure out what really makes you tick. By the time they realize you're not on that plane, we'll be safely across the border. Then we'll cut back into Alaska. I have a place there. We can continue our work, undisturbed."

Jasper did some math in his head. It was difficult—his dehydrated brain had begun to throb with migraine-like pulses of nauseating pain.

The needle came out of the satchel. Patrick stabbed a small vial through the lid. Jasper couldn't make out the printing on the label.

"Another roofie?"

"Not this time. Flurazepam. I want you good and unconscious for the length of our drive. Can't have you making noise in the trunk when we go through the border."

Jasper skimmed the attic with his eyes. He did not see what he'd been hoping for this whole time. And there was nothing he could do. The chair was too strong. The zip ties too tight.

He had to keep Patrick talking. If he let that needle go into his vein, he'd never breathe free air again. He knew it. Patrick's ego was unassailable—he was too smart for most distraction techniques. But his clinical need to understand and to be understood . . .

"It was clever, the letters. But you made two mistakes."

"Do tell." Patrick sounded only vaguely distracted as he tilted toward Jasper's neck with the needle.

"First of all, by saying there would be one more victim, you shifted our attention from looking for you to looking for the next victim."

"I don't see how that's a mistake. It was intentional." The tip of the needle pressed against Jasper's carotid. He had to be careful here. He couldn't let his desperation show. He had to be as cold and as clinical as Bridekiller.

"Maybe. But it was also *clever*. Which was your second mistake, because Grant Whitford wasn't clever."

Patrick went still. Jasper could hear the man breathing, could feel the heat of his cheek, so close to Jasper's own as he prepared to drive in the needle.

And then Bridekiller sank back into a sitting position, still holding the needle. His expression was passionless, but a lurking curiosity raised his eyebrows ever so slightly.

"Go on."

"Once I started thinking about dosages on my way to the airport, I thought about the letters, too. And how organized the killer was, but how the letters were clearly—almost desperately—designed to make us think someone stupid wrote them. You were trying too hard to throw us off the path that led to someone educated."

Patrick shrugged with a lazy pout. "So? It worked as long as it needed to."

"It didn't. Because I realized it was you all along."

A smile that, under different circumstances, might have been winsome or welcoming. "But you realized it too late."

"I think I realized right on time."

With a bored sigh, Patrick shuffled up onto his knees and leaned in with the needle. "I'm going to teach you to stop that insipid verbal jousting if it's the last thing I do. Now hold still."

"The FBI tracks my phone," Jasper said.

Patrick paused. "Yes. Well . . . I turned it off after I drugged you. So . . ." He came closer with the needle.

"Right. So they'll know I was here."

"We're leaving anyway."

"Right." Jasper couldn't help it. He smiled. "But if they tracked my phone to your house and then lost the signal . . . It's only a matter of time before they think to track *your* phone."

Eyes dancing left and right, left and right, Patrick sucked on his lower lip. "So? I'm in my own home . . ."

"And they'll know it." Jasper sighed. "You didn't even turn yours off, did you? Oh, you'd ditch it somewhere before we got to Canada, but right now . . . Right now I bet it's on you, turned on and broadcasting."

Patrick studiously did not move, but Jasper noticed his eyes narrowing ever so slightly.

"Again. I'm in my own house. And if the FBI notices your phone *was* here and they come to question me, I'll just tell them you stopped by to say goodbye and left."

"They won't buy that. Because the signal is off. And that will raise suspicions."

"What makes you so certain?"

"Partly that I understand human nature. Partly surmise based on my knowledge of the people I've been working with. But mostly, Patrick?" And now he couldn't hold back a wide, wide smile. "Mostly it's the red sniper laser dot on your chest."

Patrick scrambled back from Jasper, dropping the needle as he did so. He clawed at his shirt, where a red dot perched unwaveringly over his heart, coming over Jasper's left shoulder after transmitting through the rear attic window.

He tried not to let his relief show as Patrick stared at him in terror. He'd been hoping the FBI would connect the dots at some point. It had been very, very close.

A muffled jingle. Patrick's phone, in his pocket.

"I'd answer that," Jasper told him.

Still staring straight ahead at Jasper, Patrick felt for his phone blindly, his entire body frozen save for the questing hand. He raised the phone to his ear.

The volume was loud enough that in the still attic, Jasper could hear de la Croix's voice.

"Hello, Dr. Olefsky! Or—I'm sorry—*Mr.* Olefsky. This is going to be a very simple decision for you. You can get up and walk away from Jasper and stand in the far corner with your back to the room and your hands behind your back, or my friend here with the sniper rifle can shoot you through the head."

Jasper managed a hoarse chuckle that didn't hurt. Much.

"I want to emphasize, Doc—*Mr.* Olefsky, that this is entirely your choice."

As Jasper watched, the red dot slid smoothly up Patrick's body, bisecting his face along the line of his nose, terminating with definitive immobility dead center of his forehead.

"Shit," Patrick said tonelessly.

32

JASPER'S WRISTS WERE abraded by the zip ties and he was thirsty and woozy from the drugs, but otherwise healthy and cogent. De la Croix herself cut the zip ties from him as a cluster of cops and agents not-at-all-gently dragged Patrick from the attic.

Olefsky had gone utterly silent after his *shit* comment, staring balefully at Jasper even as they hauled him away, until his eyes finally vanished beneath the floor of the attic and he was just footsteps in the distance.

Jasper stood and rubbed his wrists. "I guess I missed my flight," he said. "Can you get me on the next one?"

De la Croix blinked as though assaulted with bright light. "Look, you need some time to—"

"I'll have plenty of time on the plane. I'm getting the hell out of here while I still can."

She nodded slowly at that. "Yeah, yeah, I get it. Look, though . . . I guess . . . uh, I guess Seattle PD will be in touch with you if they get any leads on the guy who attacked you."

Jasper smacked his forehead. "Oh. Oh, that. Right. No, no need. I was going to tell you when I got home: I figured it out a few days ago."

De la Croix goggled at him, her expression that of someone who's opened a closet door only to find a floorless drop down four stories. "I'm sorry—you what?"

* * *

It took about half an hour to get everyone together once Conroy acquiesced and gathered all of the task force's FBI personnel in the main room.

Jasper and de la Croix stood off to the side. There were about thirty agents and support persons from the FBI before them. Counting quickly, Jasper said, "Let the women go. Have the men stand over there." He pointed to a spot near the wall.

No one moved at his command. They all looked to Conroy, who nodded wearily and actually said aloud, "Let's humor him."

Sixteen men remained. They stood against the wall like a lineup.

Jasper slowly walked down the line, de la Croix at his side, perplexed and nakedly eager for answers. He reached the end of the line, stopped, turned, and walked back, again followed by de la Croix.

He stopped again in front of the sixth man in line.

"How did you know Jennifer Morales?" Jasper asked quietly.

Grenier blinked rapidly. "What? Who?"

"Ah." Jasper nodded and smiled. "See, I wasn't entirely one hundred percent certain until just now. But pretending you don't know that name . . . That sealed it for me."

"Dent, what the hell?" Conroy said, coming up behind him.

"Wait," said de la Croix. "Grenier? It was Grenier?"

Grenier didn't wait for anyone else. He towered over Jasper threateningly, and Jasper managed not to flinch at the memory of Grenier towering over him in the hotel room, face sheathed in a balaclava. "I'm not going to sit here and be treated—"

"No, you're going to stand there, I guess," Jasper said. "You couldn't take the ultimate step and kill me, but you sure wanted me dead, didn't you? Tried to break me. Goading me to kill myself . . . What was it, Grenier? Did you partner with her at some point? Or was it personal, not professional?"

"Oh, wow," de la Croix whispered.

"Answer his question," Conroy said.

"Sir, with all due respect, I'm not beholden to some *kid*—"

"You're beholden to *me*." Conroy's tone did not waver in the slightest.

For a moment, Jasper thought Grenier was going to run. It would have been, he figured, amusing. Grenier wasn't built like a runner and there were dozens of cops and agents between him and the door. Jasper was rooting for him to make a good show of it though.

But instead, Grenier leaned forward, fists balled. "You got her killed!" he snarled, spittle flecking from between his lips. "You little piece of shit! You got her killed!"

"I did," said Jasper. "Yes, I did."

Two cops came out of nowhere and grabbed Grenier by the arms. Still, Grenier lunged forward, hauling against them, as though he could devour Jasper, needing no hands to destroy him.

"I don't expect this to mean anything to you," Jasper said quietly, "but I live with that and so many other things. Every day. Every night. Every minute of my life."

"Fuck you!" Grenier lurched forward more. The two cops managed to hold him back.

"You'll find video of a man of his height and build on the hotel security cameras," Jasper said. "You'll have to hunt for it—I'm sure he's good at avoiding them. But also, have your handwriting experts look at these."

He handed over the various notes he'd accumulated during his time in Seattle. Conroy took them with a hand that shook just the tiniest bit.

"He probably tried to disguise his handwriting, but I bet your guys can figure it out."

"Dent . . ." For the first time, Conroy's voice was weak, thready. "On behalf of . . . I don't even know what to . . ."

Jasper smiled and shook his head. "No need. No need."

They stood in staring silence for a moment, and then Conroy offered his hand. Jasper took it and they shook once. Twice.

"Look, even though it turns out your father wasn't involved, we're still going to chase down those phone calls," Conroy said. "If we learn anything at all that I'm authorized to tell you . . ."

"I'll wait for your call," Jasper said. He made Conroy believe it.

He couldn't tell Conroy what his mother had told him all those years ago. That the Crows had placed some of its members in positions of authority and power. Including in law enforcement.

Including, possibly, the FBI?

And he couldn't tell Conroy that because what if Conroy was one of them?

Time would bear it out, he knew. Time and maybe something else.

De la Croix escorted him outside and offered him a ride back to the airport. He declined.

"I'm really sorry about Grenier," she said. "I had no idea."

He opened his mouth to speak. To tell her that Grenier had not been the first aggrieved party to track him down nor would he be the last. To tell her that he would suffer for the sins of his parents his whole life . . . and that the suffering was deserved. That even as a child, he'd been wise enough to know the difference between right and wrong, that he could have told someone, called someone, done something that would have saved lives.

But something in the warmth of her eyes checked his words. She didn't need the burden and he didn't need to unburden himself. Not right now.

"Lose my number," he reminded her gently, and she nodded and said nothing more as his Uber pulled up to the door.

33

THE FBI FLEW him back coach. A window seat, at least.

He assured Howie that he would be fine on the return flight, even though he could not be certain. He hadn't enjoyed the flight out, but at least he'd had de la Croix and the coming Bridekiller case to distract him. Coming home, he had only himself and his thoughts, neither of which had ever provided much in the way of distraction or comfort.

To his surprise, the flight back was pleasant. He had a window seat and once they leveled off at a cruising altitude above the gray clouds, there was nothing but sunshine and a periwinkle vista like a child's idea of sky. He stared out the window, captivated by the utter lack of any sensation of movement. The jet thrummed all around him; he could feel the power of its engines vibrating through every cell of him. And yet without a point of reference outside, he might as well be immobile.

Howie picked him up at the Nashville airport. They hugged, gently. Jasper asked about G. William and Howie informed him that the retired sheriff had been moved to a rehab facility. It was the best news Jasper had heard in weeks.

"When can we go there?" he asked Howie.

Howie grunted as he steered. "Where do you think we're headed right now?"

The facility—Crosswind Rehab and Hospice—was about thirty minutes from Lobo's Nod. Jasper hated the ill-angled, asymmetrical building the moment he saw it, but bit his tongue and instead thanked Howie for making the arrangements and getting G. William set up.

Inside, he sat at G. William's bedside and watched the big man sleep. *Big man* was turning into a misnomer. Three weeks of illness and a restricted diet had already carved away a significant chunk of G. William's bulk. Skin hung loose and slack under his chin, and the swell of the bedclothes seemed too low an altitude to match Jasper's memory of G. William's gut.

"I think he's gonna be OK," Howie whispered, standing behind Jasper.

It was a private room and Jasper probably could have spent the night, dozing in the quite uncomfortable-looking easy chair in the corner. But he couldn't do anything for G. William by contorting himself into the chair and waking up with his body a deformed mass of cramped muscles and dull nerves, so he let Howie drive him home.

At the front door, he steeled himself for the frigidity he would have to endure within, but when he opened it, a blast of warm, humid air engulfed him.

The house was sweltering. He could have sworn he'd turned off the heat before leaving, had anticipated the house freezing cold when he returned. And yet the Dent house had— as always—done as it preferred, not as he wanted or needed. Was it the thermostat? Was it the furnace? Was it the wiring? Was it his grandmother's cursed, demented spirit, gabbling eidolic curses while flipping switches and conjuring technical glitches from beyond the grave?

It was north of eighty degrees in the house. He dropped his bags in the living room and spent a good half hour in the basement, trying to figure out what had happened. Ultimately, he ended up disconnecting two wires and swapping their positions, which seemed to shut down the furnace and still kept the thermostat active and connected.

In the kitchen, he opened his laptop at the counter and fiddled for a few minutes until his phone bleated for his attention—Connie. He flipped on FaceTime and watched her snap into focus.

"Hey, there's that face!" she said without preamble.

From the background of ropes and darkness as well as her hushed tone, he knew she was calling from backstage during rehearsal. And sure enough . . .

"I just have a minute," she said, glancing around at who and what he could not see. "But I wanted to welcome you home."

"It would be better if you were here," he told her. Lightly. No sense starting an argument.

She smiled with half her face. "Opening night is right after the first of the year. We're in full-on panic mode."

"So you missed Thanksgiving and you're also not coming home for Christmas, then?"

"This is home now." Gentle. No reproof. He imagined some people's parents probably spoke that way to their small children.

"How do your parents feel about that?"

"They understand. And besides, they'll have my brother. And you'll go over, right?"

He tried to chuckle, but it came out a sigh. "Maybe."

"Maybe? You know they need their token white boy for the holidays."

He stared down at his laptop, open on the table before him. The website for an airline glowed up at him. A search for flights from Nashville to JFK.

"Maybe. We'll see. I don't know yet."

Her eyes searched him over the Wi-Fi and the miles, but she said nothing more on the topic. "You look a lot better. Healed."

"I think . . ." He stared down into the screen. Such fidelity. The best technology in the world and it looked like Connie, but it wasn't Connie. "I think I'm a little better."

She smiled at that. With her whole face this time.

*   *   *

Later, he closed the laptop. A ticket would be easy. So easy.

He wasn't sure. Not yet.

He went into what had been his grandmother's bedroom, when she was alive. He'd cleared it out years ago and went into it almost never.

Now he unfolded a map of the United States and taped it up on the wall. Then he drove pushpins in at five points on the map:

Baltimore.

Newark.

Memphis.

Houston.

Seattle.

Above the map, he thumbtacked one last item. A photograph of his father.

Billy had begun calling FBI offices before Patrick began killing brides. Maybe Conroy was legit and would help.

Maybe not.

Either way . . .

Jasper stared at the map, at the photo.

"What are you up to, Billy?"

*   *   *

In the morning, he drove to McCutcheon's house. The man himself stood in the doorway, and Jasper flashed back to

Patrick waiting in his doorway, mugs waiting on the kitchen table. Somewhen during Jasper's time in the Pacific Northwest, McCutcheon had had his hair cut—it lay neat and sleek against his skull like a tight gray cap. Jasper didn't know quite how to react to the lack of a mad scientist coif.

He'd made a lot of mistakes in Seattle. It wasn't the mistakes so much that bothered him as the idea that he'd somehow convinced himself that he was done making mistakes. Such foolishness enhanced the shock of gazing into the mirror and recognizing his fatuity, his senselessness.

His humanity, McCutcheon would probably say.

"Welcome home." McCutcheon's voice was gruff but contemplative. Jasper had called him before he'd left Seattle and given him the basics.

Maria, McCutcheon's long-suffering wife, stood just inside the door with a cup of hot coffee. Jasper demurred as pleasantly as he could. He didn't want the caffeine jitters. He didn't want the blast of endorphins. And he also thought that it might be a good long while before he trusted any beverage not prepared before his own eyes.

He and McCutcheon repaired to the remodeled family room that served as McCutcheon's home office. When they'd begun this journey, McCutcheon had worked out of the barely renovated garage. Now, with his kids out of the house, he'd taken over the old family room and turned it into a beautiful, expansive home office.

Jasper tried not to imagine how much of the remodel he had personally paid for.

McCutcheon sat in a buttery leather chair across from a gray upholstered love seat. Jasper knew it well. Sitting felt like a homecoming.

"I fucked up," he told McCutcheon, unable to meet the man's eyes.

"Just this morning," McCutcheon asked, "or . . . ?"

His chuckle laden with regret and self-deprecation, Jasper managed to look up. "Pretty much every day for the past couple of weeks."

"But you caught him."

"Yeah, but . . ." He shook his head. "Never mind."

McCutcheon sipped from his mug, eyes never leaving Jasper.

"How long have we been doing this?" McCutcheon asked.

"Years," Jasper whispered.

"And I've told you from the beginning—it only works when you tell me *everything*."

"'*Never mind* is *I give up*.'" Quoting from one of their earliest sessions.

"So tell me. Tell me everything."

And Jasper did. Even the hard parts. The parts where he admitted his attraction to Patrick's methods, his rejection of McCutcheon's. The parts where he doubted himself, where he allowed himself to be manipulated. The wounded pride that he, trained in manipulation by an expert, raised to be the very best, allowed himself to fall under Bridekiller's spell and have his innards twisted into a new configuration.

And worse—he'd asked for it. He'd approved it. He'd liked it.

McCutcheon listened without comment or condemnation, even when Jasper described deliberately ignoring the man's texts, blowing off his beseeching for contact.

When Jasper was finished, his body felt fluish and drained. He'd vomited it all out, every stupidity and fear and misgiving of the past weeks. He left nothing out.

And McCutcheon said nothing. He drank from his mug and then he stared down into it and then he slowly put it aside, balancing it carefully on a coaster poised near the edge of his nearby desk.

"I probably shouldn't say this," said McCutcheon at last, "but I'm proud of you."

"Did . . ." Jasper drew in a deep breath. "Did you hear what I said? Did you hear all of it?"

"I heard every last word. You made every mistake imaginable and you still figured it out."

"But I was wrong about everything."

"Were you? You were right about some of it. And you were being manipulated by a master of the art. And you *still* caught the guy."

"Jesus Christ!" Jasper exploded, throwing his hands in the air. "I'm not supposed to be catching these guys! I'm not supposed to be doing any of this! I'm supposed to be putting away the past!"

"Says who?" McCutcheon asked mildly.

Jasper choked on his own breath, unable to form coherent words. He spluttered and gasped for too many seconds before finally yelling, "You! *You*, you fucking imbecile!"

"Really?" McCutcheon actually *scrutinized his fingernails and yawned.*

"Yes!" Jasper flailed about on the love seat and shoved himself to his feet. "For *years* you've been telling me to *get healthy* and to *figure myself out* and to *move forward!* For *years* I've been trying to make my life about something other than goddamn serial killers!"

He realized he was looming over McCutcheon, panting, sweat beaded along his forehead and the back of his neck. Breathing hard, he glared down at his therapist, who sighed without drama and tilted his head to look up at Jasper.

"None of that—getting healthy, figuring yourself out, moving forward—is at odds with what you did in Seattle. I never told you that *getting healthy* meant a life about 'something other than goddamn serial killers.'" He made quotation marks in the air.

What the living hell . . . ? Jasper clenched and unclenched his fists. "Then what the hell have we been *doing* all these years?" he wailed.

And McCutcheon smiled. "We've been getting to this point. To this moment. Where you are maybe—maybe—ready to understand and possibly even accept that you don't have to deny who and what you are in order to be happy and healthy."

It made no sense. He'd spent so much time with McCutcheon, unearthing all the pain and the horror of his past. If not to discard it all, what was it all for? Why dredge it all up if not to set it on fire?

His knees quivered; he staggered backward and fell onto the love seat.

"I don't get it," he whined. "Now you *want* me to hunt killers? I thought I—"

"I want you to do whatever fulfills you, Jasper." For the first time, there was a hard edge of annoyance in McCutcheon's voice, an honest anger and disappointment that reminded him of Patrick. "I want . . ."

McCutcheon balled up his fists and glared around the room, as though an answer had been inscribed somewhere in the decor by the contractors who'd renovated the place.

"Have you ever . . ." He thought another moment while Jasper waited in impatient agony. "Have you ever read anything by Shel Silverstein?"

It came out of nowhere and both surprised and exasperated Jasper. "He's a kids' writer, right? I didn't read a lot of kid stuff."

"No. Of course not." McCutcheon leaned forward. "I guess it doesn't matter. Look: Silverstein's editor was a woman named Ursula Nordstrom. She was a lesbian in an age when it was difficult for a woman to wear pants, much less love other women."

Jasper rubbed his sweat-wet palms on the arms of the love seat. He figured he'd give McCutcheon another minute to get to the point.

"There's a wonderful collection of Nordstrom's correspondence with her authors," McCutcheon went on. "At one point, in the 1960s, she has lunch with Silverstein, talking about her general malaise and unhappiness. And she knows Silverstein is doing just great, is happy and fulfilled, and she can't figure out why. She asks if he's been in therapy . . . which at the time was not common, not well understood. Looked down upon."

"I wonder why," Jasper said grumpily.

McCutcheon went on, not acknowledging the snark. "So she asked Silverstein about therapy and he laughed and said he hadn't been and she asked him about his happiness and how and why he was so content, so fulfilled.

"And Silverstein said it was simple: He had learned to accept himself. In fact, he told Nordstrom that if he came to realize he was attracted to goats, he wouldn't become anxious or worried. He would just find the sweetest-tempered little goat and go settle down somewhere in the hills and be the happiest goat-fucker in the world."

Clearly McCutcheon did not want Jasper to take up with goats. And the way he stopped talking, laced his fingers over his belly, and leaned back in the chair made Jasper realize that it was *his* turn now, that the epiphany was right there for the taking, if only he could stretch out his arm and grasp it.

He thought of the reservoir at Volunteer Park. At the cool blue peace separated from him by a chain-link fence.

"So what are you saying? Are you saying . . . Are you saying I need to figure out who I am and then be that?"

He paused. McCutcheon's expression was inscrutable.

"Is that what you're saying? No matter what comes of it? No matter what kind of hell . . . Just follow my . . . Just follow my gut? Even if it leads to chaos and death?"

McCutcheon's lips quirked into something akin to a smile. He made a show of pushing up his sleeve to look at his watch.

"I think that's our time for today."

34

HE DIDN'T WANT to go home. He drove into town instead. The Nod had changed not much since his childhood. Some of the store signs were grimier; some of them were newer. But the shops were all generally still the same—drugstore, hardware store, gun shop, tattoo parlor . . .

At the end of one block, there it was: the Coff-E-Shop.

He parked at the curb and sat in the car for a while, staring.

He hadn't been inside in years.

Once upon a time, a woman named Helen Myerson had worked at the Coff-E-Shop. She'd been good-natured and efficient, always quick to whip up Howie's most densely perverse concoctions, no matter how convoluted and perplexing. A smile, a jot on her order pad, and she was off to the races.

She'd been murdered by the Impressionist while imitating Jasper's father's early crimes. The very first killer Jasper had caught, though too late to save Helen Myerson.

Not too late for so many others, though.

With a sigh, he unbuckled his seatbelt and—before he could stop himself—marched into the Coff-E-Shop. The place hadn't changed much in the intervening years. The booths still had the same cracked brown leather upholstery and the counter was still chipped butcher block. The biggest upgrade he noticed was an iPad on a turntable in place of the cash register and a sign advertising free Wi-Fi.

He waited patiently in line. When it was his turn, he smiled as naturally as he knew how at the barista who was not Helen Myerson. He handed over Shanna's slip of paper and said, "Hey, is there any chance you could make this for me?"

*   *   *

Minutes later, he emerged from the Coff-E-Shop with a steaming hot takeaway cup. He stood on the corner for a moment, inhaled deeply.

Then he thumbed open his phone and called.

"Special Agent Maxine de la Croix," she said in a no-nonsense tone.

"Hi," he said.

"Jasper?" Surprised.

"Remember how I told you to lose my number?"

"Yeah."

He sipped his drink and breathed in and smiled. "Don't."

<<<<>>>

ACKNOWLEDGMENTS

If you're new to the life and times of Jasper Dent, welcome! And if you are an old fan from the *I Hunt Killers* days, welcome *back*! Without any of you reading, this would not be nearly so much fun.

I want to thank everyone who helped get this book to this point, such as Kevin Callahan and Dan Ehrenhaft, my agent Kathleen Anderson, as well as everyone who made the original trilogy work.

As we dive into Jasper's future, I want to thank the folks at Crooked Lane, including but not limited to Marcia Markland, Dulce Botello, Thaisheemarie Fantauzzi Pérez, Madison Schultz, and all the folks in production, sales, and marketing who make the magic happen.

Buckle up—there's more to come!